RAID

RAID

KRISTEN ASHLEY

This book is a work of fiction. Names, characters, places, and incidents are the product of the author's imagination or are used fictitiously. Any resemblance to actual events, locales, or persons, living or dead, is coincidental.

First ebook edition: February 27, 2013
First print edition: 2013
Latest editions: July, 2015

ISBN-10: 0615766412
ISBN-13: 9780615766416

Discover other titles by Kristen Ashley at:
www.kristenashley.net

Commune with Kristen at:
www.facebook.com/kristenashleybooks
Twitter: KristenAshley68
Instagram: KristenAshleyBooks
Pinterest: kashley0155

Praise for *Gateways to Abomination* by Matthew M. Bartlett

Bartlett spins the dial to a radio jacked into the psyche, where the nightmare world unravels and a surreal dream-logic pushes the tales along with real intent in this curious and most satisfying collection that seems at all times to be spilling off the edge of the page.

– John Claude Smith, author of *Autumn in the Abyss* and *Riding the Centipede*

Completely weird sui generis stuff from an original voice in horror, the stories, snippets, tone poems and meditations herein are as perverted, strange, and nauseating as anything I've read.

– Scott R. Jones, Martian Migraine Press

Simply, this is a wonderful, clever work of modern weird fiction... every scene unit is a surprise and a delightful journey. This is the most unique material I have read in 10 years, and a must read for anyone keeping track of those pushing the envelope. Superior story lines, characterizations, descriptions, and pacing.

– Michael Aronovitz, author of *Alice Walks*, *The Witch of the Wood*, and *Phantom Effect*

Gateways to Abomination plunked me down into a place where the grotesqueries of François Rabelais and the nightmarish imagery of a Thomas Ligotti tale frolic about like demented wildlife whose proportions are not quite correct. Things slither and squelch and drip in Bartlett's world. Doorways and perspectives tilt at incorrect angles; goats and seething masses of worms wear suits. Nothing is as it seems, and even less is explained, because the oneiric realm Bartlett creates has a strange logic all its own. Here surrealism is cloaked in ambiguity and is just as likely to beat you to death with a walking cane as it is to confound you… Bartlett's creations are more than a little bit naughty, and yes, often repulsive and disturbing. But they're also as haunting and mischievous as something giggling from deep within a dark forest.

– Christopher Slatsky, author of *Alectryomancer and Other Weird Tales*

The writing is sparse but lovely while the imagery, page after page, is savagely disturbing. The overall effect is one of a phantasmagoria, a nightmare from which one is both thankful to awake and strangely eager to revisit.

– Daniel Mills, author of *The Lord Came at Twilight* and *Revenants*

Creeping Waves

Matthew M. Bartlett

Muzzleland Press
Golden, Colorado

"Master of Worms" first appeared in *Wicked Tales: The Journal of the New England Horror Writers*, Vol. 3, NEHW Press, 2015.

"Rangel" first appeared as a chapbook published by Dim Shores, 2015.

"Night Dog" first appeared in *High Strange Horror*, Muzzleland Press, 2015.

muzzlelandpress.com
Twitter: @muzzlelandpress
Facebook.com/muzzlelandpress

Editing, cover design, and layout by Jonathan Raab
Photo art by Thom Davidsohn
Leander font by Michael Tension
"Anne Gare Occult" logo by Standard Design. Used with permission.

ISBN-10: 0-9970803-1-0
ISBN-13: 978-0-9970803-1-5

This book is dedicated to the memory of
John R. Saulnier.

CONTENTS

STATION IDENTIFICATION: WXXT

By Nathan Ballingrud

Nobody saw this guy coming. The small and indie press horror scene is a pretty self-aware bunch. Everybody might not know everybody, but everybody certainly knows *of* almost everyone, including a lot of the up-and-comers. With the proliferation of online magazines, subscription chapbook series, genre-focused podcasts, and the clutching grasp of social media, there aren't many surprises to be had. But in the summer of 2014, without fanfare and to small notice, a self-published book called *Gateways to Abomination* by Matthew M. Bartlett—a name most of us had never heard before—crept into the world. And it was getting ready to make a big noise.

Slowly, it started to get passed around. There was no ad campaign, no book trailers, no social media blitzes. What *Gateways to Abomination* had was something much more valuable: it had word of mouth. People started talking about this book. It kept cropping up in conversations, links started peppering social media feeds. After a while it seemed to have become part of the atmosphere. If you were part of the horror and weird fiction community, you couldn't turn around without seeing the folk art aesthetic of its blood-red cover posted somewhere, that title seemingly stripped raw from the scuffed box of a cult-horror VHS tape.

In any small and passionate literary community, the desire to discover and foster success, while inarguably noble, sometimes leads to books being exalted beyond their actual merit. Because of this, when I sat down to read it, I did so with no great expectation. I expected a pleasant diversion, at best.

I might as well have wandered onto a freeway while staring at my shoelaces. I was that unprepared.

What I encountered was a writer in full flourish, in complete command of his art. I encountered a savage dream which moved with the lethal confidence of a great white shark. Bartlett was no dilettante; here was someone channeling a vision. The book seemed to vibrate.

In *Gateways to Abomination*, Bartlett introduced us to Leeds, Massachusetts, a town under the thrall of a witch cult broadcasting from a radio station—WXXT—found on the far left regions of the dial. Those call letters, I am confident, will echo through the years in discussions of great early 21st century horror fiction, sending a glad shiver through the blood of anyone who's read it.

And so now we come to *Creeping Waves*: the full aesthetic flowering of that vision. Promises made are delivered upon, secrets hinted at are—if not revealed—then given deeper layers of mystery. Like its predecessor, *Creeping Waves* is a series of stories and vignettes, clippings and broadcasts—so that the experience is one of steady accumulation. Characters disappear for a while only to crop up again unexpectedly; threads are presented, hidden, and revealed again in new contexts. The larger story does not play out before you so much as it reveals itself around you: incrementally, suffocatingly.

Leeds is a modern town. Indeed, there are several overt examples of corporate horror, of a kind that would do Thomas Ligotti proud—but the looming presence of the Dark Wood, and all the witch-haunted New England folklore which accompanies it—is ever-present. That the voice of this presence is articulated through the radio is one of

Bartlett's canniest innovations. The radio is a modern instrument, yet just quaint enough that it seems a bit archaic to the modern reader—a relic from a simpler time. It is a kind of halfway point between the present day and the dark days of old, when the wind was smeared with the greasy ashes of accused witches. This is no accident. Bartlett draws a hard, bloody line from the past to the present, the echoes of ancient cruelties spilling blood into our own bright afternoons. The character of Leeds shapes the characters of the people who live there (sometimes literally, and always with violence). In this way, *Creeping Waves* functions as a work of psychogeography, in the tradition of Alan Moore's *From Hell* and *Voice of the Fire*. It is the story of a place before it is the story of people.

But let's not be coy. You've come here for a horror story. And what you get is one of the purest and most audacious expressions of horror in the modern day. There are more tantalizing ideas per page than you'll find in most full-length novels. Here you will encounter faded cult leaders returned to prominence and infused with bloody purpose; old grimoires, diaries, and cookbooks of unsavory provenance catalogued and priced for the corrupted bibliophile; passage to the Night of Black Tents and to the blood-drenched carnival at the rancid heart of the dream. There are missing children and missing souls. Every past sin and every forgotten defeat returns to you here, dressed in the terrible glamor of an animated, ravenous death.

There are times you will want Bartlett to stop. You will think, "You've gone too far. You shouldn't say this. You shouldn't write this." And that's when *Creeping Waves* is succeeding at its deepest levels. I believe horror operates at its best when it functions as a transgressive literature. It achieves its full majesty when it places itself in opposition to the reader. *Creeping Waves* is transgressive because it is fearless, crossing boundaries with a hungry intent and with full aesthetic integrity, pushing the horror so far that it ceases to be a source of fear or revulsion and instead passes over into the sublime. This is Hell's beautiful, bleeding face.

A part of me is a little jealous of Bartlett, and of what he achieves in this extended category of nightmares. But it's pointless to be jealous of him, in the same way it's pointless to be jealous of David Lynch or Lars von Trier. He is an artist in service to a vision; there is no replicating it. Nor should there be a desire to. You just thank whatever accident of fate allowed you to witness it.

You're listening to WXXT, the worm in the heart, the maggot in the skull.

WXXT

Prologue

Like all New Englanders, I await the spring with anticipation and impatience. More people venture into the woods in spring. More sad souls wander by lonely rivers. Some get lost and never return. Some fall from great heights onto craggy rocks. Some encounter bears. And some unfortunate souls encounter William Dither. Were I a wanderer in these woods, I would fair face a bear than I would old Will when he's in his cups.

I walked tonight. I broke the neck of a bird. I ruined the heart of a child. I drank beer after beer in The Dirty Truth and took a bar girl to the woods and built a birdcage from her ribs. I locked a frightened squirrel in the cage and shot it with a pistol from 10 yards away.

And then, faithful listeners, I cast my mind back to days of antiquity.

There were no call letters in those days, no frequencies, save the ones that rode the air inaccessible to man. We had no name. We were a ragtag band of miscreants, dopers, murderers, witches, bitches, boozers, smugglers, thieves, bandits, veterinarians, panty-sniffers, harlots, pederasts, perverts, dim-wits, and sneaky-Petes. Obliquely-worded and anonymously-distributed pamphlets led us into the woods on a providential September day, pamphlets written by no-one-knows-who but designed to draw precisely the crowd they drew.

There was opium that day in the woods, and there was tobacco and wine and cider and fresh fruits. There was laughter and plotting and bashing and more than one stabbing and an impromptu orgy that left one poor tot armless in its aftermath. I emerged as clear leader and hand-picked Dither and Ronstadt as my acolytes. Dither, his ass-hole still sore from the rigorous rogering, glared at me balefully, his eye slit horizontal like a red sunset. I knew we would be fast friends.

Young Master Ronstadt, a dead teen-aged strumpet slung over his horse, scratched his pimpled forehead with long, black fingernails. Dither spat a venomous red. I slid a knife across my tongue. We made a blood oath.

Over 100 years later, well beyond our bodies' meager lives, we broadcast the Word from the woods of Leeds.

I arrive at the station at 4 a.m. Rexroth Slaughton is there already, sorting through carts and scribbling the day's monologues on a tablet whilst pulling the worms from his waistcoat. I find Dither weeping disconsolately at the microphone. Ronstadt's limp body hangs by the neck from a thick branch that has plunged through our modest roof, his neck impossibly folded, his tongue a black bug peeking from a pink letter slot, a coffee mug that says "I Don't Like Mondays" gripped in his curved rigor mortis finger.

"Mornin' Old Ben," he says, a thick string of black spittle swaying hypnotically until it finally lights across his pus-stained musty shirt.

I light a candle and flip a switch.

"WXXT," I say into the microphone. "This is Benjamin Scratch Stockton signing on. There is no hint of sun yet this morning, and there is still time to hunt. Soon light will creep amongst the trees that line our studios, obscuring, for but a few hours, the plagues and the blights and the ants and the maggots. To-day the FCC will be lost on the way to our door, a cat will scratch the eye of a virgin, a dead man will touch the cheek of a newborn and turn it black. But first, here is Jebediah Blackstye with the weather report."

SPRING THAW

And the last brown patches of snow melt away. The bodies planted in autumn reveal themselves. A blackened thatch of bones intertwined among briars, bristles, and burrs. A mummified infant, curled like a bug, wedged under the root of an ancient elm. A long, lean cadaver, white as marble, winding gracefully through the rocks in the swift waters of a reborn tributary. A fresh kill caged in thorn-busy vines, a man of indeterminate age, his head cracked open at the jaw, a bouquet of mushrooms growing from the gaping maw of a mouth like a swollen fungal megaphone.

Harken: a liturgy of flies.

Rampage

That was it, then. Elisa had gone and told her parents. Now it would be falling dominoes, parents to principal, principal to police, police to Candace, all tumbling towards him until the biggest, heaviest one crushed him like a foot stepping on a flower. Nothing worth going through lay in his future; there was nothing he could even countenance. A trial? Facing his accuser? *Never.* Prison? *Absolutely no fucking way.* And he'd never be employable again, except maybe as a supermarket bagger, the kind people barely look at, the kind whose prison stint was scrawled over his face like graffiti. Toothless and wrung out.

Rich sat in the Honda on the shoulder of North King Street, rain beating on the windshield like colorless blood. The gun sat on the passenger seat next to him. He put the radio on. Something bombastic and classical shook the speakers. He turned it up all the way and he screamed and screamed and beat his fists on the wheel.

When he was done, he turned the volume back down. The classical what-have-you had segued into something that sounded like bagpipes being played by people who had no idea how to play bagpipes. Over the music, the drab voice of a newscaster repeated over and over the phrase *A dark bruise ran the length of her leg.* Fucking college radio experimental nonsense. He shut the radio, put the car in gear, executed a U-turn, and headed back to downtown Leeds.

Elisa lived with her parents in a small blue Cape Cod house on Summer Street. Rich pulled up to the curb, grabbed the gun, and headed up to the porch. His legs felt heavy, difficult to lift, as in a dream. He tried the doorknob. Locked. Holding the gun at his waist, he knocked four times. A man opened the door, thinning hair, rumpled sweater, jeans faded and sagged. When the man saw that it was Rich, his eyes narrowed and his face curled in disgust. Before he had a chance to see the gun, Rich put a bullet through that scrunched up face.

Screams from back in the house, females, more than one, only one whose voice he recognized. Rich walked in the direction of the screams. His mouth felt very dry.

A dark bruise ran the length of her leg.
A dark bruise ran the length of her leg.
A dark bruise ran the length of her leg.

When he had completed his work, he put his hand under Elisa's neck and pulled her face to his. Her eyes saw nothing, but he still found them beautiful, even given the hollowed out, smoking cave of her chest below. He kissed her mouth, put her bottom lip between his lips and pulled at it. He kissed her teeth.

He stood and looked at Elise's mother, who had sunk into the sectional, half her head scattered across the couch's arm and the wall behind her. Her chest lurched, settled, lurched again. With each lurch, her jaw opened and closed, ejecting small bursts of air.

HuuuUUhg, the corpse said, its voice barely more than a snort. *HuuuUUhg... HuuuUUhg.* Fat pink fingers clutched at nothing, like the fingers of an infant. He shot two more bullets into her torso, watching the aquamarine and periwinkle dress puff out with each impact, watching her half-head jolt and bounce. He was surprised to find it made him laugh. He shot another time, then thrice more. He laughed and laughed.

Rich emerged from the front door to find that the sun had come out. Between the two houses across the way ran the curve of a very bright rainbow. His shoes made squishing sounds in the wet grass as he walked back to the car. Littler rainbows leapfrogged along the lawn. He sank into his seat, avoiding his face in the rearview mirror. He put the barrel in his mouth, the spittle on his tongue sizzling. The passenger door opened and someone sat next to him.

A hand reached into his view, white haired and pink as a baby ferret. It turned on the radio. Voices humming low. Over the humming a voice spoke. Rich understood somehow that the voice coming over the radio was spoken by the man sitting in his car.

"I don't think you're quite finished," the man said.

"I'm finished," Rich said.

"No thoughts of hell, then? I have to say I'm *most* relieved. People do put such a high stake in belief systems that are no longer tenable. So. If this is the end for you, would you be terribly aggrieved if I took possession of your body when the act is complete?"

"I guess it makes sense that I went crazy," Rich said.

The apparition in the passenger seat waited.

"What... what would you do... with my body?"

Rich actually *felt* the man smile... the car sank slightly on the passenger side, as though the man's plans for his corpse *weighed something*. Fear wriggled through his gut and bubbled up as acid in his throat.

"Are you certain that you don't have more to do?"

"More?"

"Well, there is your wife. Candace, yes? My assumption—and do tell me if I'm being gauche or overstepping a boundary—is that she was indifferent to your needs. Ah. You needn't reply. I can see the answer in your eyes." His voice sank to a whisper. "Must she go unpunished?"

"I didn't catch that," Rich said.

The hand reached out again and turned up the volume.

"Must… that… go… *unpunished*?"

Rich spared the man a glance. A goat's horns spiraled up from split-skin wounds on either side of his high, acne-scarred forehead. They scraped the fabric of the car's ceiling. His face clung tightly to his skull, cave-cheeked, eyes in dark hollows, his nose an afterthought, not much more than two holes above a lipless mouth. A black suit sat loosely on his long, thin frame. His knees, high and bony, hovered just above the level of his lowest rib. He turned to Rich and grinned a Satanic grin. Maggots spilled from his mouth in wriggling clusters, carrying the stench of neglected dumpsters, intestine-choked sties, sun-heated ovens of rot and deterioration.

Screams from all around, wailing sirens, headlights flashing. Police cars swarmed in from all sides, bouncing over curbs, carving brown ruts into neatly-tended green lawns. Cops bursting from their doors, guns pointed at Rich, shouting, bellowing.

A dark bruise ran the length of her leg.

"Oh dear," the apparition said.

A booming voice from a police loudspeaker: POINT YOUR WEAPON.

Rich looked at the apparition. It gave an exaggerated shrug.

DO IT NOW. QUICKLY. POINT YOUR WEAPON. POINT YOUR WEAPON.

SHOW US YOUR WEAPON.

The apparition said, "Mother once told me that it is always best to obey without question the commands of the constabulary."

Rich held up his gun in a trembling hand and extended his arm.

Chaos, conflagration. The bullets powdered the windshield. One of the apparition's horns exploded in a cloud of dust, causing him to cackle madly. The rearview mirror shattered and spun away. The car bounced on its wheels. Blood painted the interior.

I exited the car, walked between the cops, their red faces, their coughing pistols. I had not gotten what I had wanted, and I was angry for the loss. I wanted revenge. I wanted blood, more blood, never enough blood. Brothers and sisters and radio listeners, I walked away. I walked into the true heart of Leeds.

ANNE GARE'S RARE BOOK & EPHEMERA CATALOGUE #304935-A

Bastions of Disquiet by Rangel Bantam

A rare treasure indeed, this one-off book's authorship is a matter of fierce debate among collectors. The book is thought by many to be a hoax, being that the author's name is the very same as that of a young girl who disappeared in the woods of Leeds, Massachusetts in nineteen eighty two.

The book, thought to have been written in the early nineteen nineties, was discovered in two thousand fourteen, one of several tomes dropped off in a weather-ravaged cardboard box on the shop's front stoop. Papers in the box indicated that the books within were part of an estate sale at the Bantam residence. That residence has been abandoned for the better part of a year.

The book itself contains parts of poems, drawings of obscure symbols, and a series of fractured aphorisms such as, "In a cage of muscle only the bosom-beaked killdove collects gristle." The last pages are a fever dream of accusations, phantasies, quasi-sexual ramblings, and unspeakable blasphemies.

Stapled illustrated wraps in fine condition. One hundred eleven pages. Eight thousand, nine hundred and ninety nine dollars.

THE DISSOLUTION OF NATHAN WHITESHIRT

Nathan Whiteshirt staggered down the steps of the venerable church, the sky wheeling above him, the clouds jabbing down like daggers, the trees whirling and hissing, their roots lashing at the earth. He lurched among the sighing gravestones, passed through the gate, crossed the common, attained the walk, pushed open the door of the furrier's and put both hands on the counter to steady himself.

"Banished!" he said. "Banished, like some devil!"

The goat-like man behind the counter parted his lips and curled them upward to reveal a mouthful of yellow, overlapping teeth—one could not in good conscience have called it a grin. A fat grey worm crawled up from below the gum-line like a grave robber scaling a cemetery fence. The goat-like man's long grey tongue appeared at the corner of his long mouth, slid over his bottom lip, and scooped up the worm, depositing it between gnashing teeth. A wet crunch followed, and a thin stream of fluid shot out, hitting Nathan Whiteshirt square in the eye.

Oh, ho, ho, said the furrier—one could not in good conscience have called it a laugh. He proffered a stained white cloth from the folds of his coat. Snatching it from the goat-like man's filthy hand, Nathan Whiteshirt cried out in disgust and surprise as he wiped with great vigor and little efficacy at his afflicted eye.

What do you want?

"I want it back."

You want what back? Be precise.

"Everything."

I can help you, the goat-like man said, and he gestured for Nathan to come behind the counter, where a black curtain secreted the stockroom and office. The goat-like man went out, locked the door, and returned. He opened the curtain and bade Nathan entrance.

Behind the black curtain, shelves lined the walls all the way to the high ceiling. The lower shelves grinned under the weight of strapped bundles of documents and slim books bound in brown and black leather. One electric light provided the only illumination, flickering at the ceiling, causing angled shadows in a thousand variations of gray to endlessly climb the uneven surfaces of the paper. The goat-like man stood on his tiptoes, and in the flickering light it appeared to Nathan as though the man's body stretched to an unnatural height as he pulled down one of the books. He lowered his glasses and flipped the pages until he found what he wanted. He began to read aloud, the words sounding like English, but somehow defying understanding; a litany of disconnected syllables, with sounds that seemed incapable of having been produced by the human chorus of palate, glottis, and tongue. Beneath it all, a sound like meat sizzling on a griddle.

Nathan became increasingly aware of a sensation behind his assaulted eye that intensified along with the sound—a combination of itch, burn, and ache. He put a hand over his eye and watched the goat-like man's own eyes as they swept from left to right and back again over the page, his voice bouncing around the room like the buzz of a trapped housefly.

Nathan pulled his hand from his face and his eye popped from its socket like a squeezed pimple. He shrieked.

Two long-nailed hands gripped Nathan's collar, and the goat-like man pulled his gaunt face right up to Nathan's, then clamped his right eye over Nathan's sizzling socket. The man's breath was hot as glowing coal against his cheek. Nathan struggled, but the man's grip was powerfully strong.

"Ah," said the goat-like man, his voice a glottal creak, breath hot as steam against Nathan's face. "I see! I see! The Shaman brings The Morning Man. And soon. Or soon enough." He shoved Nathan away.

Nathan felt hot, though it was late November and the shop was drafty. He felt a rising sensation in his stomach. He turned and bolted through the curtains. The goat-like man followed, his voice rising as Nathan shouldered open the door and careened into the street. The door opened behind him and the goat-like man bellowed his endless liturgy.

Nathan knelt and vomited, and what came out was a writhing mass of segmented worms stained with streaks of blood, and he saw with terror that the worms bore faces at both ends—eyeless faces with wet mouths that pulled vainly at the air like the mouths of fish. He retched again, and up surged more, clogging his airway. His other eye popped like a bubble, then he fell into the mass of worms, who surged toward him for a taste. Their bites were as needles plunged deep into his person. He shrieked, and a horse echoed his shriek and threw its rider to the packed-dirt of the road. A group of children spat in unison and raised their hands in strange gestures. The bell on the town hall tower began to peal, striking eleven. Nathan stood, pulling the worms from his face, his sides heaving, and bolted blindly away.

And his vision began to return. And everything was color and blur and black lightning and wheels that contracted and swelled and interlocked, flying together, bouncing apart.

He found his way to his home, a doddering Colonial at the corner of Orchard Street and Hill Road. For days, the rumors roamed from house to house like living things, and the people of the town began to gather at Nathan's porch. For the cost of a dime, some even dared look into the caves of poor Nathan's eyes, and marveled at what they saw.

UNCLE RED READS TO-DAY'S NEWS (1)

Local poet and mystic Michael Dooley reported the presence of the ladies of the Leeds Women's Society in the field adjacent to his house last Sunday evening. Clad only in wind—according to Mr. Dooley—the ladies, all of a certain age, swayed in the starlight like alabaster bells, with their black souls clanging against their walls of skin and sinew. Their hands traced the spaces between the stars. Their eyes glowed like fireflies. Their ululations and their terrible cries put him off his books and he contacted the constabulary to urge them to put a stop to the ladies' most unruly noise. Mr. Dooley was strongly advised to remove himself to the reaches of his house farthest from the field.

MASTER OF WORMS

It was by any measure a modest procession: a black hearse leading two stately silver sedans, evenly spaced, making their way down the winding cemetery road. Gravel crunched. Birds tittered. The wind gave an enthusiastic, sibilant ruffling to the treetops. It was early April, early morning, the sky somewhere between grey and blue, the clouds white and wispy. Shadows' long fingers stretched across the monuments, the grasses, the silent paths.

The hearse braked with a jolt, as did the sedans in turn. The hearse's reverse lights came on like white eyes blinking open, and the vehicle jerked backward, spraying gravel and kicking up a cloud of dirt. The procession abandoned the pretense of grace as the cars reversed, one almost hitting another, the last swerving slightly to avoid backing into a reverently poised, blank-eyed stone angel. Brake lights flashed, splashing angular red lights onto the faces of the stones.

From the passenger door of the first sedan rose a middle-aged man, bald, bucket-jawed, mustachioed, bearing a walking stick with a goat's head handle in blackened jade. He approached the hearse as the driver, grey haired, in mirrored sunglasses, clambered out. The wind rose up as the two exchanged words, the hearse driver's face contorted with fear, pointing with a trembling finger at the point just ahead of where he had stopped the hearse.

The man with the cane looked at the spot, squinting. Uncertainty flickered on his face, and was swiftly subsumed by a contemptuous sneer. He said nothing, then turned on his heel and limped back behind the sedan. He opened the trunk with perhaps more force than necessary, pulled out a shovel, looked back defiantly at the driver, then walked over to a tall, brown headstone.

Douglas Archibald Harbor
1945 – 2014
Man of Peace

The flowers—white roses—had been removed, placed to one side of the headstone. The man stabbed his cane into the petals, twisting them, crushing them, grinding them into the earth. His face betrayed no emotion but his knuckles were as white as the roses he defiled. Then, letting the cane fall, he raised the shovel and stabbed the earth, using his foot to force the blade in deep.

Presently he was joined by the driver, who had retrieved from the hearse his own shovel. They worked. Dirt flew, the first ragged chunks bearing wigs of green grass. Birds on branches flapped their wings but remained perched. The wind sighed. The shadows began to recede as though chastened. The men worked without speaking, their only sounds grunts and exhalations.

An hour later, as the men wrested the coffin from the gaping earthen gash, the driver's side door of the second sedan opened, revealing a slender woman, hidden in flowing black linen, veiled, very likely on the younger side of her thirties. She exited the car and turned to pull the seat forward. Out climbed two brown-haired twin boys in little suits; and a blonde girl all in yellow. They walked a few paces from the cars and waited, the children standing in front of their mother, hands clasped in front of their stomachs, elbows out, faces neutral.

"Charles," the woman called out in a practiced mid-Atlantic accent. The mustachioed man with the goat's head cane propped his shovel against the tombstone and walked over. From the folds of her dress, a small white hand pulled out a small silver pistol. Charles kissed her brusquely on the cheek, slid the gun into his overcoat pocket, and returned to the coffin, which the hearse driver was in the process of prying open. He had managed, after some shovel work, to get the top open, exposing the head and suited chest of an elderly bald man, his eyes sewn shut, his mouth an angry pink line. Purple, furrowed hands, still as stone, were crossed at his chest. Scattered across his chest and stomach were baubles and trinkets and strangely shaped coins bearing inscrutable lettering, gifts that had rested behind the corpse, on the open lip of the casket's cap, at the wake.

The hearse driver struggled with the bottom half of the coffin lid, then gestured with his chin towards Charles. The men went around behind the head of the casket, each grabbing a handful of shoulder pad from the cadaver's brown suit jacket, and, with some difficulty, wrested the body from its oak cocoon, spilling the baubles back into the box.

Under the now-bright blue sky the body lay on the grass, arms stiffly up, grey slacks jerked down at an angle, revealing a crooked expanse of white hip peppered with brown acrochorda. The body frowned heavenward. It looked small, without weight, the shell of some hideous crustacean. Charles looked at the face. Did the eyes move under their sealed lids? Was it possible? His stomach dropped as though from a great height. He raised his shovel and brought the broad blade down on the forehead. The family and the hearse driver winced. One of the boys burst into tears and the mother lifted his tiny chin to shush him.

The forehead caved in at an angle, a capsized island in a pool of pink and grey, under which the face still frowned, its eyelid bruised and raked, one corner of the mouth unglued, showing a yellow tooth. The hearse driver marched over, raised his shovel like a golfer, and then swung the broad side of his shovel into the cadaver's face. A puff of dust flew up and the other eyelid sprung open, revealing a chipped, plastic dome. Charles pulled out his pistol and shot once, twice, three times, bloodless holes springing up in the corpse's cheek, forehead, and neck.

The woman stepped forward, leaving the children standing behind her, their faces—even that of the child who had been crying, though his cheeks were still red—neutral masks, the faces of cherubim painted on a church wall. The men stepped back, bowing their heads and looking at their shoes. The woman raised a finely muscled leg and jammed the heel of her shoe repeatedly into the corpse's eye, its nose, its mouth. She raked the flesh of its cheek, crushed and mauled its large ears. With each impact, she grunted, piglike, she spat, she made sounds that were not quite words and not quite not. Then she knelt, grabbed the cadaver's collar, and yanked the ruined face up towards her. Her face contorting, she cajoled, she whispered, she let forth a black stream of curses in an unknown tongue. The cadaver's head lolled. A stitch popped at its white lip, then another. It seemed, horrifically, as though it were preparing a reply.

At length, she shoved the cadaver to the ground and walked back to take her place behind her progeny. Once her breathing had returned to its measured rhythm, she touched the childrens' shoulders in turn. They grinned demoniac grins. They set upon the body. The woman wiped the grass from her pink knees and then watched them, pride blazing in her eyes.

After a time, Charles approached the frenzied scene, wedging the childrens' little bodies away one by one with his walking stick. They ran to their mother, who from her handbag pulled pristinely-folded white towels. She set to wiping their mouths and their hands, cooing as she did so. Then she moistened her fingers and used them to fix their hair.

Charles and the hearse driver pulled from their pockets sets of gloves and donned them, wriggling their fingers in. They each grabbed a part of the cadaver and flung it into the hole, then set to putting earth back into earth. When the work was done, Charles removed his gloves, used them to wipe his brow, folded them, and put them back into his pocket.

He pulled from the inside of his coat a slim book, black, leather-bound. He found his page, pulled the tassel.

"Let the worms have him, who was Master of Worms," he read. "Let his betrayal be written as history. Let it be known that he alone broke the covenant, that he alone invalidated the contract. Let us be forgiven. Let our actions be understood."

He closed the casket and the two men lifted it into the hearse. The woman and children were back in their car now. Charles joined them. The hearse driver got in his vehicle and started it. The procession left the cemetery as it had come, quietly. Noontime fell upon the empty cemetery. A bird began bouncing on its branch. It spread its wings. It screamed and screamed.

In the ground, the stitches at the cadaver's lips continued to pop, one by one.

In the third car sat Raymond Harbor, gaunt face hidden behind dark glasses, the collar of his overcoat up over his cheeks. What had occurred he had ordained, but in the end, to his shame, he could not bear to watch. He followed the procession out of the cemetery and onto Barkman Street, with its rows of huddled two-story houses.

"It is done," he said aloud to the empty car. With the old man now gone, now truly and really gone, he might consider his studies complete and assume leadership. No longer the acolyte, no longer the gofer, the fetcher. What he wanted would be brought to him by lesser men, and if it was not right, it was he, Raymond Harbor, who would dole out punishment, bestow damnation, without pity, without feeling.

He would blacken cells and cause hearts to wither and dry like gourds in rotten soil.

Raymond pulled the car around to the garage deep in the wood. The other cars were there. He entered the first bay. The casket sat in the center of the room, opened wide like the toothless mouth of some wooden god. It was surrounded by men with veiled faces. Charles was there. The hearse driver was there. The butcher was there and the arborist. The groundskeeper was there and the pastor. The schoolteacher was there and the nurse. The wig maker was there and the mill worker. The men put their gifts into the casket. A desiccated and hairless four-legged thing. A torn hat. A cloth bag of bird's beaks. A burnt locket. A small, corked glass tube filled halfway with a sickly orange liquid. The men knelt. The men chanted. The casket hummed and buzzed. The world turned around. Evening crept along, lowering the sunlight, and eventually the men rose and departed wordlessly.

The casket, sated, grinned a toothless grin at the empty garage. The windows beamed back, coloring the casket the yellow of a mostly faded bruise. In the rafters, unspeakable things slithered. In beams of light, dust motes swarmed in a frenzied orgy.

The family gathered at the Black House, candles lit and curtains drawn. A long table bore a great feast: a blister-blackened pig on a perversely large platter, in its pried-open mouth a brown, pimpled gourd. A great wooden platter of celeriac; fat, deformed faces under verdant crowns. A basket piled high with steaming fresh rolls, surrounded by ramekins of warmed butter. A great ocean of applesauce in a white blistered bowl, cinnamon dashed across its surface like dirt across the lid of a casket. A basin of noodles, curled in clusters and sprinkled with curds of green-tinged cheese. A green salad with a grisly outbreak of furred sprouts and cranberries burst like picked blisters.

Around this feast the family stood and jabbered, laughed and slapped shoulders, drowning out the rising wind outside. The room was watched over by family portraits, grim-faced matrons coddling walking sticks in hands preternaturally small and pink and delicate; stern men with pinched faces nested in jowls like pink pillows. The only other furnishing consisted of 12 chairs, which seemed too shallow and ornate for sitting in, and were indeed empty, save for one, which propped up Mr. Raymond Harbor, still in sunglasses and overcoat. He hunched like an animal, pulling meat from the pile on his plate and putting it between his teeth, pausing occasionally to take a great, rasping breath and to look with trepidation at the door. Over the clamor he could hear the wind shrieking around the eaves.

Finally someone spoke aloud what Raymond had been thinking:

"What do you suppose," the voice said, rising above the hum of conversation, "is keeping Charles and his kin?"

"Home for a pint and milk for the little ones," guessed the arborist, followed by several more affirming the hypothesis, and glasses clanged and silverware glinted and teeth tore at pig meat and Raymond felt a cold terror spring up in his belly and then to his esophagus, where it converted to a fiery bubbling heat. He dumped his plate to the floor.

As Godfrey and Wills and Georges leant to pick up the mess and tend to the stricken man, a knock sounded at the door. The boy of the house opened it to reveal the hearse driver standing on the leafy landing, an arm bent against one of the white columns for support. He was white as the linens, even to his lips, even to his eyes, which were rolled back, or perhaps down. The men carted him to the chaise lounge, where there began a fruitless interrogation, punctuated with slapping and a vigorous shaking of the man's collar. As the attention was so thoroughly diverted, Raymond rose from his seat, stepping in his abandoned repast, to the mild chagrin of Godfrey and Wills and Georges, and he climbed the stairs to the quiet guest room which had been his bedroom in childhood.

The room was unaccountably chilly. He shut the window, the weightless husks of dead flies bouncing on the sill, and fell backward onto the bed and pulled pillows to his sides and under his head before gathering the coverlet around him. Then, at once, he felt too hot. He shoved at the coverlet with his hands and his feet, pushed away the pillows. Then the light was too bright, a spotlight, a thousand suns. The switch seemed unbearably far. He stretched out an arm to grab a pillow and put it over his eyes. He used one shoe to kick off the other, used his foot to kick off the first. Having not felt in a full week the sensation of sinking into sleep, when it began to happen, he felt a surge of exhausted hope. He might yet escape into a dark tent of unconsciousness.

When the window opened, and the sounds of footfalls landed on the parquet floor, Raymond Harbor, every inch his father's son, jammed his cold hands against his ears and bellowed into his pillow with rage and despair and fear. And when the rough hands pulled the pillow from over his face, he saw before him two tall men in robes and veiled faces, between them on the floor something under a crushed velvet blanket. He backed up to the headboard as the gloved hands of the silent men grabbed the shoulders of his coat and pulled him up. He blacked out, his last emotion a baffling mixture of terror and gratitude.

Raymond Harbor awoke in a dark, hot place, seated on an uncomfortable cushion in a threadbare chair. He undertook a brisk physical inventory and found that he was not bound, but he was blindfolded. He heard about him the sounds of rustling, perhaps of chewing. Under it all was the occasional creak of the floor, as though somewhere before him a person was periodically shifting his weight.

A voice spoke out and he jumped in his chair.

"Did you think you could prevent his return?"

It was a voice Raymond did not recognize. He opened his mouth to speak, not knowing what he might say, but found his throat too dry to facilitate the passage of words. He tried to summon a wash of saliva into his palate but failed. It was silent now in the room, save the creaking of the floorboards, the shifting of weight.

It was not a surprise that the voice was unfamiliar. Douglas Archibald Harbor collected men: acolytes, servants, attendants. Thin men and fat. Barefaced and bearded. Slope-snouted and fist-chinned. Men just *brimming* with ambition. Needful men, lost men. Leeds was a bastion of this kind of man.

Rough hands landed on his shoulders and another hand pulled from his head the blindfold. Raymond Harbor looked all around him, at the heaps on the floor, the singed and battered flesh, the skin of faces pulled to the sides of skulls, or down; noses stretched over chin bones, skeletal hands gesturing from ragged sleeves of torn flesh, the pools of blood, clusters of plucked eyes, and in and around and among them the things slithering wetly, the thin, vibrating tongues like blood-slicked blue thread.

Raymond Harbor knew he would never attain his rightful position, never attain his rank, never make his covenant, and he knew that no one need break him in his grave and leave him faster to the worms, for he hadn't the power. Barely had he possessed even the semblance of power.

And then Raymond looked before him, on the table, in the center, surrounded by upturned bowls, rockslidden rolls, glops of applesauce, stove-in pig, smithereens of goblets in a nest of crushed velvet, and he saw, he saw everything, everything, under the stark light, and Douglas Archibald Harbor, all the parts of him, lurched forward, and the room went red, and then redder; then black, and then blacker.

VERNON GOLDEN

From five years before my birth until my third birthday, my parents worshipped as the Messiah a 32-year-old insurance salesman named Vernon Golden.

The curious can find footage of this earthbound, bloodless, thick-middled messiah on a series of three six-minute YouTube clips culled from an early '90s television news feature about The Order of the Eighth Hand. I remember television in those days looking crisp, clear, like you were watching with a pair of new glasses. Now, on YouTube, the broadcasts look like some grainy, rippling artifact. I watch them compulsively, as my memories of Vernon and the Order are largely lost to me now, blotted out by time and distance.

On that wavering, tiny screen (only on the smallest resolution can you watch without an obfuscating degree of pixilation), one can see Vernon Golden hold forth to a reporter whose face never appears on camera. He claims to be the Lord God in human form, come to earth at a time of great tumult to provide an express-route to salvation for the hopelessly lost. This claim is not exactly uncommon among the ranks of would-be messiahs, though invariably they themselves are a veritable catalog of human inadequacies: obese, weak-chinned, near-sighted, pinch-nosed, fence-toothed, sallow. Vernon was all of these, the apotheosis of the lesser gurus. His face is bracketed by huge-framed glasses and he's clad in one of his vertically striped shirts, this one white and blue. He always wore the same kind of striped shirt, always white and one other color, along with brown suspenders (one of them twisted, usually). His hair is naturally black in the videos, so black it shines.

Little in those clips suggests Golden would have the ability to hold people under any variety of thrall. He was truculent, poorly spoken, just the other side of unkempt. And yet—his eyes. His *eyes*. Even in that artifact video, with its grains and ripples, those eyes—they reach out and grab hold.

A combination of those hypnotic eyes and a fractured, grumpy kind of charisma got Vernon accepted in the unlikeliest of circles. Not long after my parents were generously permitted to leave the Order (a rarity, at the time nearly unthinkable; in fact, they might have been the first) Golden was invited to speak to the students at East Hodgson High School. The exact contents of his speech are lost to time, but it certainly speaks to the skills of the Confidence Man that he was allowed anywhere near such a roiling cauldron of malleable youth. It is chilling to imagine that the students who listened to Vernon are out there in the world somewhere, a little dose of Golden's intellectual toxins still inhabiting some speck of real estate in their cerebral systems. It is also rumored that he and his wife Betty (never seen by members of the Order) hosted lavish parties whose invitees included the mayor and some of the city council of East Hodgson, as well as prominent business owners, entrepreneurs, and moguls.

My parents were, at the time of their tenure in the Order, alcoholics, though they hid it from Golden, lest they incur his wrath and, worse, suffer the confiscation of their bottles. Alcohol was their vocation, the sticky glue that held together their fragile marriage, their sustenance and their succor. Upon my father's becoming sober, he and my mother split. I was 12. My father remained a teetotaler until the day he died, one year ago yesterday, in fact. On the day of his death, he was able for the first time to tell me he loved me. We wept and embraced.

Though he seemed shrunken, as though he had ceded power to the god of sobriety, his embrace was fierce. It carried the weight of wasted years—I thought he might literally break my ribs.

My mother is still an alcoholic, albeit a functional one. Daily, she has her first beer at six a.m. Mom tells me she loves me all the time, but her words are slurred, a recitation—quite possibly a lie. I can't trust her. And me? I cannot claim to have escaped my birthright. My poison is vodka, oh, dear, clear vodka, if you see it in a glass it might as well be water, but me, I can see a glass of vodka and tell you the brand and the proof.

I was deep into a bottle, deeper than a deep-sea diver, on a moribund October night, when my phone lit up and buzzed with UNKNOWN NUMBER on the display. Sober or even tipsy, I never would have picked up. But I did pick up, and the voice I heard was that of Vernon Golden, the off-the-rack savior, the father of untold young, the man who bestowed upon me my name, the man who had disappeared in the glare of television cameras and prosecutorial ambition, the focus of a protracted search by the FBI and INTERPOL, Vernon Golden, on *my* phone, asking *me* for help fighting the devil in some godforsaken New England city. And even in the absence of those persuasive, calming eyes, hearing only that voice, that voice I hadn't heard since I was a boy, except on cheap computer speakers, I said yes.

HAVE YOU SEEN THIS MAN? (1)

Have you seen this man? He wandered off in 1898 and we miss him dearly. He answers to Matthias Deadstreet. He walks with a limp. He frequently cries out to Jesus and has a lazy eye. He may be carrying a doll smeared with lipstick. He may be soiled, or quite possibly unclad from the waist down. He might smell of grape wine or of something earthen. His ears are jammed with waxy plugs. He sings spirituals and obscene songs and might drool uncontrollably. He paws at infants. Do not sing to him. Do not run from him. Do not remark upon his clothing or hair.

ANNE GARE'S RARE BOOK & EPHEMERA CATALOGUE #1395944-F

The Dither Family Cookbook

This fifty five page book of recipes is unusual not because of the recipes within, which consist mainly of standard New England fare such as Fried Mush, Red Flannel Hash, Johnny Cakes, and Oyster Stew, but due to the handwritten notations in the margins. The book was inherited by Priscilla Dither from her father Flood Dither, and it appears that over the course of the time it was in her care she underwent a severe psychological breakdown of unknown origin.

"Something in the steam," she scribbles next to a recipe for Portsmouth Fish Chowder. Under a Steak Tartare recipe she writes, "I feel but do not see them gather at my bedside at night." On an end page: "I would fair face a bear than old Will when he's in his cups."

William "Old Will" Dither was Priscilla's Great Great Grandfather on her father's side, and he expired on the very day of her birth.

The last seven pages have been stitched shut.

Stuffed with additional recipes clipped from newspapers, handwritten on plain paper, and carbon-copied from family archives.

Hand stitched, with some wear to edges. Substantial staining. One hundred fifty dollars.

MY MOTHER LUCILLE

My mother, according to several local townspeople, had a voracious sexual appetite, and would often be seen rubbing up against goats at the Whipotte farm, much to the dismay (or jealousy!) of Edwin Krunkle Whipotte, who regarded Mother with a heady mix of disgust, respect, and naked lust. Mother also seduced several young boys at the schoolhouse and had become rather a local legend. In those times, sexual dalliances between a woman and schoolchildren was not entirely frowned upon, and my mother was often extravagantly thanked by other local schoolteachers or parents, whom she would then bed.

This did not affect me negatively, for the other boys saw my mother as a kind of nurse or saint, and I was given a respite from the regular tannings my hide would receive at their cruel hands. Well, I was fine, I guess, but for the fact that the whole affair made me and my brother Earl join the rest of the town in disdaining and abusing my poor, ineffectual father. Clearly disturbed by my mother's frequent and brazen dalliances, Father would often lay on the floor next to the bed, having been pushed off by one drunken suitor or another (or a fair squadron of them), and sob while Mother thrashed and squirmed and wailed in ecstasy. Often times Earl and I would lie outside the bedroom door in the hall and see if we could shoot spitballs into Father's gaping mouth.

My brother and I were quite handsome, and townsfolk praised Mother for keeping her voracious hands off of our pale, scrawny bodies. But, unknown to nearly everyone, Mother beat me regularly, pushing my face into the toilet when I had done my business and taking me quite by surprise occasionally, when I would return home from school, by walloping me straight in the face with the latest Sears Roebuck catalog.

Yet it was she who got me interested in music: morose Druidic dirges and Polish songs of lament and/or rancor filled our house at night, often at top volume. Mother taught me the ins and outs of the lute, and occasionally soaped up the reeds from Father's old, neglected oboe and jammed them ceremoniously up my hindquarters. Since this was the only attention I received from mother save the beatings, I came to look forward to it and miss it if she'd fall asleep before completing the soaping.

Mother was eventually killed by one of her suitors and hanged upside down outside the tavern, where she was used as a sort of urinal/spittoon. Father had never had a drink before then, but since her hanging he made it a point to hit the tavern every morning and not leave 'til deep in the dark night. He never lost that haunted look, though, and, one night, having failed to set Earl on fire, he took his own life with a volatile mix of turpentine, motor oil, and peanuts, to which he was terribly allergic.

He is said to haunt the houses of only the unhappiest marriages. When a husband sits awake at night, terrified of the foul creature that cringes next to him, it is my father's shrieks that curdle the milk in its jug, my father's hoarse sobs that accompany the sound of dragging footsteps endlessly circling the filth-strewn attic.

This is WXXT, radio for the spiritually weary. Up next, the latest tune by Michael McDonald. And don't forget to join us at midnight for *Chants and Rants*, our latest field recordings of monks gone hopelessly and irretrievably mad. The time is 11:14 a.m. and you're listening to 87.5, WXXT, home of the Two-fer Tuesday.

Night Dog

On numberless midnights, swatting away the night dogs leaping at the hem of my coat, their teeth flashing like crescent moons, I went in for night work at the flagship office of Annelid Industries International in the profusely wooded easternmost environs of Leeds, Massachusetts. Numberless midnights with the moon spilling its milklight down the forested mountain, numberless midnights crossing the parking lot to the gentle music of the cricket song and the fabric whisper of my pant legs. I'd badge myself in a half-hour early, fingernail the security code into the keypad, follow the lights of the red EXIT signs to my desk, where I would wear the light from the computer screen like a mask—a mask composed of spreadsheets and schedules—until 3 a.m. Then I'd rise, stretch, head to the kitchen, release from the vending machine a squashed, frosted thing to eat, brew a pot of coffee to wash it down. Mug in hand, I'd walk to the pedestrian bridge to watch the cars passing under while the coffee spread its warm fingers through my system. Then back to spreadsheets and schedules, mail alerts and messages, until 5 a.m., slouching through the double doors with the other night shift slouchers.

On one of those midnights, during an early March warm spell, one of the night dogs, a wiry, cat-like thing with an elongated snout and teeth like Hokusai mountains, got a curved claw caught in my jacket pocket. It whipped its body back and forth as I knelt, knee joints popping, and grabbed with my right hand the dog's long ear, feeling its eye moving wildly beneath my palm. I tucked my thumb under the upper lip, closed my hand into a fist, and with my left hand wrested free the paw. Then with both hands I flung the beast into the reeds and rushed to the door. The other night dogs, bellies low to the ground, bared their teeth and inched at me, but none was foolhardy enough to lunge.

In the main hall, three offices from my own, I stopped to attend to a loosened shoelace, when I heard somewhere behind me the sound of a baby gasping and wailing. In the instant the sound registered, it was suddenly muffled, then cut off altogether. Leaving the lace hanging, I rose slowly, as silently as I could. I turned back, and peeked around the corner at the hall that led to the President's Office. The corridor was dark, shadowed, interrupted with rhombus-shaped sections of weak light from the windows, its terminus black as pitch. I inched down the hall and, when I reached the President's Office, I saw a rounded shadow spreading from under the door. My eyes began to adjust to the darkness, and the shadow revealed itself to be an expanding oblong patch of blood-soaked carpet. It glimmered in the half-light. Just before it reached the tip of my shoe, I turned and walked briskly back down the hall and around the corner, my breath popping from my lungs in little bursts.

I had learned quickly in my early days with Annelid Industries that intervening—even, perhaps especially, in the spirit of being a Samaritan—was not looked upon favorably by management. In May of my third year there I had happened to glance into a warren of cubicles and saw a man's legs jutting from one of the open walls. I hurried over to find a youngish man, slender, nose flattened against the carpet, arms and legs splayed. I knelt, patted him on the shoulder with the palm of my hand, gently turned his head to the side. He was breathing. I called 911 from the man's desk phone, told the operator to send the ambulance to the side door. When the EMTs arrived I opened the door and led them to the scene.

As the man was being lifted onto the stretcher, a coterie of frowning executives arrived, and one of them called the driver aside. They formed a tight circle, speaking in low voices, their faces tense and furrowed, while the EMTs loaded the man into the ambulance and, absent their driver, began to minister to him, talking him awake. A few moments later the driver, red-faced, was released from the convocation and called a brief but equally intense conference with his co-workers. Then two of the EMTs climbed into the ambulance and unloaded the stretcher, still bearing the stricken man. The driver and the one of the executives each grabbed a side rail and guided the stretcher through the double-doors that led to the executive offices and the auditorium hall.

About ten minutes later, the men brought back the tenantless stretcher, folded up the wheels, and deposited it back in the ambulance. The EMTs left without further ceremony. A few hours later I checked back at the man's cubicle and saw it had been emptied of everything but a computer monitor, wires dangling from its back. The next day I was called to Human Resources.

Wright Knowles, the HR manager, a prim, mirthless man whose unironed shirt collars stuck up like toast points, handed me a written warning; vague, but biting, the intimation was that matters of perceived emergency were to be dispatched only by approved personnel, a club to which I absolutely did not belong and, if I continued on my present course, a club to which I would *never* belong. He signed it, pushed it over to me so that I could do likewise. I had never in my life received so much as a talking to, and I remember feeling chastened.

Now, I hurried back to my desk. I could feel my heart drumming, in my shoulders I felt it, and at my pulse points. I sat, caught my breath, did my best to try to settle into my work. The building was always quiet, but that night it was unusually so. From time to time the fluorescent lights in the hall flickered and the image on my monitor contracted briefly, shot a few lines of static across its lower section, then recovered. The phone rang shrilly once, and not again. When the red voicemail indicator lit up, I grabbed the receiver, typed in my code. I could hear only the sound of wind and faraway voices, calling in urgent tones. I strained to make out what they were saying, but it was no use. I hung up, dug back into the night's tasks. I thought about the blood. I thought about that baby's choked-off cry, and I thought about that warning from HR.

When my shift was nearly done, I checked the company email. There was only one new message. It was from the CEO himself, Wren Black.

To: AII-Corporate; AII-RDSci; AII-LSci; AII-ESO; AII-XXT
From: Wren_Black@AII.eso
Subject: Changes for A.I.I.

Good men and women of A.I.I.,

The time has come. Watch your email over the next few days for an invitation to a spectacular company event. The last of its kind took place forty-five years ago, in a different world. Come celebrate the latest step in the ever-unfolding saga of Annelid Industries International. Refreshments will be served. Attendance is mandatory. We can't wait to see you there.

Together we will walk into the future.

For a reason I could not name, I was unnerved.

I put my finger on the mouse to close the mail window and an instant message popped up. The sender field was blank. The message was the address for the 24-hour Pan-Asian Buffet a quarter mile up the road. That was all.

The Asia-India-Ichiban Buffet was dimly lit and all but deserted. Red curtains and swirling neon representations of bowls and bottles adorned the rain-bubbled windows. The furious looking hostess, all in black, sickly slender but for the jutting protuberance of her pregnancy, was texting rapidly with both hands, her thumbs moving like the front legs of a fly, tears shining on her cheeks. In a red-cushioned booth by the sushi station, a young couple sat side-by-side, laughing in an unmistakably malicious manner, at what I could not tell. Across the room an old man in a fly-blown cardigan sat at a table by a window, alternating between looking glumly out at the grey boulevard and scraping noodles from his bowl with his finger and nudging them into his mouth.

I was just sitting down with my plate when a man slid in opposite me. Startled, I knocked over my water glass, and the man grabbed a pile of napkins and started to mop up. I grabbed his arm. He was bearded, slender, dressed in a light jacket and dark blue jeans.

"Wendell," he said. He sounded sad. "Let me look at you."

I let go his arm and winced. I don't like to be stared at. He said, "The email came today, didn't it, from Wren Black?"

"I'm afraid I don't know who you are."

"Wendell, we knew each other, a long time ago. I'm Byron Holeman. Look at me."

The name meant nothing to me. I stared at his face, but I couldn't reconcile his features. They were morphing, blurring, blending, eyes going square, then narrowing, their color changing from blue to brown to green and back. His mouth widened, pursed. His nose changed shape again and again as though animated with clay. My stomach clenched as though I was falling from a great height, and I fell back into the cushioned seat.

"That's all right. I guess it's not important, not now, anyway. The important thing now is this: the company event at A.I.I.—you don't want to be there for it. You don't want to be in Leeds. Wendell, you don't want to be in *Massachusetts*. Go to Maine. Go to New York. When it's all over…"

Who was this madman, I wondered, with a face that would not stay still, telling me I knew him, insisting I abandon my livelihood. "I… I need my job," I said, ashamed at my obsequious stammer.

Holeman put his hands in the air, palms out.

"Just listen to me for a few minutes, then I'll leave you to your meal."

I looked at my watch.

"Go ahead," I said.

"I worked there, at A.I.I., Wendell. In tech support. One day about four years ago I was going through old company footage, and I hacked my way into a password-protected file. I saw it, Wendell, the film of the 1969 meeting. I've never seen anything like it before. It was more of a ritual, a rite, than anything else. Wendell, I saw impossible things, terrible. Some of it… I'm still not sure it was real, but I don't think it could have been faked. But it's about to happen again. Annelid Industries International is old, far older than this country, older than you know. It started out as… as a *different* kind of concern. It was formed and founded by men with their hands in all sorts of forbidden things. They conjured up… Wendell, I hate to tell you, but I fear you're under their thrall… under *its* thrall. Most everyone there is, too."

And that was more than enough for me.

"I'm sorry. I really am. But I have no idea what you're saying to me. I think I'm going to leave."

"Let me ask you a question," he said. "Where do go when you leave work, Wendell?"

"I…" My mind conjured up blurred images of streets, houses, apartment buildings, high-rises, lawns, hedges, fences. They melded together into a chaos of glass, brick, wood, concrete, stone, and dirt. I could picture myself getting in my car, starting it, pulling the seatbelt across, driving out of the lot… and then? And then? Trying to focus made me dizzy, dropped a ball of nausea into my gut. I leaned over in the booth, grasped the edge of the table. "Why are you doing this to me?"

"You helped me out when we were boys," was his reply. He then pulled from his pocket a rolled up newspaper, spread it out on the table. "Read this," he said, pointing to the upper left corner.

"It's blank," I said.

He looked down at the paper, looked back at me, stricken. "It's…it *was*…the article about your disappearance."

I had come to A.I.I. in those faraway days when applicants desirous of employment typed up their resumes on 24-lb paper, carefully constructed an accompanying cover letter, tri-folded the two into a business envelope, and deposited it in a metal mailbox to be taken away by blue-suited workers in white trucks, submitted to an extensive and complex process of culling and sorting and coding, nestled in bins with hundreds of thousands of other envelopes, divided and dispatched, and finally delivered to the hands of Personnel managers who would slide them open with small knives, examine their contents, and determine whether the sender warranted a personal audience.

Mine, apparently, had done the trick. I was called in for a night interview.

The A.I.I. Leeds campus consisted of two stone buildings that stood across a forested road from one another, connected by a pedestrian bridge. Behind the peaks of Building A rose a tree-covered mountain, forbiddingly caliginous and dark as pitch, except toward the peak, where pale yellow lights shone here and there, adorning the high trees with a suspicion of sepia. Behind Building B sprawled a crumbling, weed-split concrete wall about 8 feet high, its eastern and western edges obscured by thorny brambles. Beyond the wall rose the silos and pylons and staircase-encircled towers of some manner of factory, all of it lit up stark and bright like a mockery of daylight.

I drove under the bridge, turned into the lot, gave my name to the man in the gatehouse, and parked my Corvair between two hulking Jeep Cherokees. The receptionist bade me sit in a small waiting room, and then, after an interval, she called my name. When she stood, I noted that she was pregnant, very far along, too. She led me to the room where my interviewers waited.

"Boy or girl?" I asked cheerfully.

She looked stricken and did not answer.

The conference room was sufficiently long to accommodate a long table with 18 chairs, a dry-erase board, a ceiling-mounted projector and screen, and nothing else. The hiring manager, grey-haired, slender, in vest and jacket, and the head of the recruitment division, a young woman, blonde, in a tasteful business suit, also, I noticed, pregnant, sat at one end, each with a copy of my resume. I sat at the opposite end, clutching my own copy next to a mug of rapidly cooling coffee. The questions were standard, and my answers generated nods of assent and impressed looks between the two. At the close of the interview, the hiring manager took me aside and asked me whether I would assent to a polygraph examination and a routine physical, to be scheduled within the next seven days. I agreed. Having worked almost exclusively in manufacturing, never before in a business office, I assumed these preliminaries to be standard. Four days later I drove back in a frothing downpour for the three-hour testing period.

The personality test was long and unexpectedly stressful to navigate. Some prompts were repeated several times throughout, each time with slightly varied wording. Some were invasive. Of them, I still remember these:

You often consider humankind and its destiny

You feel involved while watching soap operas

You often contemplate the complexity of life

You willingly involve yourself in matters which engage your sympathies

For each I had to select agree, somewhat agree, neither agree nor disagree, somewhat disagree, or disagree. The desired answers were not in every case easy to determine, but I did the best I could.

One week and one day later I had a job.

On my first day, I was supplied with several binders of lined notebook paper. Each page contained handwritten names, many nearly illegible, perhaps a phone number, a partial address. My task was to locate complete contact information and enter all of the data into a spreadsheet of my own design. These bits of information, I was told, represented Contractors. Their disciplines remained a mystery. Each could have one of 28 codes assigned to him or her, codes that upper level managers would enter into my spreadsheet, and codes were also assigned to each of the company's laboratory technicians, whose names I was not allowed to know.

I was to use the codes to match contractors to technicians and arrange meetings and set intermittent work schedules. I arranged hotel rooms, made dinner reservations, provided company as necessary—that is, if persuasion were needed or goodwill necessary to garner—based upon the contractor's sexual preferences, no matter how odd or verboten, which were also noted in the spreadsheet.

As the main liaison and contact, I was also responsible for transporting Contractors from reception to the Laboratories. It worked like this: The red bulb on my desk console would flash three times. I would tap the pound sign twice to indicate I'd received the message, lock the computer, rise, and walk to Reception. The Contractor would be standing—there were no seats—perhaps studying the painting of lightning-lit caves that spanned the wall, perhaps looking out the window. His features would be obscured by a black hood that covered his head, obscuring his features but allowing him sufficient sight to navigate. I would walk the Contractor through the main hall, up the stairs, and to the pedestrian bridge. On the bridge would be a Laboratory Technician, features obscured in the same fashion. He would favor me with a slight nod, take custody of the

Contractor and lead him through the door into Building B, where office staff were not permitted, just as Lab workers were denied access to the corporate offices of Building A. I would return to my desk and mark the Contractor's arrival in the database.

This was my work. I did this for years. It was all I knew.

Holeman paid my bill and we left the buffet.

Over dinner he had told me about the contents of the article: A man, Wendell LaPorte, had left his house to go to the market, and did not return. His wife Laura filed a missing persons report. A lengthy interview with detectives indicated nothing about the family life that might have precipitated a sudden departure. He could not have simply fled, the wife insisted. He loved her, adored their son. He was in all outward appearance content. She would spend every resource she had to find her husband. She was certain something terrible must have befallen him. The police were keeping the investigation open, but one might easily infer from the article, Holeman told me, that it was not going to be aggressively pursued. After all, no one truly knows what is in a man's heart.

Holeman told me about a follow-up article published a few months later. The man's credit cards had not been used since his disappearance. His one living parent, his father, had received no contact from him, nor had his friends.

He was gone.

We stood under the awning in the rain. He took out his wallet, pulled from it a business card. He handed it to me. It read:

Byron Holeman
Programmer
Deprogrammer

It had a phone number, an email address, and a street address in Stamford, Connecticut.

"Get in your car," he said, "Head south on 91. When you get to… let's say New Haven, call the number on the card. My secretary will provide you with an address. Go there and get yourself settled. Once I'm finished with my business in Leeds, I'll join you and we'll talk about getting you back to your family."

A family, I thought. *A family I… don't remember.* I promised him. And then I got in my car and drove straight to A.I.I. I was running late. I prefer to be early for work.

I parked my Corvair as I had done on a million midnights, innumerable midnights, infinitesimal midnights. The night dogs were unusually aggressive. I shouted at them, kicked them away, smacked at them with my hands. They whined. They yowled. When I got to the double doors, I turned to find them hunching, their tails curled up under their legs. They looked miserable, like they were witnessing some tragedy and were helpless to prevent it. In some strange way, I felt sorry for them.

Going back to my desk, I took the route that led me through the East Hall. Lining the corridor in that hall is a gallery of framed portraits of the CEOs over the years. The first is from the late 1800s. A silver-tinted daguerreotype, copper-spotted at its corners, it depicts a steely-eyed, white haired man, broad of face, with runaway brows and a tight frown. On down the line, there are gaunt faces, fat faces, beards, waxed mustaches. Some of the men—all men, all white to the point of pastiness—are grinning blankly, others stern and serious. Apart from skin color, there is a unifying feature in all of the portraits. Something, maybe, about their eyes—not their shape or their color, but the fierce imperative implied in their stares. Walking down the hall is something akin to time travel, but with an audience, all the eyes following you, like you're in an office-themed variety of some malignant spook house.

I logged into my computer and looked at my email. There was one new message. It was addressed to me only, and the "From:" line was blank. The email consisted of a URL ending in a long string of numbers and letters and, under that, the number 77. I moved the cursor to the link, watched the arrow morph into a pointing white-gloved hand. I clicked.

Four video feeds appeared on the screen: the reception desk, empty; the main hallway, down which two security guards walked in apparent silence, looking straight ahead; the mostly empty parking lot; and the long, sky-lit atrium. I became unaccountably afraid that something awful, something grotesque and misshapen, might enter one of the frames. Dismissing that unwelcome thought, I noted that each video feed had a number at its bottom left, alongside a digital counter. I clicked the arrow at the bottom of the screen until I reached the 77th feed.

The display was crisp but for the occasional eruption of pixilation. It showed a well-appointed office, two walls filled top to bottom with glass-fronted bookshelves, the third a massive window that looked out to the wall of trees. Before the window sat a desk, massive, expansive, gilded, with grey-veined black marble panels on the side and a gold-tooled black leather surface that reflected the soft light from the green-shaded lamp atop it. The desk was clear save a few scattered papers and a feathered pen and inkwell. Then a man walked in under the apparent location of the camera. From just the back of his head and his assured walk, I knew him to be Wren Black. He pulled back the chair, sat in it, and looked up at the camera, through it, straight into my eyes. I flinched and reached to close the browser, then stopped.

Wren Black leaned back in his chair. I could see only the man's chin, above it the peak of his nose. The screen went red at the center of his shirt like a bright bulb under velvet. A flaw in the camera. No. His hands flew up and his long fingers pulled apart the shirt. I reared back. On Wren Black's chest were two long, horizontal slashes, red and swollen. They opened to reveal large eyes, blood vessels burst in each one, splotches of red, pupils dilated. They blinked. Tears streaked down the man's rib cage, and then the skin of his face went taut. His lips spread apart in a grimace, revealing clenched teeth. One of the teeth sprung out like a bullet, flying at the camera, hitting the lens, causing a curved crack to appear on the screen. Wren Black's face went red, darker, purple. His neck flexed, spasmed, and then his head began to crumple. The skin of his face pinched inward and tore at the hairline, revealing a red expanse of muscle and skull. The chin and jaw were consumed by the neck, which was greedily chewing like an upturned mouth. A tongue, large and pink, lashed up over the nose, and the skin tore again at the forehead and the whole of his face was slurped down, leaving a bare skull whose eyes were now dull and lifeless. The skull bubbled as fissures formed all over its surface and it crumpled like sodden plaster. The now-headless Wren Black rose from behind his desk and walked toward the camera. The horrible eyes in his torso looked at me. Right at me. I closed the browser, kicked back my chair, and ran out into the hall.

I *intended* to turn right and run. My legs disobeyed me. They slowed, turned left. Ahead of me at an intersection, a throng of workers shuffled east. *Everyone is here*, I thought, *the whole company is here*. I twisted my torso from side to side, trying to turn, but it was no use. I joined them as they moved along the bridge. The doors to the forbidden laboratories swept open, the crowd poured through like milk.

The laboratories! I saw such things as I moved with the crowd!

Through one doorway I saw men shining penlights at a winged leech the size of a baseball glove buzzing madly about the brightly lit interior of a glass enclosure. Its wings were a translucent blur. Through another I saw a great conveyor belt teeming with all manner of teeth. Workers in surgical masks reached in from time to time, pulled out a tooth, threw it into a wheeled cart with canvas walls. Down a long hall to my left I saw a goat, upright, limping along on hind legs, using a cane with a brass human head to steady itself. I moved with the crowd, marveling at it all, into the auditorium.

The chairs were arranged in 12 curved rows each a half step up from the one below it, all facing a great marble rostrum that looked like it wouldn't be out of place in some grand cemetery. On either side of the rostrum stood three oak podiums. Behind those depended a massive screen, silver in color, which spanned the whole of the wall. From the high ceiling hung a lighting rig worthy of some grand concert hall, spotlights at the front facing this way and that, like snipers whose aim covered the whole of the stage. Unseen hands guided me to a chair near the back.

I sat, gripping the sides of my chair, my fingers, the only part of me I could control, tapping out arrhythmic beats of distress on its undersides. My colleagues and co-workers, half of them hooded, filtered into the room, murmuring. Then the room filled with a long, lowing sound, like that of a euphonium. The room rumbled. My chair shook, my heart jostled madly in its cage, my brain rumbled in its quarters. The lights dimmed and the conversation hushed, then went silent.

The large screen depicted a crowded forest of thin trees, their branches bare and sagging. The camera swept across them, a cut, and the camera repeated its journey, faster and faster this repeated, creating a strobe effect. It was illusion, maybe, that in the sweep of the camera, the trees seemed to bend at previously undetectable joints along their scratched surfaces, bend and bow and dance. Somewhere in the blur of bending and bowing and dancing, shapes formed in the trees, hulking, pulsing, many-limbed. Toothless maws opened and closed on their rippling surfaces. The trees grew bubbling pustules, chancres, buboes. They dribbled pus and blood and gurgled lava.

Wren Black, the CEO of Annelid Industries International, strode through the room, down the center aisle, his head gone, a fire guttering at his neck, the flames red, purple, green. A plume of black smoke trailed behind him. His skin glowed red. The great eyes on his chest swept the room. Heads turned to mark his passage, and the crowd's murmurs coalesced into a rhythmic hum.

He climbed the podium, stood before the crowd. His voice came in from the speakers around the room, introduced by a shriek of feedback.

When I came to this company and gave it its name, Annelid Industries International, the voice said, *I felt like an interloper. In a sense, the company had existed for years, but without a home, without a name, without a singular vision. But all of its disparate divisions were profitable. Profitable and thriving. Their interests in the life sciences, in education, in entertainment, and in the esoteric, were interlocked like the interior of some great and vast and new machine, a machine that pulled in consumers and wrung from them gold. They summoned me to give them their name and to expand their power to this world and worlds beyond.*

I vowed to honor their wishes. I expanded the company. I sought out powerful people, and I bought them, at the expense of profit, at the expense, I know, of profit-sharing checks. There were some who seethed about that. But those people are gone. The rest of you can laugh at them, at the naysayers, the same way that we laugh at a church that tries to thwart and stifle us, at the malignancy of a press that disseminates vituperative lies like the seeds of poison trees.

We grew. We took footholds in Germany. In Russia. In London. In Prague. And last month construction began on a Mideast headquarters in Qatar that will, when it is complete, rival the great palaces, the great temples of the world.

Wren Black stepped down from the podium, a wisp of smoke still trailing him as he began to walk up and down the aisles, his voice still emanating from the speakers.

A corporation is a man with many arms. Its reach may extend to a multitude of arenas: education, commerce, communication, biology, macro and micro, even into affairs of faith and of worship, of belief itself. But the essence of a corporation lies not in those arms, not in their reach, not in the grasp of the hands at their terminus. The essence lies in the man at the center. It is his vision that directs those hands, sends the nerve impulse down the arm, having the wherewithal to say grasp more firmly, *having the wisdom to know when to say* let go.

Consistency is the cornerstone of Annelid Industries. In those great glorious days when A.I.I. became a force in the world, I shone a light before me, a light that beamed from my immortal heart. That light revealed in the seemingly impassible tangles of the world a path. And you are the workers who clear that path, who cut and sweep aside the weeds, who push aside those who might hinder our progress. If not for you, that path might be overtaken by the branches, woven and barbed, that threaten even today to diminish and extinguish that light.

It is time now that this body moves to the side of that path, lays down in the thicket, and passes from this life. I pledge to you that in my new incarnation I will continue to push this company into unheard of realms. My eyes will look out from a new face, and from its mouth will come forth my voice, the voice spoken through many mouths over many years. A corporation is a man with many arms, with many faces, but with one man at its center. It has been my life's work to honor that tradition, to speak as one voice through many mouths. My time is past, but I am again and always part of the future. May it be so for all of you, when your time does come. Thank you for your true hearts, for your courage, and for your consistency.

A shriek tore through the room. I thought at first it was some sort of shrill cheer. The room exploded in applause. Down the aisle, two security guards were dragging a man. As he was brought by me, he raised his face to the ceiling. Slender, bearded—it was *Holeman*, his features no longer shifting, but distorted by terror. He was clawing at the guards' sleeves, crying. *I have three daughters*, he said, *I have three little girls.* They dragged him before Black and pushed him to the ground. He lurched forward and grabbed the hem of Black's coat in both hands. The crowd gasped. Black pulled from his jacket a large serrated knife. He fell to one knee and jammed the knife into the side of Holeman's throat. A great glut of blood shot out, spattering the front row. They wiped the blood from their eyes. Holeman was making a terrible sound, a ragged, gurgling wheeze. Then Black began to saw.

Holeman's body sank to the carpet, his hands clutching at air. I saw his wedding ring. I saw the hangnail on his index finger. I saw the birthmark at the base of his thumb. Black grasped in his fist a clump of Holeman's hair, raised the sawed off head to the crowd. I had never before seen a dead man's face. It was white, slack, still. The mouth hung open. Wren Black placed the head on his shoulders, and the torn, mottled skin spat forth a cloud of pink smoke. There was a sound like bubbling. Holeman's eyes popped out like jelly and fell in globs on his cheeks, replaced by eyes I knew, eyes I recognized—the eyes of all the portraits of the CEOs through the years: blazing, pitiless, yet dead.

Look upon me, said Wren Black.

We look upon you with devotion as you favor us with your eyes, the crowd murmured. Two seats to my left a woman in a black dress pushed her way to the aisle, fell to her knees, and began tearing at her eyelids, ripping them completely from her face, flinging them to the carpet. A man in the row in front of me began to do the same.

Favor us with your eyes, the crowd chanted.

Look upon me, commanded Wren Black.

Favor us.

Look upon me.

The image of the trees on the screen fizzled, went to white noise. The static seethed, then revealed the blurred and pixilated image of a family. Before a green, bucolic backdrop a kind-eyed brunette woman in a green blouse smiled serenely. Her left hand was on the shoulder of a small towheaded boy in front of her, in a sweater vest, with gapped teeth, an embarrassed smile. Next to the woman, hand on the boy's other shoulder… was *me*. I had *hair*, too, more brown than grey, and a healthy middle-aged weight that obscured my cheek bones. Coldness shot through my insides, from my stomach to my joints to my extremities, like an internal jet of water meant to rouse me from a faint. I felt the profound need to find the woman, to protect her and be protected by her. And the boy—I wanted to gather him into my arms to shield him from danger. Something loosened its hold on me. I struggled to my feet. I may have been calling out, calling names I now cannot recall. People began to turn to look at me. Wren Black turned his horrible new head in my direction, glaring. I turned and bolted from the room as fast as I could go.

A corridor where there couldn't possibly be a corridor, angling off of the pedestrian bridge. Looking out the windows from the bridge, you see black on black through a prism of kaleidoscopic black, cars floating like spotlight-eyed undersea creatures along the rain-drowned road beneath, but then, walking a few feet further, there it is, unmistakable, a lit corridor leading off into the night. I ran past it to the door to the corporate offices, flashed my badge, two quick beeps and the red light blinked. They'd shut off my access. No choice, back the way I came was an army. I fled onto the impossible bridge. It was harshly lit, with a black linoleum floor and walls of large brick, painted over bright and brand-new white. Recessed lighting in the ceiling shot down in glinting cones, drawing pale circles on the floor. Ahead, the hall turned to the right, and when I turned the corner I found myself on a wet road, impenetrable tangles of bushes on either side. My feet skidded, and I landed hard on my back and slid. I got to my feet. Ahead of me, maybe less than a quarter mile away, I saw the lights of the A.I.I. Campus, of the bridge between the buildings. I scrambled to my feet, turned and ran. The faint ends of red searchlights wheeled in the sky like devils. The trees above me, leaning in, seemed to be placed in patterns, cloned, and re-cloned, stroboscopic, like a cartoon with repeating backdrops. Then I looked down, saw a cluster of eyes moving toward me, and stopped. I put my hands on my knees, stared back. The moonlight reflected off of those eyes, dozens of them, giving them the appearance of small green tunnels with echoing, unknown depths. White teeth glinted below each pair of eyes, emerging like the tips of knives stabbing out from the darkness. The night dogs loped into view, blocking the road before me. I could hear their eager breaths, almost smell the foul ichor puffing out like smoke from their gaping jaws. But then they turned, all but one, and faced away from me. The one night dog jutted his head in my direction, then turned and pointed his nose down the road, and looked back at me. The gesture was unmistakable.

Follow, it said.

The dogs began to run and I began to follow, but then I glanced up the mountain and froze. The yellow lights that ringed the mountaintop were blinking, blinking and pulsing, growing larger and shrinking back, as trying to break free of their moorings. Great cracks like rifle fire echoed down the mountain, and the lights *did* break free, whatever massive beings that bore them wrenching themselves from the earth, black shadows peeling away from blacker shadows. Trees buckled as they began to descend. I looked back at the road. The lead dog again beckoned, the others began to trot, and then to run, and I fell in among them and ran.

A half-mile or so down the road I had to stop to regain my breath. I looked up and ahead of me I saw the dogs skid, scramble and stop. A grey door hovered in the middle of the road, flickering, contracting, glowing—willing itself into being. The dogs growled at the apparition. I kept running, right at the door, then jogged quickly to my right to bypass it. The door followed, and opened, revealing a blue tiled room—one of A.I.I.'s lavatories. Wren Black stepped into view, grabbed me by my collar, and flung me into the room, slamming the door even as the night dogs hurled their bodies against it.

Wren pushed at my chest until I was backed up against the sink counter. Those blazing eyes glared from that dead but pinkening face. They glared… and then they softened. Wren Black released my collar, wiped his hands on his suitcoat.

"Wendell," he said. "I have a job for you, a job working closely with me, a job very important to the advancement of the company—we will provide you lab access, access, in fact, to the whole campus. This will, of course, involve a promotion and quite a substantial pay raise. You'll be working directly with me, and with the top echelons of our division."

Approved personnel.

Into my vision, blocking out everything, blocking out Wren Black, pushing away the blue tiles and the grey door, into my vision came the woman, her face, her hand resting gently on the shoulder of a boy, a man at her side, grinning blankly, a smile for the camera, a neutral smile. Was that man happy? Was he strong? Did he work among the top echelon? Was he *approved personnel*? I did not know. Those people were strangers to me. They might as well have been the picture that came with the frame, the one whose empty beaming faces you crumple and toss into the trash.

Look upon me.

The tiles began ungluing themselves from the wall and the floor, rising skyward, the roof tearing away to facilitate their passage. All around me, all around Wren Black they rose as he grinned at me, Holeman's teeth gleaming in front of a swirling serpent's tongue. The ceiling rose into the sky, a white rectangle spinning into the black night, just a speck, and then gone. I felt rain on my upturned face. I tasted it with my tongue. And then I too rose with the tiles, following them up, the blue-black night flaking and falling away around me, revealing in stipples a hint of the blinding-white infinity beyond it.

On numberless midnights with the moon spilling its milklight down the forested mountain, numberless midnights crossing the parking lot to the gentle music of the cricket song and the fabric whisper of my pant legs, a million midnights, innumerable midnights, infinitesimal midnights, I go in for night work at the flagship office of Annelid Industries International in the profusely wooded easternmost environs of Leeds, Massachusetts.

REUNITED

I sat in the conference room with my supervisor across from me. On the particle-board table in front of him sat his open leather-bound notebook, its forked tassel hanging out like the tongue of a serpent. From where I sat I could just make out his fussy, constipated handwriting. He had sandy blonde hair, plastered to his forehead. His mouth was small, lipless, like a paper cut.

"Look," he said, exasperation in his voice, or, rather, condescension masquerading as exasperation. "You and I are going to meet again in a month's time. Between now and"—he flipped to the front of his notebook to look at the calendar insert—"November 28, a… a Monday, you are going to have to show me that you are willing to do the work this position requires of you."

I snatched up his notebook.

"I'm going to tell you right now," I said, "because why waste a month? I am willing to do the work. But not for you."

He stared at me. He managed to maintain a smug façade. That irked me.

"You're going to want to give that back to me," he said.

"I just read the news about this study they did, new study, about work. Says a boss, a bad boss… an *uncivil* boss… can not only spoil a man's ability to do his job, but can ruin his health. Mess with his sleep.

Fuck up his heart. It can literally kill a man. You think this job is worth that to me? I've waited out bad bosses before. They come and they go. But they like you. I can tell. You're going to be here a while. Me? I'm not."

"Stellan," he said, his voice softening, becoming almost paternal. "You're going to destroy yourself long before I could ever destroy you." He lurched forward and tried to grab his notebook from me. I yanked it back and stood up, kicking back my chair. I felt like I was 15 years old, cocksure, burning to tussle. I leaned forward, catching his eyes with mine.

"I'm going to kill your daughter." I said it in a voice barely above a whisper.

He leaned forward.

"What?"

"You and Jo did have a daughter, right? She's what, four months old now? Sweet and loving? Her name is Madison, yeah? Cute. Kind of typical for the time, though. A million Madisons. This one loves her dada? Daddy's girl?

"I'm going to get her, William. I'm going to make it my life's mission. And it's going to be ugly. Poor thing won't know what's happening to her. She'll wonder where her daddy is. I mean, you're supposed to be the protector. Oh, William, it's going to be slow, agonizing. I'm talking weeks, buddy. *Weeks.*

"First, I'm going to chew off her ears."

He started to come around the table at me, and I pushed my chair at him and left.

I told myself I didn't know where that came from, but I did know. It was pure Vernon Golden. Corner him? Threaten his throne? That's when Vernon's true ugliness would come out.

The difference was that Vernon might follow through.

I spent the afternoon at Ripp's, getting plastered, and I drove home. Proving William right, in a way, I guess, that thing about destroying myself. I didn't think of that at the time, though. I still don't remember the ride.

When I got home, Vernon Golden was standing on my front porch.

But for the eyes, the man was unrecognizable. The weight was gone, for one, and his hair was a beautiful silver, white at the ears, slicked back neatly. The frames of his glasses were black Browline, stylish and clean. A trim white mustache topped his now colorless, thin lips. He had dressed in a black suit without as much as a speck of lint evident. The coat was draped over one arm, making him look like some kind of deranged waiter. Instead of his whatever-and-white stripes, he wore a grey shirt with no collar, ironed and neat, buttoned to the neck. He wore suspenders, as he always had, but they were slender and black. On his feet were steel-tipped pointed shoes. He smiled and I saw he'd had his teeth capped. He still had no chin, but he looked far more human than he does in those videos. He had color in his cheeks and an almost-tan. I might even dare say he was approaching handsome. He held out a hand to shake mine, and I took it. His nails were long, but clean, his skin dry and warm. He pumped my hand up and down.

"What the hell has become of us?" he said.

"Unfit to be seen in public," I said.

He grimaced, wrinkles crowding his face. "I mean, absolutely disgusting."

"Walking cadavers. It's… it's *unnatural*."

We stood there a while, grinning at each other like fools.

And as I grinned, a voice deep inside me called out:

Remember, it said. *Remember who this man is. Remember the money he took from his followers, and the innocence with which he stuffed his fat pockets. Don't forget the dark places he led his hapless flock. He claimed to be God, or a messenger of God, come to cleanse mankind of sin. And after divesting these people of their families and their friends, after isolating them, he led them, these wandering, needy people, into a dark, dark wood, clothed them in his* own *sin, brought them to the brink of what human beings should and could endure, and instead of cleansing them afterward, he told them in a fiery final sermon that* they *had sinned against* him, *and that he was here to bring the world to a deserved end… to swaddle it in fire and pull human beings from its burnt dermis like so many deer ticks. And only then did he vanish. Like a wraith. He left in his path a tattered string of human wreckage and damaged lives.*

And yet, as he stood before me, his eyes twinkling, gazing at me warmly, protectively, I felt safe.

"My boy," he said.

His voice sounded different from what I remembered, different from the YouTube clips, different even from how it sounded on the phone. It was cigarette-seared and jagged, but softened, the voice of a late night jazz DJ. It was the kind of voice you wanted to hear more of, a voice that lent eloquence even where the content might lack it.

"Vernon," I said. "What is it you need me to do?"

The humor fled his face.

"Pack a bag," he said. "I have heard the voice of the Devil himself coming from the radio speakers"—he pointed an angled thumbnail to his black Hyundai—"as I drove through Leeds, Massachusetts. We have to find him and kill him. It's my repentance and your cure."

"My cure for what?"

Again, that smile, those eyes.

"I intend to inspect your baggage," he said. "And there is to be no alcohol." His mouth widened. His canine teeth had been filed into points. "None."

SUCCUBUS

When the dark clouds lie over the valley, appearing to be held aloft only by the tops of the mountains, sometimes I feel like a child in a fort, where I can do my foul and mortal deeds hidden from the eyes of God.

But I like the sun almost as well. When men drag the lake and pull a bloated body into the light. When a knife opens up skin and reveals to the stark sun all the glistening purple secrets of man's insides. When the trunk of an abandoned car is wrenched open like a blue-black eyelid.

What I hate is night. I met Martha at night. I met Martha at night in New York City.

I woke as she was wrenching herself all herky jerky upon me in my very bed. Her ass was like two taut fists, her breasts like the third joints of your pinky fingers. Her breath was coffee, canchres, and cabbage. My body buckled in confusion and revulsion. As I reached climax she punched me square in the eye-sockets with two sharp sets of knuckles. After, as I curled myself into a clenched comma and wept, she sang foul songs about my mother, her fingers moving over the guitar strings like segmented snakes.

She was expert with a bowie knife and had a voice like blood poured over broken glass.

I loved her but she told me from the beginning she belonged to legions of lost men. I stayed true to her though she cuckolded me a thousand times over, floating sickly and spindly over bald men, muscular men, car mechanics, athletes, murderers, pimps, and queers, stealing their souls and throwing them away over musty trinkets in bowery alleys and flophouses. She slit their tongues like snake's tongues. She tattooed them with black blossoms of bruises. She destroyed all their love and sucked up the ashes, her mouth a gaping oval rictus ringed with bursting blisters.

I was but one. I was a lesser one. Maybe I was a mistake: I was never lost. I knew my destiny as I winked into the womb.

Whenever I murder a woman, I think of Martha and her black shark's eyes. I think of the shiny scabbards she wore as shoes. I think of her pointed nose tracing my ribs. I think of her long nails sinking into my temples and her sharp, slick tongue probing my ear.

I have been asked to offer advice to my listeners. I say only this. Never sleep on your back. Never look too sharply into the darkness over your bed. Always keep an eye on your door and an eye on your curtains. Block your ears with cotton.

You are listening to WXXT, the chuckle in the churchyard on a cloudless midnight.

ANNE GARE'S RARE BOOK & EPHEMERA CATALOGUE #823343-Q

Violent Rigor by Phillip Rippingcoat

A most curious volume, Violent Rigor is a list of rules for killing, but not only for killing. In numbered lists and sub-lists and sub-sub lists accompanied by charts and graphs and elaborated upon in exhaustive footnotes and endnotes, Rippingcoat (surely a nom de plume) lays out a mad rulebook for teasing, torture, mockery, murder, desecration, display, and evading the cold hand of authority. The prose is bloodless and antiseptic, void of passion or enthusiasm. It is workmanlike. What makes this book stand out, however, are the illustrations. They contain all the passion missing from the text, but they are amateurish, the work of someone impish, infantile, or severely unhinged. It is as though he held the pencil in the fist of his unfavored hand, imbibed a quantity of rum, slammed his head into a brick wall, and then began to scribble.

Leatherbound. One hundred fifty dollars.

UNCLE RED READS TO-DAY'S NEWS (2)

Wednesday's storm was a howler, reported Williford Frickey of Round Hill Road. It snuck around the corners of his house like a burglar seeking a vulnerability, finally finding its way under the side door, up the staircase, and under the skirts of his beloved wife Eunice, causing her to shudder and shriek and finally to utter a litany of foul language and harangues and threats against her aghast husband. Finally she revealed her knowledge of Williford's most private of secrets, a secret, Williford claimed, that she would have had no earthly way of knowing. This, insists Williford, is why he did the Wicked Thing. As always, the matter will surely be resolved in the courts, and Williford will swing on the end of a rope for his unseemly and unspeakable crimes against her person.

Griffon Raker, local purveyor of fine furnishings, was found drowned in his bathroom sink on Saturday evening last. There was naught but the merest trickle of water, yet Mr. Raker was bloated to such a degree that he was nearly unrecognizable, much to the despair of his three daughters, and wedged rather cruelly under the faucet of the shallow tub of the sink. Removing him was the work of the better part of a day, and grim work indeed, according to local police. One might hear the lamentations of the Raker daughters all about town, for they are known to be most demonstrative in their mourning.

A great bird swept down upon the mastiff owned by Lucille White and made away with the friendly beast, up into the sky, unheeding of the wounds it suffered at the hands of Mrs. White, who fired her pistol empty in order to try to save her beloved Rufus. The dog was found in an unsalvageable state, presumably released from a great height over the main thoroughfare of the city. Residents of the city claim to have seen the great bird reeling and crying out in anguish atop the tower of the Edwards Church, its talons causing great damage to the structure and its droppings staining and eroding the bricks of the edifice and the walks below.

THE MEN

A group of men in moldering topcoats, deep crags in their faces, crags out of which curl tendrils of grey dust. Impossibly vibrant blue eyes at the bottom of tessellated wells of skin. One of the men, tall and slightly bowlegged, runs a thin, long-nailed fingertip from eye to jaw, extracting a string of black grime. He flicks it dismissively into the snow, where it wriggles a few yards and then burrows under.

They are old and bent and they seem frail, these men, surely harmless, but they exude menace in almost palpable waves. They walk and leaves dive from trees, trash swirls in furious eddies, pedestrians lose their footing on flat walks.

One grey November day I saw them in front of the abandoned theater. The previous July they stood in a circle in the midst of a vast tangle of brambles behind Waxman Elementary. Not long before that I saw them in the waist-high brown waters of the brook behind the skeleton of the textile mill.

I sometimes dream that I open my front door to find them in a line on my covered porch. Their eyes burn. They turn to dust, collapse, their eyes separating into sparks, and are pulled up in clouds into the ceiling fan. I, too, dissolve and join them. The ceiling fan mixes us together and sends us wafting in clouds over the town. Our rain will be searing poison and will wash away everything good and pure.

Leedsian Graffiti

And now, rockin' your day away as the sun slowly sinks is Gene Daniels with "A Hundred Pounds of Clay."

Sally tugged at the neck of her seafoam green Sloppy Joe sweater, took a pursed-lips sip from her malted, leaving mottled red kissy lips on the straw, her brown hair bouncing as she tapped her fingertips on the steering wheel. Johnny slid in next to her with a tray bearing two hamburgers tucked into folded wax wraps. The door shut with a ca-chunk.

"What gives, kid?" he said. "*I'm* driving."

She turned up the radio, staring at him, affecting the smoky, dim-bulb stare of the magazine models, poking his shoulder with her fingernail along to the beat. He stared at her, admiring the shape of her jaw as he ran his hands over his pompadour, kept extra-long so as to cover the shameful bald spot he'd inherited from the male Grogans down through the decades.

We've just been boppin' to A Hundred Pounds of Clay, ten decades of dismay, millennia of decay, let's lose that negligee, this is Big Boppin' Clodhopper Clem, spinning the hits, squeezing the zits, bruising the tits, bring on the worms, bring on the nits, the cadavers, palaver, the skin unzips, the skin sloughs off along with the slip…

Sally grabbed at Johnny's cheeks, hooking her thumbs into his mouth and pulling up hard. Flesh tore free from muscle with a terrible sound, and a waitress watching from the snack window screamed as the worms poured from the young man's mouth and began to fill the convertible fast as floodwater. Even as the young woman pulled the mask of the young man's skin off of his skull and there was a great rumbling in the distance and from up on Tremens Terrace came… what was it? A landslide? A flood? No… heads, severed, streaming blood and torn flesh from the necks, thousands upon thousands rolling down the road, some fresh, some cobweb-strewn skulls from ancient eras, all tumbling, weeping, shrieking, thundering, under a bruised and battered sky, the clouds in tatters, bouncing down the sidewalk, shoring up against the fire hydrants and streetlights and the parked cars, in their wake a trail of brains and saliva and blood, staining red all of Leeds.

Now we've got the haunting voice of Roy Orbison, that sweet, sweet poison to pour into your ears, oh teens of Leeds, oh Leedsian teens, Running Scared, run, kids, run. You're listening to WXXT, the Screaming Brain in the Bloody Basin of the Pioneer Valley.

THE GATHERING IN THE DEEP WOOD (CONCLUSION)

The wind whipped the trees without mercy, without respite. The lights that had lit my way into the wood appeared to have been extinguished, but the forest was bright with the light of the supermoon, a giant cataract-clouded eye peering over the wind-lashed, cringing treetops.

At my right stretched a long line of tables draped in white. Red plastic cups and scattered pizza boxes, open like gaping mouths, empty, grease-stained, sporting asterisks of cheese on their corrugated tongues. I used my fingertips to scrape a line of cheese off and chewed on it. It was good, salty, and adequately seasoned. I saw a cup with an inch of amber beer and a cigarette butt within. I pinched out the butt and downed the beer. It was warm and free of carbonation, more spittle than anything else. I slurped it down to the soundtrack of wood cracking and splitting. I turned my face to the tree-line.

A tree in front of me leaned forward as though about to fall. I cringed and jumped back, and then two of its upper branches reached down, twigged fingers tearing at its bark, ripping it in a jagged horizontal line. It lowered its bark like a pair of pleated pants, then lifted the upper section like a shirt. The bared wood was fleshy, goose-pimpled, flushed pink. Sections were dotted with a proliferation of brown nipples. Swollen, purple genitalia pulsed and glistened at its many crotches. The other trees followed suit; the tearing and discarding of bark deafening. I clamped my hands over my ears. The trees set upon each other, shrieking and creaking as the rain came, slicking their bodies and wrenching from them the shrieks of wet wood drawn hard against wet wood.

I turned to run, only to face a massive oak right in front of me. It bore a huge knot, a navel tied by a mad midwife. It began to pulse. Then it burst, showering the ground in front of it with a pile of rusted transistor radios. They all clicked on at once, spilling a torrent of green light onto the fallen leaves. Jaunty '20s piano music filled the forest, backed by the moans of men and a sound like someone retching noisily into an echoey bucket.

Through the trees, hands tracing designs in the air, pranced a slender troupe of female ballet dancers, clad only in purple thongs and clinging white tops, their tiptoes leaving tiny turrets in the ground. Each had her hair tied back, pony-tailed, jaw-line carved and taut, lipstick a dark, deep, alluring red. I tore at my shirt and flung it to the ground and danced toward them, my fat arms beckoning, for perhaps the first time in my life utterly unselfconscious, unaware of my hanging midsection, my white, sunken chest, the rueful patch of hair at its center. They were around me in a second; their fingers trailing lightly over my chest. I looked down, grinning madly, but saw with horror that what I had at first taken for purple thongs were in fact bulbous leeches—swollen, pulsing, slurping leeches. From behind the women followed a group of dancing men, wiry and muscular, naked, stepping high-kneed through the creaking orgy of trees, whose little genital nests bounced gelatinously. The men held above their heads the rubber-gripped handles of huge metal apparatuses. Blades whirred, bisecting leaves as they fell from the lustful trees. They fell upon me, the men and the women, and I screamed until I had no more to scream.

The next morning, damp and drippy and grey-blue, I stood outside the Look Diner, my brain in my cupped hands. I felt an itch at my temple, and briefly tucked my brain between my ribs and my left arm, using my right to adjust my scalp. I pulled my brain back out—it was warm now, in my hands—and I went in.

At the counter on swivel-stools, watching the toil and tussle of the cooks, sat a group of old men, tall and pale, in musty black topcoats. The coats roiled and writhed, as though the men's backs had sprouted masses of wriggling fingertips. As I passed behind the men, I heard bubbling, hissing sounds, like radio static, as though they were talking back to the sizzling bacon on the griddle.

In a booth sat a bearded man in a brown corduroy jacket, a plate before him emptied of food, save a twisted orange slice garnish and a knob of grey gristle. I sat opposite him and he gaped at me, a bit of egg falling from his beard down into his lap. I put my brain on his plate. I put the plate on the floor. The old men rose from their stools and descended upon it, their faces those of gaunt, befanged jackals.

"Are you looking," I asked the man, "for a good time?"

You're listening to WXXT. The hand reaching out from the barrel of blood. The call from the sewer pipe. The fang in the eye of the Pioneer Valley. Now, here's Guy Ronstadt with the Traffic Report.

INTERSTATES

It is my custom each summer to stand on Interstate 91 at dusk when the streetlamps flicker to life like a tentative waking of a regiment of impaled fireflies.

I dance out from the median and cars swerve as their headlights glance off my pince-nez and the shiny buttons of my waistcoat. Some see the face I wore in my youth before they bounce, end on end, into the trees by the highway. The unlucky see what has become of my face. I have always favored the smell of a car wreck: gasoline, burning plastic, flame, and fear. I can still imagine it in these desolate caves that were my nostrils. I like also when the smoke mingles with the darkening sky until everything is a blue-black bruise.

Before the rescue and fire vehicles arrive, I step amongst the wreckage and turn off the car radio. Then I can hear the crickets and, later in summer, the cicadas and their monotone complaints. I can hear the soft whisper of the wind in the trees. I can collect my trinkets and step into the woods, where I am enveloped.

This is WXXT, home of *Thursday Night Death Jazz* with General Jack Cosmo and "Saucy" Marcus Blot. WXXT. *Our Knofe is Nice and Sharp.*

THE TELEPHONE CALL

FCC: Is this Ms. Martin Tousey?

Tousey: It is. May I ask who's calling? I don't want any more...

F: Ms. Tousey, my name is Kenneth Cottons, and I'm calling from the Federal Communications Commission's Consumer Help Center. You recently utilized our online form to contact us about an obscene, indecent, or profane broadcast?

T: Oh my, yes, I did indeed. Thank you for getting back to me so promptly.

F. We take very seriously complaints of this nature. It is my duty now to ask you a few questions, if you are willing to carve me out some time in what I can only assume is your *very* busy day.

T: (pause) I have time to answer your questions, Mister Cottons.

F: Splendid. Firstly, was the broadcast in question between six o'clock in the morning and ten in the nighttime?

T: It was right before lunchtime, sir. Between 11:30 and 11:45, if I'm remembering right. I was slicing cucumbers and happened to look up at the kitchen clock...

F: Second question. Would you, Ms. Martin Tousey, consider yourself to be an average person, that is to say, a person who adheres to... indeed, embodies, contemporary community standards?

T. Mr. Cottons, I am a Christian woman...

F: Say no more, my dear. To continue: did what you heard describe sexual or excretory organs?

T: It did.

F: Did what you heard describe the interplay of the two? Oh, tell me true.

T: Yes. And there were *sound effects*. Any child, Mister Cottons, any child could have tuned in and heard what I heard.

F: And your reaction, madam, is precisely that of a child, an innocent! Sweet woman, I am as stricken as you must have been. My word! Oft times I wonder if my poor heart can bear the strain! But we must pull ourselves together, mustn't we, if we are to resolve the matter at hand. Now. What were the call letters of the station in question?

T: The what, now?

F: Four letters. In the eastern part of the country, the first letter would be a 'W.'

T: W-X-X-T.

F: De*light*ful. And the frequency?

T: I can't say that I know... that I know what that refers to.

F: To which that refers. That, madam, refers to the position on the dial starting in the murky, shadowy depths of 87.5 and ending in the lofty, supernal heights of 108.00. Somewhere between those two, if you please.

T: On the lower end.

F: Ah, the lower end. The source of much of our pleasure and, in some unfortunate cases, terrible, terrible pain. Now, Ms. Tousey, I must ask of you a decidedly unpleasant undertaking. As best you can, that is, to the very best of your memory, describe for me what you heard on that Sunday morning broadcast, between the hours of 11:30 ante meridiem and 11:45 ante meridiem, on WXXT, located at the southernmost end of the Frequency Modulation Band, perhaps closer to 87.5, or to 88.1 or to 89.3. Be specific. And remember, it is not you saying the words; you are simply providing for me the ammunition I, acting on behalf of the government of these beloved United States, require to remove from the airwaves the person or persons or, rather, *ghouls*, responsible for the dissemination of such vomitus, such egesta, such repugnant carnal...

Forgive me. Please. I do tend to go on. I cede to you the telephonic stage, as it were.

T: I was listening to Sunday morning polka, and I kept getting interference, a voice from some other station. He was talking nonsense. It sounded like he was reading from a textbook on the preparation of a body for a funeral, something like that. But then he said something like, "Blast that damned accordion," and there was a sound like people were fighting. A man cried out, "*he's got a knife!*" and then there was this raspy breathing. I... I don't know if I can describe this.

F: Oh, do go on. It's very important. Speak slowly, and enunciate. Breathe.

T: There was a sound like a zipper being unzipped, a rustle of clothing. Then... then these *squishy* sounds... and moaning. And then he began to describe what he was doing. Doing to the wound.

F: And you didn't turn the radio off, or switch the station?

T: (stammers)

F: It felt so good, Sandra. So good. The lungs, they gripped my manhood like a wet fist. They were trying for breath, but went unsated, unlike me. The chest hairs ticked my...

T: I'm hanging up! I'm hanging up!

F: *Wait, Sandra, please!*

T: M... Martin? No, it's not possible, *Martin*?

F: *I don't know. I don't know where. I don't know where I am.*

T: Martin, listen! Martin... do you know that I loved you? Could you hear me at your bedside at the end? Could you hear what I...

F: Thank you for playing, Ms. Martin Tousey! Whilst we cannot in good faith award you the Grand Prize, we do have for you a lovely parting gift.

T: Let me speak to Martin! Oh, please, oh Lord, I have to tell him... hello? Wait a minute. Just a minute. Someone just came in my front door. Please, sir, keep Martin on the line. Please keep him. Please hold him…

F: (static)

T: Who is that? Who...? Martin! Martin? *Martin!* You're… Martin, no. Martin, *no*. Oh, no. NO!

(line disconnects)

RANGEL

Leeds, Massachusetts lived in Gaspar Bantam's memory as a city of perpetual gloaming, of eternal October. In every memory, in every dream, the faces of jack-o'-lanterns flickered from cornhusk-garlanded porches, treetops glowed orange and red under a sky of charcoal clouds, leaves crunched under your shoes like the snaps and cracks of radio static. The baskets at the farmer's market spilled over with red and yellow peppers curled like beckoning fingers, and bulbs of garlic hung from knotted strings like clustered nests of pupae. You'd pull the comforter around you for warmth in the mornings but throw your jacket over the bike rack in the sun-seared afternoons before playing Pirates of the Woods. The whole village thrummed and hummed to the constant soundtrack of the peepers and the crickets and the whoosh of trucks on the rush and rumble Interstate. Autumn is said to solemnly herald a kind of dying, but in Leeds, in that shadowy little city tucked into a curve of the mighty Connecticut River, the season is an ecstatic celebration of the fury of death's rebirth.

It was the height of autumn when Gaspar's baby sister Rangel disappeared into the woods, never to return.

Gaspar, now 40 years old, the whole of the country between him and Leeds, stared up from his bed at the morning-grey ceiling. His wife Laura lay curled beside him, lightly snoring. He had awakened from the latest iteration of a dream in which he was walking through the Leeds woods at dusk, his sister's voice calling to him from the treetops, from the tangled brambles, from the thorn-spiked deadfalls. Trees began to burst up out of the ground, spraying dirt, opening like gargantuan umbrellas as they rose, blocking the light in steady increments, turning the woods into a coal-black prison thick with woody bars. He had stirred awake, gone for a piss, returned to the warm bed. Now, cocooned back in, he allowed himself for the first time in months to replay in his head the Halloween just after Rangel's disappearance, 30 years ago as of this coming Saturday, back in faraway Leeds.

As dusk crawls along State Street, the porch lights come on one by one, on all houses but number 131, the Bantam house. In that shadow-swaddled Victorian cottage, decorations are folded and boxed somewhere in the darkness of the cellar, where Gaspar is not allowed. No candy graces the table by the front door, and bedtime is 8 p.m., no arguments, no negotiations, buddy. Against the strict rules of the Bantam household, Gaspar slips from his bed on the second floor and soft-foots it to the window. He kneels and watches as the little ghouls and princesses and Frankenstein's Monsters, led by doting parents, go in lantern-lit clusters from house to porch-lit house. Kneeling there in his darkened room, he cries, pushing his fists into his eyes, his mouth curled into a grimace. He cries for his lost sister, yes, but mainly he cries for himself, selfish, selfish Gaspar, because Rangel, snot-nosed friendless and lost little Rangel, has stolen from him his last Halloween as a child.

The next Halloween, his 11th, is drenched in downpours, and if it were any colder, it would all be coming down snow. As it is, his werewolf costume is hidden under a puffy blue winter coat (which his mother won't let him rip open to heighten the effect), his furry mask moist and stinking despite the umbrella that hides it from the world. The festivities are further dampened by the smug insistence of his friends that Halloween is for kids, and dressing up? Well, you might as well be a queer, for middle school kids, the worst thing you could possibly be. The year after that, he barely acknowledges the holiday, though he does take his place at the window to watch. That year there are no tears. He has learned to stifle them.

Gaspar rose quietly so as not to rouse Laura, showered, as much to wash away the dream as anything else, put the coffee on, fried and plated a couple eggs, and sat, looking out the window of the ground-floor condominium. In the city there were no falling leaves, no October aromas, only bus fumes and acrid smog. L.A.'s attempts at being seasonal seemed to Gaspar half-hearted and overcompensating, and maybe they weren't, but to the provincial New Englander that smoky, fire-lit season can't be fully realized anywhere else. At that thought a city bus slid by with a green, grinning witch on its side, winking, mocking him, a wart protruding from her nose, a distorted white square on the surface of the wart to suggest that it shone. A hand landed on his shoulder and he started, nearly spilling his coffee.

"Jesus!" he said.

"Keep it together, kid," Laura said, jostling his shoulders like a boxer's trainer. Again his coffee started riding up the sides of the cup. He put it on the table, shot her a narrow-eyed look. "How are you holding up?" she said.

"Thirty years," Gaspar said. "*Thirty*."

"I know."

Gaspar stood up, turned, and hugged Laura close to him. He pushed his fingers up into her long, brown curls, held the back of her head and kissed her gently. When he had first met her nearly 15 years earlier, having only recently arrived in L.A., at what was otherwise a dud of a party, there had been an immediate attraction and an easy rapport. They had talked about movies, about food, about politics (both leaned left), and about religion (she was agnostic, he an outspoken atheist). She had lost a baby brother to cancer, and so they had talked about loss. At the end of the night, she said she wanted to see him again. The last thing he wanted her to do, he told her, was leave. She left anyway. But he knew she would come back, and she did, again and again. She was the first woman to whom he did not cling, afraid that out of his sight, she might disappear, abandon him as in a dark wood. There was something about her—an ineffable aura of permanence, of solidity. She was hard-edged while he was dreamy and sentimental; she was forward thinking while he traveled through the past like a tourist fixated on sites of historical atrocities. She kept him in check.

"I'm going to go back this year," he said, before he knew he had decided, before he knew he was going to say it.

But the moment he said it, he knew he had to do it. Why it seemed so important, so *imperative* that he go, and go this year, he did not even bother to consider. It had been enough, before now, to remember the Leeds of his childhood, suspended in autumnal amber, to willfully deny the existence of the changes he knew must have taken place. It was time to face Leeds as it was *now*, just a city, not a tainted place of nightmares and secrets and loss.

"You should call your parents, let them know you're coming," Laura said.

"Maybe I'll surprise them."

"Do you need me with you?" Laura asked.

Laura and his parents had met only once, when his folks had flown to L.A. for the wedding. They had all gotten along well, trading embarrassing stories about Gaspar until he had all but begged them to block their mouths with wedding cake. But his parents would likely be away traveling and, in some deep, shadowed part of his brain, he feared that if Laura came to Leeds, she, too, might wander into the woods and be taken from him forever.

“I don’t think I do,” Gaspar said. “I think I’ll need to be alone, to, you know, walk my old paper route, check out the town, look at the old house…”

“To pretend that time hasn’t passed?” Laura began scratching his head with her long fingernails, looking at his prematurely graying hair.

Rangel won’t touch her broccoli. She pouts. She cries crocodile tears. She clasps her small, pink hand over her mouth.

“Come on,” says Gaspar. “It’s good with pepper on it.” To demonstrate, he twists the pepper mill over his plate with a dramatic flourish.

“I’m with her,” says Red. “That shit is disgusting. She can skip it this meal.”

“Absolutely not*,” Shirley says, her voice shrill. “She can pretend it’s monkey brains.”*

“Mmmm, monkey brains,” Rangel says. “Wait a second, cauliflower is monkey brains. Not *broccoli.* Cauliflower*.”*

“Have a no-thank-you helping,” says Shirley. She is done with this argument.

“Hey Gaspy, why did the monkey fall out of the tree?” Red says, his mouth full of steak.

“Because it was dead,” Gaspar answers.

“That’s goddamned right. Dead as a fucking doornail.”

“Language,” says Shirley.

Meanwhile, Rangel has started in on her broccoli.

That night, after Laura had gone to bed, Gaspar pulled from the high closet shelf in the guest room a wooden box with a metal clasp. He placed it on the marble coffee table, sat on the couch, and pried open the lid. The picture on top, caked in dust, was of his parents at a party in some large, twilit room. It had to have been taken in the early ‘70s:

Red was wearing checkered pants, and his sideburns and his collar were comically large. Shirley wore stylishly pointy-framed glasses and a green polyester dress with a self-belt. Her hair was swirled atop her head like soft serve ice cream. Both were grinning widely, their teeth slightly out of focus, white and blurred, as though their mouths were full of clouds. They were toasting the camera with their wine glasses.

He pulled that one out and started going through the rest one by one, piling them to the side of the box. Not a quarter of the way down, he found what he had been looking for, the one picture of Rangel and him he'd allowed himself to keep. In it, she sat on the sheared stump of a tree in her grey wool jacket, her pink and purple scarf wound about her neck. She was pale, ginger-haired, freckled. Her expression was inscrutable as she squinted into the fall sun. A miniature Gaspar stood behind her, his hair in a bowl cut, a study in brown corduroy and narrowed eyes, much too cool for picture-taking. He could not remember having posed for the picture. He focused again on her, at the vertical lines between her brows, the fine, almost translucent hairs there, the long, horizontal freckle on her left eyelid.

What would she look like now? Would her hair still be that same glowing red, or would it have faded to a strawberry blonde, as his had? He couldn't even remember that much about their interactions beyond earnest conversations of childlike confusion, of underdeveloped minds trying to make sense of a puzzling world of adults and their inscrutable doings. Beyond that, she was what most every little sister is in the eyes of a 10-year-old boy: a nuisance. What Gaspar had lost was not as much a person as a mystery—the full person his sister was going to be… or, if she was alive somewhere, *was*.

Ah, it was all just conjecture. He was not going back in order to storm into those dark, dense woods in search of bits of clothing stuck on tree branches or a small shoe stuck in the mud of some remote embankment. Which is not to say that in his dearest dreams he didn't imagine spotting her looking in shop windows on Pleasant Street, turning her by the shoulder to face him, the shock of recognition, of years shorn away... but in his waking hours he knew those thoughts were a little too close to *hope.*

Hope was among the most destructive forces Gaspar knew, a force that had nearly laid waste to his already fragmented family. Hope could stab you with its cold blade. When the phone rang but once. When you saw a redheaded girl down the wrong end of a one-way street. When a car pulled into the driveway, that crunch of tires on gravel, a sound that should herald a homecoming.

Five years after Rangel's disappearance Shirley and Red had seen that it was time to stop hoping, so in their hearts they effectively declared Rangel dead. They arranged for a funeral with an empty casket, purchased a plot at Leeds Memorial Cemetery. Gaspar was determined to remember, though: he stored Rangel deep within him, and in the middle of the night he would take her out and turn her over and over in his mind like a rare coin. He wondered if his parents still did that too, in those infrequent times when their lives were silent and still, awake in those pitch, hourless vistas of time that stretched beyond their midnights.

If they did, there was not the faintest hint.

Gaspar rarely spoke with Shirley and Red now. Before Rangel's disappearance, they had been a happy pair, or at least they had shielded him from any discord. They would both show (or lovingly feign) interest in his youthful obsessions, no matter how dull. The change had been sudden and final. It was as though they imagined Rangel was in some unearthly realm, some parallel universe, and they spent all their time and attention wishing themselves there. Not only had Rangel robbed him of his Halloween, she had robbed him of his parents, turned them into strangers. No, he would absolutely not let them know he was in town. He would not surprise them.

Before going to bed, he logged on to the computer and booked a flight and a room.

Four policemen and his parents conferring by the tree stump. Raised voices, his mother's sobs. Questions, rephrased and repeated, and then a search of the house, unknown men, tramping in and out, smoking, occasionally laughing, as though there could possibly be something funny. The next weeks are a haze of unreality: lines of townspeople, hand in outstretched hand like paper cut-outs, eyes to the ground, slowly making their way through the fields and the forest. Dogs, all lolling tongues and eager eyes, summoned to sniff at Rangel's scarf, then cast scrambling into the countryside to seek the scent. It seems to go on forever, and forever, and forever, and then it just… stops.

Gaspar is surprised to find that he misses the attention as the real, hard ache of loss begins to settle among his family like some great, crouching monster proffered by the callous gods to take Rangel's place.

It is a time of loneliness and fear, the Bad Time. His parents have stopped going to work, and when he asks why, they evade the question. They evade him, *as much as they can. When he wakes screaming, an occurrence that is not infrequent, no one sees to him, no one cradles his head, no one sings him back to sleep. When he walks to the bus stop or to Danny Trask's house for a sleepover, he takes care to avoid the edge of the woods. What exactly he fears will happen he does not know.*

He finds ways to spend more and more time at school, seeking extra help he does not need, joining the Dungeons & Dragons club, any excuse to put off coming home, at least until it is time for a quiet and mirthless dinner, then bedtime, the relief of sleep, of letting everything go in exchange for a too-brief taste of oblivion.

The plane landed at Bradley a little before noon. Gaspar had found himself unable to sleep, so he'd spent the time reading some vacuous airport novel to distract himself, half-watching the bafflingly unfunny in-flight movie, putting the SkyMall catalogue over his eyes to rest them. Now he walked bleary-eyed through the concourse, got an egg sandwich and a coffee from the Starbucks, rented a little red Civic, and found his way to the Interstate, heading northward to Leeds. Absently, staring off at the layered vistas of foliage like the leaf-peepers his parents used to joke about, he put the radio on for a semblance of company.

"This Halloween," boomed an antiquated sounding announcer, who sounded as though he were echoing in some great hall, "You could do worse than to gather at the Leeds Town Common! Trick-or-treats start promptly at Five! Pee! Em!, followed directly by the ceremonial presenting of this year's Halloween Queen!"

"What are you going to go as, Mister Ben?" asked a creaky-voiced DJ who Gaspar thought sounded rather too old to be a radio announcer.

"Why, I'm going to go as an old buck goat," bleated Ben, who then proceeded to affect the wavering cry of a goat. "And you, Stanton?"

"I'm going to go as unresting death itself," replied Stanton.

A female voice spoke out, a familiar voice, the voice of a child.

"Aren't you going to ask *me* about *my* costume?" the voice said.

"Why of course, I'm so sorry, Rangel," said Ben. "What are *you* going to go as?"

"I'm going to go as a little lost girl."

Gaspar started from sleep, fumbled madly for the wheel, foot jutting out in search of the brake, only to find that he was in the back seat, his jacket draped over his body. His beard was wet with saliva. To his right was a guardrail, a gully, and a long line of unchecked vegetation, to his left the cacophonous northbound traffic. He couldn't remember having pulled over, couldn't remember having gotten out of the car nor having climbed into the back seat. He realized he must have left the ignition switch on, as the radio was playing. There were no old men bantering, however, and certainly no Rangel, only some sort of polka music, over which someone was coughing noisily, as though the DJ had forgotten to silence the microphone.

Gaspar got out of the car, and, buffeted by the wind from barreling tractor trailers, climbed into the driver's seat and turned off the radio. He had been asleep for over three hours, but the car, miraculously, started without hesitation. He rubbed his stiff neck and waited for a break in the traffic.

A half hour later he was on the main drag in Leeds. A lot had changed in the years he was gone. In the place of Dynamite Records was a shop that sold Oriental rugs, and the corner shop that used to house Gwenn and Deb's Yogurt was now a bank, as was the former Fire & Water café. A disheartening number of storefronts now housed cell phone showcases. He was happy to see that some hardy little businesses had remained intact, in their same locations, at least superficially unchanged. Willie's hardware store was there, with its gas grills, backs to the chain-link fence, in regimented lines like sentries. The Haymarket café still proffered coffee and fresh juice and baked goods. Anne Gare's bookstore, which had been a Leeds institution for as long as he could remember, was squeezed in between an old laundromat and a new pizza joint, still with the little table of dollar books outside by the door.

Gaspar parked at the Hotel Northampton where King Street met Main, checked in, hauled his bag upstairs to the room. He took a long, hot shower and put on some fresh clothes. His stomach performed a brief but jaunty aria. Clearly the egg sandwich hadn't been enough. He left the hotel and walked up King past the supermarket and the car lots, hoping that the Bluebonnet Diner ("The Bloob," his dad used to call it) would still be there. And so it was. The place hadn't changed in the slightest. The dining room, to the left, was a wide, booth-lined corridor, 10 shades of tan, that bee-lined for the bar area. To the right was the traditional diner car set-up, a counter lined with stools, opposite which sat six booths with a little wall-mounted jukebox in each. Gaspar took the stool across from the register. A frosted blonde waitress addressed him as "hon," took his burger order, and disappeared around the corner.

"Hey," a voice called. Gaspar looked up. Grinning at him from the order window was a bearded cook in an apron over a tie-dyed Red Sox tee. Green and white guest checks hung above him like garland. "You're Red's kid," he said. It sounded almost like an accusation.

"Gaspar."

The man clapped his hands.

"That's *right*," he said. He ducked back into the kitchen. "Hey Billy—tend to them taters," he shouted. A mumbled reply. "Billy. *Taters*."

A moment later the man was sitting on the stool next to his. "Sammy White," he said, offering a big pink hand. Gaspar shook it, glanced down at the man's arms, which were dotted with burns. His face was dimpled and red, his teeth as straight and white as the pickets of a new fence. "Your dad and I went to high school together. Don't see him here much these days. He still in town?"

"They travel, him and mom."

"Ain't that the life?" Sammy said, leaning back on his stool. "Me, I'll be slinging potatoes and flipping pancakes right here, like, forever. Probably just pitch over onto the grill when I die. They can serve me up as a hash."

"Don't take offense," Gaspar said, "if I order something else."

Sammy guffawed, stopped short, seemed to consider, and then said the thing Gaspar had feared he'd get to. "Listen, terrible thing, your sister."

"Thank you," said Gaspar.

"Hell of a thing. *Hell* of a thing. Not the first, you know?"

"Not the first… what?"

"Kids in this town have a way of disappearing. Cops eat here, you know, not just at Dunkin'. I listen. The cops… they know what's going on, do a little, you know, perfunctory inquiry, then the matter's closed. The papers keep quiet about it. You ever hear how this buncha kids got lured away from Langford Elementary?"

Gaspar had not. He was still wondering what exactly it is that the cops know is going on.

"Jesus, must be 20 years gone by. I don't remember how many kids, but some maniac just… *called* them into the woods. Teacher who'd been watching them, they found her flat on her back in the soccer field. She's up in Cooley Dick now, insensible."

He paused, then put his hand on Gaspar's shoulder. "Where *are* they, y'know?"

"Do you think they're still alive?" asked Gaspar. He told himself that Sammy's answer wouldn't matter, what does he know, but his nerves were vibrating.

"Tell you what I think," Sammy said, leaning in close. His breath was peppermint burned with booze. "I think they're up there in those woods, with *them*, and one day they're gonna…"

"Your burger." Frosty slammed the plate down, the burger and fries bouncing. She shot a look at Sammy. "Your potatoes are charred."

"BILLY!" Sammy shouted. He slapped Gaspar on the back. "Never mind what I think," he said, and hurried back to reclaim his temporarily abandoned dominion.

The students had returned to the women's college whose buildings gazed upon Leeds from its promontory like vine-swaddled Arguses. Girls and beaming parents bantered happily under umbrellas at the sidewalk cafes, straining to be heard over the buskers and the occasional swarms of stuttering motorcycles, while tourists and townspeople promenaded this way and that, getting in the last bit of outdoor time before another winter snarled in and swept them back into their curtained and cushioned homes.

One substantial change Gaspar noticed right away as he walked the familiar streets was the proliferation of trees. In his youth they had been slender, leafy, well-kept, spaced evenly along the walks. Now there were more, and they were thicker, untrimmed and unruly, their canopy coloring with shadow the streets and the sidewalks and the storefronts. Even though they shone with the rust and butterscotch colors of autumn, they cast a pall over the downtown, as though they were trying to deny passage to the sun's rays.

Gaspar walked down Center Street, which curved away from Main, passing the police station and the French restaurant, and turned right at the family market. Just beyond the commercial district, the sidewalks were carpeted in leaves like an overabundance of rose petals scattered in honor of his return. Finally he stood in front of the red Victorian cottage in which he had spent the first 18 years of his life. The driveway was empty. The house seemed smaller now, shrunken and somehow sad, barricaded with hedgerows tight as corsets, its interiors secreted and shielded by heavy curtains. Gaspar stood on the walk and stared at it, the broad porch that bracketed the house on three sides, the bargeboarded arches, the windows, nearly floor-to-ceiling, the pots of marigolds lining the steps as though queued up for a house tour. Up to the right, his former bedroom window reflected trees stippled with the blue of the sky.

Gaspar spends hours of solitude in that eave-shadowed sanctum, afternoons playing with matchbox cars or propped up in bed with a Hardy Boys book and nights sitting up awake as his parents and their friends laugh and drink and sing downstairs. His parents' parties frighten him: the men are obstreperous, with booming voices, and the women's laughter sounds no different than the shrieks of

terror from the Dracula movies on Channel 38. Not long after Rangel's in absentia *funeral, the parties intensify, screaming, singing, stomping, and a new feature, something that sounds like group prayer, which Gaspar finds particularly odd, as his parents have never been churchgoers. Finally, Gaspar pushes his pillows over his ears to drown out the noise.*

Feeling the coffee start to catch up with him, he headed back to town to use the men's room at Thorne's Marketplace. Thorne's was Leeds's answer to a mall: three stories of shining oak floors and open-fronted boutiques and specialty shops. He descended the small set of stairs behind Rao's coffee and pushed open the door. There were two sinks and two stalls, no urinals. The stall on the right was occupied. Gaspar entered the other. It was a wooden, cramped little cubicle, with blue walls and a door painted industrial green. As he relieved himself, he looked out the small window at the apartments and fire escapes that backed a row of shops, over whose rooftop he could just make out the peaks of the Norman towers that topped the ancient city hall. Black birds were circling the turreted tops, landing, taking off. He was surprised to discover that he had missed old Leeds.

Reaching for the lock to let himself out, he noticed carved into the green wood a series of initials and years: J.S. '74, K.S. '76, R.B. '82, B.V. '87, and so on, forming a crooked vertical line down the center of the stall door. He stopped, his hand still on the latch, and read them slowly from top to bottom. R. B. ... *Rangel Bantam*? Gaspar's stomach seized. Rangel had disappeared in 1982. Were the other initials those of the lost children Sammy had talked about at the Bluebonnet? Or... it could just be graffiti. Just coincidence. He should get a record of it, though. Just in case. He could head over to the Forbes library, find out the names of the missing kids. He pulled his phone from his pants pocket and snapped a picture.

At the shutter sound, there came a rustling and a rasping groan from the stall adjacent to his. Gaspar quickly exited, as did a shambling figure from the other stall. The man was tall, thin, his head mostly obscured by the black hood of his sweatshirt, though wisps of straight blonde hair, as light and wispy as corn silk, were evident at the ears. The man carried himself oddly, as though there were a stitch in his left side. His right knee jutted out to the side as though the hinge was 90 degrees from where it ought to be. He positioned himself between Gaspar and the door out.

"You taking *pictures*? You taking pictures in the *bathroom*? Pictures of *me*?" His voice was hoarse, high pitched. He took an aggressive step toward Gaspar, who stepped back, shocked, his tailbone hitting the counter. The man's face was that of a child, maybe 10 years old, 12 at the oldest. His skin was unblemished, his eyebrows slight and thin, his cheeks flushed pink. His eyes, a bright, searing blue, were dilated.

Gaspar held up his hands, palms out, fingers splayed.

"No, no!" he said. "I was taking a picture of the initials carved into the wall."

The man-child peered at him.

"J.S. That's me, pal," he said, thumping his rib cage for emphasis. "I am Jeremy Scheer. I was nine years old when they took me into the woods. Nineteen seventy and four." He said it as though reciting it from rote.

Gaspar tried to speak and found himself without a voice.

"They showed me *everything*," said Jeremy. "The great rift, redder than the reddest valentine. Bellies of blue light. Horizons of carrion. This…" —he spread out his arms and Gaspar saw that his hands appeared to be prosthetics, plastic, or rubber, with seams down the sides— "is *nothing*."

Gaspar found his voice. "Did you… did you see my sister? She had red hair…"

Jeremy grinned, revealing his teeth, small and white and pristine. "You don't *deserve* your sister," he said, and suddenly, before Gaspar could absorb what he'd said, he was out the door and gone.

Gaspar ran after him. Jeremy was jerky and awkward, but he was *fast*, which belied his apparent infirmities. When Gaspar skidded into the corridor, Jeremy was at the exits. When he pushed his way outside, Jeremy was through the crosswalk. Gaspar kept up for as long as he could, struggling to keep him in sight. Just outside of the city center, Jeremy rounded a sharp curve, and when Gaspar got there, the man was nowhere to be found.

Gaspar doubled back a block to the police station—if Jeremy had been abducted, if he knew the fate of those other lost children, Gaspar had to tell the police, provide a description. He entered through the front doors and found himself in a mid-sized waiting room ringed with wall-bolted chairs, with a long table in the middle. To his right was a window that spanned the length of the room. He cupped his hands and peered in. Just on the other side of the window was a counter piled with papers surrounding a desk-mounted microphone. It looked like the habitat of some disorganized disc jockey. At the far right corner were couple of desks in an "L" shape, a darkened computer monitor on each. To the left was an empty coat-rack, its small arms reaching to the ceiling as though, in the absence of any policemen, it was reacting to an impending holdup. All was lit red by an EXIT sign at the back of the room above a blackened doorway. He looked in vain for a buzzer or a bell, then he turned and spied a ragged scrap of newspaper thumbtacked to an otherwise empty corkboard.

"***LEEDS HALLOWEEN PARADE***," it read in a dripping font. "*As dusk falls on the town center, venture into the fray by gathering around the Haunted Common. Follow the parade along Prospect Street in your scariest get-up! And stick around for the crowning of the Halloween Queen and King! The woods are watching!*"

Gaspar left the empty station in a daze and walked back over to State Street. Crowds of people—it looked like half the damned town—

were walking north on either side of the road, turning about two blocks ahead onto Prospect Street, which bisected Leeds on the diagonal, and, further along, formed the easternmost length of the half-mile long town common. He fell in among the townsfolk, feeling conspicuously alone, disjointed, still shaken by the encounter in Thorne's and by the empty police station. His head buzzed and he found himself unable to marshal his thoughts.

The trees here were more profuse, as in the city, and thicker, all mammoth trunks and elongated branches, even more so the further down Prospect he got, as though the forest was in the midst of some glacially slow insurgence. At the last block, it was as though someone had superimposed a picture of an ancient forest over one of a present-day neighborhood. Many of the houses had trees growing right through them, sticking out from their rooftops and carports, and those houses and all the others were lit up brightly and bursting with the noise of parties, screaming laughter, thudding music, squeals of joy and of pleasure, as though all manner of bacchanalia might be going on within their walls. It sounded like those parties back at the red Victorian cottage, all around him now, the shrieks and the prayers and the booming voices of the men.

Gaspar emerged from the forested neighborhood into the crowded common, and all of his unease fell away. He was instantly back in his childhood, when Halloween was the province not of the malls and city centers, but of the shadowed suburban streets and cul-de-sacs. Children were marching in great, chattering bunches among the houses that ringed the common. The costumes, unfettered by winter clothing, were just as Gaspar had remembered: little black-caped vampires, fuzzy wolfmen, leaning zombies, gamely gauze-wrapped mummies, all carrying orange sacks and plastic pumpkins piled with candy. At 10-foot intervals, staked into the ground, were torches, orange flames gamboling in cages of iron. As the blue of the sky darkened, the flames cast capering shadows onto the old oaks, the façades of the houses, the faces of the crowd. And like *that*, like the result of the flick of some celestial switch, twilight came to Leeds. The sky was blue-black and orange-veined, and the trees and the clouds were still, dead still, as though anticipating an apocalyptic storm. In the distance was the sound of drums, insistent, almost liturgical, now nearing.

The crowd lined up on either side of the green, murmuring with anticipation. Then a sudden burst of applause as the procession rounded Prospect Street. At the front, two blonde girls in cocktail dresses, faces obscured by black veils, held aloft a banner that read HAPPY HALLOWEEN in letters composed of strung together sausages, rotting, bursting, crawling with fat, curled maggots. Below the banner capered a skeleton, bowing and crossing from left to right and back, and waving wide its bony arms, presenting the crowd to itself. The costume was a marvel: Gaspar could see between and around the bones, hear their clack as they tapped on the concrete.

Behind the skeleton and the girls rolled a large, white, bloodstained pickup truck bearing on its door an inscrutable heraldic insignia, military, maybe, or pagan. The truck's bed was crowded with epicene youths in black and red robes like those of altar boys. Some of them danced, their arms undulating in front of their bodies, their gloved hands tracing shapes in the air; others threw baubles and what appeared to be communion wafers into the crowd, which parted as children ran in to claim them. One landed at Gaspar's feet and he bent to pick it up. It was a tooth, like a human molar, but the size of a man's thumb, elongated and coated in yellow-brown plaque. Gaspar, mystified and disgusted, threw it back to the ground, and a kid dressed as a cowboy ran by, scooped it up, and fled back into the crowd. Gaspar wiped his hands on his jeans.

Next came seven rows of men in red vestments, their hands clasped as though in prayer, but pointed downward, their faces also cast down, chins on chests. On their bald heads were painted demon faces with slitted eyes, curved noses, and grinning mouths full of curved and glistening fangs. Some had pony-tails that served as mustaches for the painted faces. The painted mouths looked disconcertingly real, and Gaspar thought he saw a tongue emerge from the top of one man's head and lick lasciviously at the teeth. Then came a small, wheeled wooden platform on which capered a goat that brayed and bellowed, the sled pulled on red ropes by two obese, diapered oafs, their pink bellies distended, their navels red knots, their eyes a touch too close together, who with their other hands tootled on long, metallic flutes that glinted orange in the fire's light.

It had begun to dawn on Gaspar that he was witnessing something forbidden, that the crowd, which now was full of cheer and merriment and raucous laughter, might, if he tried to leave, turn ugly, dangerous. They might tear him apart. His stomach twisted as the parade continued by, a seemingly endless juggernaut of obscene pageantry: scarecrows with glistening human organs visible through the hay, grey-skinned cadavers hoisted on the backs of policemen wearing Holly Hobbie masks, gnarled, staggering forms that sizzled with festering pustules and buzzed with flies. Among them was Jeremy Scheer, limping along, muttering madly to himself, swatting at the flies that assailed his face and chest. A bruise on his forehead the size of an apple pulsed in the firelight.

Then the Queen's float, the last float, the culmination of the parade. It was a giant sleigh, curled up at the front like an elven shoe, of dark wood, ancient, creaking. Six hooded figures walked with it, three to a side. In a throne at its center was Rangel, and warmth burst through Gaspar's stomach, up his spine, into his head. He was flooded with the resolution of the hope that thought he'd denied himself. She still had the face of a child, the face he knew and loved, the face from that old snapshot, but the body of a grown woman. One elbow rested on the arm of her black throne, her hand aloft, her forearm stilled, her freckled hand waving, blue veins standing out at its back. She spotted him and gasped theatrically, then smiled, the jaw-locked, teeth-together smile of the beauty pageant winner. There were so many teeth, small teeth, crowded in. Rangel's face contorted with effort, and she began to wriggle from her woman-costume, pulling her small arms from the sleeves. The costume-hand continued to wave as Rangel, just a child, the very child that had gone into the woods thirty years and four days earlier never to return, pushed herself out, clambering down over the lap, down the long legs, trailing behind her a bulging, scarred, red-grey sack of afterbirth. As she climbed from the float, it caught on a spike and burst, releasing horrible oozing fluids and a swarm of buzzing insects that flew into a section of the crowd, prompting some to scramble and flee.

Gasper opened his arms as Rangel neared, and she opened her arms as well. They confronted each other silently, their eyes hurling messages back and forth like lightning bolts. She wrapped her small arms around him, pushing the side of her face into his belly, and he squeezed her. The homey smell of her—soap and strawberries—brought everything back to him in an overwhelming torrent that weakened his legs. She grasped his index finger with her small hand and guided him up onto the float. As he took his seat, one of the hooded figures approached and affixed upon his head a crown gilded with opals and tourmalines and jewels for whose colors and shapes he had no names.

As the figure turned, Gaspar caught the merest glimpse of the hard face of his father—*their* father—in the dark hood. His father jumped from the float and joined a smaller figure. His mother. *Their* mother. The two turned to a third hooded figure, at the edge of whose cowl Gaspar spied a familiar curl of brown hair. Something somewhere in Gaspar broke off and was pulled away into oblivion. Rangel ascended her throne, climbed back into her costume. The crowd began to murmur, and the murmur separated into words, a chant, a black and blasphemous psalm. The drummers resumed their ritual drumming. The orange fissures in the sky began to crack and open, and whatever was left of Gaspar wondered in terror what had been hidden behind and beyond the façade of sky, what would be revealed when the great starry costume fell away. And then he saw.

It is a blazing bright autumn evening. The setting sun pushes its red-orange rays through the orange-red treetops, turning the world the color of cider. A young boy and his younger sister stand at the edge of a great dark wood.

"My friends are in the woods," says the young girl.

"You don't have any friends," says the boy.

"I do!" she insists, pursing her lips. "They give me gifts. They teach me songs." She pauses, deciding whether to say the next thing. Finally she says it. "They gave me a costume."

The boy's eyes narrow and he puts his fists on his hips, his bony elbows jutting like less-than and greater-than.

"Horse crap," he says.

"They did," she says. "It's in the woods, and it's the best costume I've ever seen, better than the princess. Wait here. I'll show you."

The boy watches her go into the woods. Further and further down the path she goes in her white sweatshirt and her skinny little faded jeans. The woods rustle and sigh, and the treetops huddle in together, the tree trunks cracking gently as they pull inward. The boy can now only just make out the white of her sweatshirt as the night approaches. The earth fully claims the sun, shadowing the land, banishing light from the devil-haunted streets of Leeds, turning the forest to a towering empire of night, protecting its many secrets, and the boy looks, and he looks, and he looks, and the girl is gone.

OSCURITÀ

Police Report – December 12, 2015

LEEDS, Massachusetts. Police investigating reports of a noise disturbance at Leeds wine bar Oscurità say that the restaurant was open after hours, and that several of the workers, including owner Reginald Mayhew, were standing in a circle in the dining room naked and covered in blood. The restaurant was lit only by candlelight, according to police. None of the crowd was injured, and Mayhew claimed that the blood was from a butchered animal being prepared for a meal. Oscurità serves only vegan meals. No animal remains were discovered on the premises.

The first officer to arrive on the scene, Lt. Robert Marinell, was hospitalized for exhaustion after the incident. In a letter to the editor that the *Gazette* declined to publish in full, Lt. Marinell claims that the tables at the restaurant were crowded with elderly men attired in clothing from antiquity, and that the tables were piled high with the bodies of children, some alive, most in varying stages of decomposition. Marinell went on to say that the tables bore goblets of pus and of saliva; that the room smelled of blood, cordite, and rosemary; and that there was something large, charred, and alive muttering grim prognostications from the far reaches of the brick oven.

DRIVING TO LEEDS

Have you ever been in the midst of a conversation that seems perfectly sane, normal, even mundane, and without warning it takes a turn into starkly surreal territory, and you realize you are in the presence of a madman? I imagine this is a thing that happens to the solitary hitch-hiker picked up by a stranger with big glasses and a crooked stare; just as the car enters a long and dimly lit tunnel; the talk turns to alien abductions and global cabals… and the locks engage.

That's how it was that late October day, and I was trapped in a car with the mad bugger. I should have known. Even though the conversation at the outset was crazy, the narrative had a semblance of sense. An early adapter to social media, Golden had used an encrypted MySpace page to contact certain favored followers who arranged to secret him in a succession of safe houses, even as the forces of order and outrage aligned against him. He preached not in full auditoriums nor packed theaters, as he had at the height of the Order's membership numbers, but to followers in groups of eight or 10 in cabins and tree-forts and sheds and caves. Arizona to Utah to Prague to Kyrgyzstan, he hid out.

They almost got him in Quebec, he told me, and the jolt of nearly being caught led him to an epiphany. He had been wrong all along, and he'd been *doing* wrong. His belief that he was the messiah, chosen to lead and to breed and finally to *punish*, had been a mental bugaboo, the result of a glitch in brain chemistry. He began to retrace his steps on a mission of deprogramming and repentance.

Understand that I did not for a second believe he bought his own line of bullshit. I think he was hoping to be able to prove before a jury that he had made an effort to undo, at least in part, the damage he'd inflicted, that it might reduce his sentence when he was finally apprehended. Of course, he never was.

I have to pause here to clarify: when he had said he needed me to help extricate the devil from a small city in a crook of the Connecticut River, I assumed he meant that we were going to expose a charlatan of the variety that he used to be—to pull victims from the thrall of another pseudo-messiah. To rid the world of a competitor, if I were going to choose the route of cynicism, a very familiar route indeed.

I wasn't even close.

The story he told veered into madness. To hear him tell it, Leeds was a hive of abominations, goatish demons in the shadows, and strange chants echoing in the parts of the woods from which daylight had long been banished. Creatures that swarmed the roof-beams and lurked in the basements, lorded over by an abomination, a long-dead magus who had returned through an unspeakable ritual. A man who had been reborn from the carcass of a goat.

As he rambled and ranted, I watched his hand on the steering wheel. The tips of his fingers were twitching in time to his monologue. It was an ancient hand, the hand of an octogenarian, with a spray of blue veins across the back, a sinewy subcutaneous set of fingers working his hand like some kind of grotesque puppetry. His right arm was wet. The dampness darkened the sleeve of his jacket just over the elbow. Even as I watched, the stain grew. He gave me a sidelong glance, eyes narrowed, suspicious. *I want to go home*, I thought, and then I thought about home, stodgy, shitty East Hodgson, with its condominiums and cul-de-sacs, its mazes of chain stores—CVS,

Buffalo Wild Wings, Staples, Target—situated in clusters in vast, poorly designed parking lots; of my apartment, my things, weighing on me with their bulk and their tiresome familiarity. Wherever this mad path might end, it had to be preferable to my post-Order life in all its prosaic greyness. I was very curious to find out exactly what Golden had up his sleeve.

THE LEEDS WORD AROUND TOWN (1)

by Ms. Margaret Maughbrook
From Ms. Maughbrook's column in the *Leeds Weekly*

My shrewd and trustworthy sources inform me that Mrs. Willa Grench of Strant Street called upon Mrs. Martha Arthurson of Castle Road last Wednesday at 4:00 p.m. Their falling out, presumably precipitated by Mrs. Arthurson's dalliances with the Eyeless Man who dances in the churchyard at dusk, appears to have resolved itself, within a week of the Eyeless Man's having been mauled to bits by Town Councilman Anderton's mastiff Old Henry.

* * *

Mr. Sanford Blanch of Bedford Terrace is recovering from a dreadful case of pneumonia but was seen recently in Childs Park consulting his Book of Birds. He is still rather pale and was unkempt and possibly insensible, reports my source. Moreover, the birds fled at his arrival, and worms rose from the ground like pink revenants to follow Mr. Blanch even as he became alarmed and fled for home.

* * *

The lament of lean times has not sullied our stalwart and inventive shopkeepers! Robert's Rugs has instituted a policy wherein once a patron has spent a sum of two thousand dollars, she receives in return a four per cent discount on any four items purchased within four hours of that level having been reached. Four-for-four is the name and it is sure to catch on!

* * *

Mister William Kart and his sister Jocelyn have returned from a trip to Northfield, Massachusetts which lasted a duration of six days. It was reported that they only brought with them one small valise and a suspiciously full-to-bursting handbag!

* * *

The newest gadget is called the "i" phone and it talks to you! My phone talks to me too! It says the bills are due and when are you going to pay up!!

* * *

Miss Ashley Wollet of Shallowbrook Lane has fallen again into ignominy, it seems! Where she walks, the verdure crumples and wilts and turns brown, and the vulnerable take to their beds, reports my source! She has severed relations with Jeremy Blank, and the boy is quite blue and loudly pines at the edge of Folly Pond.

* * *

Mister Tall is up to his old tricks again! My source tells me he walks at night and makes the dogs bark, and he is up to no good when the kindergarten recess bustles in the late morning at Jackson Street Elementary School! Little John Orange was taught words in a foreign tongue and recited them to his mother Violet, who took the boy by the ear, straight to morning mass.

* * *

Father Ezekiel Shineface has been without warning relieved of his duties at The Youth Church on Prospect Street due to his homilies being inconsistent with the Doctrine of Gospel. He promised in secret that he would continue to preach, and has been holding candle-lit clandestine sessions in the attic of the decrepit, abandoned house at the corner of Verret Street and Washburn Road. My source tells me that attendance is quite high, and the sermons unexpectedly persuasive.

HAVE YOU SEEN THIS MAN? (2)

Have you seen this man? He was gone from his dear wife's bed one morning. He responds positively to abuse. He answers to Nathaniel Flood. He has a wooden leg and is missing his right eye. He is epileptic and long ago bit off the tip of his tongue. He clutches at the sky. He breaks windows and enters houses. He favors sausages and bitters and likes to be tickled on the small of his back. He may carry a dog-eared Bible and a sharp knife. He may cry into public telephones whilst fiddling with himself. He likes nursery schools and cots and may attempt to sell you twigs for a pittance. Do not touch his arms. Do not look into his eyes. Do not accept food from him.

ANNE GARE'S RARE BOOK & EPHEMERA CATALOGUE #4950394-C

"The Stockton Pamphlets" - author unknown

Thirteen pamphlets housed loosely in the original paper wrappers. Some creases and damp marks. The pamphlets, printed in seventeen twenty in Leeds, appear to be coded calls to some manner of meetings in the quadrant of town known at the time as "Hog's Bladder." There are illustrations of three-tongued devils, winged leeches, and of a box that, quite impossibly, appears to be a rude drawing of a home radio receiver that would not be invented for another two hundred years.

Twelve of the thirteen pamphlets are divided into three groups of four, each with a paper wrapper, and with the series wrapper enclosing the complete set. The thirteenth pamphlet is encased in a rectangle of amber like some ancient moth. Carved into the amber on the reverse side is a warning to keep the pamphlet in its yellow-orange prison. Most of the individual pamphlets were published in editions of only one hundred, and complete sets are uncommon.

Six hundred and forty nine dollars.

THE ROCKING HORSE

In my sleep, down low, down deep, I rode that rocking-horse for miles. Miles upon miles and more miles on top of those. He bolted when I jammed the pointed steel of my boot between two ribs, running like the devil's salty tongue was rasping at his hind. It was all I could do to hold on. He leapt over the gravestone of my mother, his hind hoof chipping off a chalky fragment. He galloped through my uncle's musty shack, kicking aside bones and skulls tethered not by sinew and muscle but by spider webs and browned, decaying twine. He stomped through the rivers on whose banks I first discovered the grim intersection of sex and murder, and the water that splashed my face was warm and metallic on my tongue, like blood. He flared his nostrils at ghosts, his eyes wide and bulging, and they flashed away, leaving ozone and burnt rose petals in their wake. Free of the oak arches to which he had been nailed, he was no longer a frail, hollow husk. His breath was fire. His tantrums were earthquakes and his tears hurricanes. I was nothing so grand as a rider or a jockey; I was a witness.

You're listening to WXXT, home of the no-repeat workday. If you hear the same song played twice between midnight and 11:59 and you're the sixth caller, good for you, Johnny Shit-Ears.

My Brother Earl

Earl was a strange boy, on that most anyone would heartily agree. Even at four, he was curious. He would crack eggs upon the floor and prod at the colorless liquid with his forefinger, then rub it into his eyes and scream at the stinging. He would chew the wet, jagged shells, gagging with a red-eyed fervor.

At school he was no better, rendering crude caricatures of Miss Jade jamming an exaggeratedly large log of chalk under her petticoats or grotesquely fellating a bulging fireplug. He seemed to enjoy the subsequent punishment, cackling as the yardstick smacked solidly against his wee knuckles, giggling into his fists as the lash reddened his pale hindquarters. No one knew quite what to do with Earl.

He stolidly refused meals and instead snacked droolingly from the flower garden. For six months at the age of seven he spoke only in shrieks and obscenities. At the age of eight, he disemboweled a local drunk with a butter knife. He had a way about him, though, and he was a fixture at Abraham's brothel; to what degree he partook of the ladies' affections I was always wary of asking.

Earl ran away from home at the age of 10 and died of exposure in the woods of Montague. It was months before his body was discovered, and by that time it was bloated and twitching and humming with worms and insects and pink foam. It was I who found him. I held him, stroking his purple face even as his cadaver thrummed and buzzed and bustled against my chest. I never knew what kind of man Earl would have become, nor did I dwell upon the subject. That kind of thwarted hope leads to grave-digging and spells and murders and living nightmares.

Earl is with me every day, a forgotten warrior for the cause. When an FCC agent searches the mirror and finds the pink in the corner of his eye twitching. When he pulls at the pink and it wriggles from his head and lands pulsating on the basin. When more come, streaming from his nose and mouth and he gags with the effort of loosing them. When they fall from his eyes like tears. When his wife backs away with repulsion and his children faint from fear at his dissolving, bursting visage. I tremble and go taut as Earl bursts through me, his eyes red red roses, his hands a blossom of thorns.

You're listening to WXXT, where knife and throat meet. Join us this Tuesday and every Tuesday for the Audiotaped Torture Hour, with your host Typhus R. Brickbat.

THE EGG

"So... chickens?" said Julie, and chickens it was. See, I didn't want pets in the house, and, moreover, I was—and am—deathly allergic to cats. I had a general distaste for the idea of keeping living creatures imprisoned indoors in small cages or enclosures, therefore no little birds, no hamsters, and, ugh, no snakes nor lizards. Dogs you have to actually take outside to do their business. In the *winter.* So: chickens.

I spent a good portion of my week off fencing in and converting our old shed out back, building roosts and putting in milk crates filled with straw for nesting boxes. I drew from our savings to buy a hanging feeder, an automatic dog waterer, and an overhead lamp for heating during the cold weather months. On the following Saturday, Julie went to the feed store in search of healthy pullets. We resolved to start with six and let Jack, almost five years old now, name them. Hence Wiggy, Piglet, Chick-chick, Raptor, Zoltar, and Frankenstine (his spelling, on which he insisted. Little Jack inherited his mother's stubbornness).

It was Julie who insisted on my installing a motion detector light out by the roost. Our property backed up to the edge of the state forest, and at night you could hear all kinds of cries and howls and the sounds of things crashing through the thickets and the brush. Moreover, it had been only about two years since the Mierzewskis' poor kids had been traumatized when someone—probably little dirtbag high school kids like the ones who lived up on Tremens Terrace or Hospital Hill—had busted up the rabbit hutch in the backyard of their house on Moodybridge Road—just three streets over—and wantonly slaughtered the rabbits, stringing their intestines across the tree branches like grisly garland. I remember grimly joking about it, pretending to be a detective on the scene, saying, "Somebody must have really had a beef with these bunnies. This? This was personal."

Julie and I had both laughed. Only it wasn't funny.

"The chickens are bored," Jack said one sunny Thursday about a month later as I was washing up his breakfast plate.

"I don't think chickens can *get* bored, Bubba," I said. But maybe he had a point. They hadn't been producing at their regular rate, hadn't been as energetic, nor as eager to eat. We consulted the great oracle called Google and found the word "broody." I told Jack that I myself had got a bit broody around my junior year of high school, and that joining the Drama Club had helped me get past it. "So," I said to Jack. "We have to introduce some excitement into their lives. A chicken burlesque show? An outdoor movie night? Is… is cockfighting *always* bad?"

"How about a radio?" said Jack.

The kid is good.

I paid 10 dollars for a scuffed-up boom box down at the Goodwill, bought a package of C batteries for the first time since I was, I don't know, 16, affixed the boom box to the grate in the coop window with a couple of bungee cords I scrounged from the cellar, and plugged it into the outdoor extension cord that also provided electricity for the motion detector. Julie frittered around in the garden while Jack helped me. When it was all wired up, I looked at Jack and he looked up at me, his expression serious, almost grave.

"What kind of music?" he said.

"Let's see what we've got," I said, twirling the knob. "We have... bro country..." Jack shook his head whiplash-hard, to my not-insubstantial relief, "... a little Zeppelin here, classic rock from WAQY... no, okay... classical? No, okay, I'm with you… more classic rock... songs from the 80s, 90s and today..." I rolled the dial down into the low numbers, the land of the college stations.

"Stop!" said Jack, and we and the chickens were treated to some Joy Division.

"Now, we're not looking to make them even *more* broody," I said, but Jack's little fists were on the hips of his corduroys, his bottom lip jutting out. WMUA was to be the chickens' entertainment, and that was that.

After we finished watching our evening shows, I was restless, jumpy. I felt like going for a drive or taking a walk downtown, maybe poking around at the mall. And I didn't feel like doing any of those things. So I put on my slippers and shuffled out back to the coop to look in on the chickens. There was a high wind that night, and the light from the motion detector, splayed across the green of the lawn, was crowded with the gargantuan shadows of dancing leaves. I could hear the muffled sounds of WMUA—they were playing something kind of odd… it must have been the Experimental Music Hour. From the speakers emanated a voice reciting something, backwards; deep, sonorous, with that sort of rhythmic sound somewhere between lisping and inhaling, the same few words over and over, indecipherable, speaking over a three-note tune played on an out-of-tune piano, while far off a woman cried, occasionally drowned out by a wash of applause. For a moment, it sounded like the crying and the applause were coming from out in the deep of the woods rather than from the boom box, but I didn't dare enter the coop and turn down the volume to find out.

When I peered through the window of the coop, I had a bit of a start. The chickens were in a circle, facing one another. Their eyes were wide. In retrospect, it occurs to me that at no point did I see any of them blink. Frankenstine, the largest, turned my way, her eyes open very wide. Her stare was even, steady, imbued with some kind of alien intelligence. My first response, God help me, was to burst out laughing. My mirth supplanted by a deep unease, I decided to retreat to the house and pour myself a stiff drink. When I reached the porch door, the radio unleashed a roar of static. Somewhere in that static, a familiar voice was yelling hysterically, rising in pitch and in volume, the words indecipherable.

Back in the dark house, I made my way through the darkness to Jack's room to check on him. He was there, face smushed into his pillow, snoring lightly. I put my hand on the side of his head. It was warm. He didn't stir. I tiptoed to the bathroom, stripped to my shorts, ran a toothbrush over my teeth, and practically leapt into bed. The adrenaline kept me awake for hours. Well, the adrenaline and the fact that I was fairly sure that it had been Jack's voice crackling through the static, filled with panic and rising to a frenzied pitch.

The next morning, the chickens were out and about, clucking and meandering around the enclosure. The radio was playing some classical thing or another, unfamiliar to me, accompanied by echoing birdsong and the rustling of leaves in the mild, warm wind. I went in with a cloth bag to collect the new eggs and there it was, in a mote-mottled beam of light, like a scene cut from one of those Tolkien movies: an egg the size of a grapefruit, upright and pale pink, dotted with dewdrops. I knelt and put my hand on its side. Warm. I picked it up with both hands, cradling it between my palms and fingers. The chickens had moved to the walls of the coop, sitting with their backs to the plywood walls, blinking, their eyes darting about, looking somehow furtive, as though they were trying not to snicker at me.

"There's no way this thing came out of one of *you*."

Wiggy thrust her head into the air and ululated.

The egg had some heft to it, and as I placed it in the cloth bag, I felt something shift. I heard a rustling within, followed by a sing-song whisper. A wave of revulsion shook me, and suddenly I wanted to drive somewhere far away and fling it into the woods by the side of some out-of-the-way road. Or, I don't know, hurl it into the ocean.

Instead, and I cannot now for the life of me account what moved me to do so, I brought it into the house and slipped into my study. I cleared out the pens and paperclips and junk from the bottom of my desk drawer, the deep one that people use for hanging files, put a couple of crumpled but clean t-shirts along the bottom, and rested the egg in its new nest. I drew the key from a jar on the bookshelf, locked the drawer, and wound the key in next to the house key and car key on the ring I keep in my left hand pocket.

And I forgot about it.

The days went on as they do, mostly the same every day, with few variations, none notable. Julie walks Jack out to the bus stop and I fill my thermos with coffee and drive the 14.5 miles to work at the warehouse, Julie bicycles to the florist's to watch over the till. Home at five, dinner from one of my admittedly small and simple repertoire of recipes, television time, read Jack a little something, and then off to bed. Fresh eggs from the coop in the morning, naturally.

There was no more weirdness from the chickens, though they seemed a little—don't laugh at me—a little tense and apprehensive, a touch less productive. Back to broody, maybe. The radio played odd little ditties and strange symphonies and operas in alien languages and absurd little plays and parodies of Catholic liturgies. I looked at it carefully one morning and saw that it was no longer tuned to WMUA—the little vertical red line had shifted about an inch to the left. And the dial was stuck fast. Even with a pair of channel-locks, I couldn't budge it.

And here's the stranger part. When I was straining, my reddening fingers gripping the channel locks, my face locked in a grimace, the voice of the singer—some Dean Martin wannabe—began to clench and strain as though *he* was struggling to hold the dial in place. Finally I gave up, and the crooner began to scat, a tone of triumph and… and *mockery* in his nonsense syllables. As I entered the house, I heard the audience break into hooting and applause and jeers. It sounded for all the world like it was directed at me.

Summer turned to Fall like a flick of a switch on September 1st. The days went from hot and oppressively humid to breezy and mild, the nights cool. One night, about halfway through the month, I snapped awake from an awful dream in which one of the chickens, Wiggy, I think it was, had been terribly injured. She was on her back in the side yard, talons clutching at air. Her beak was mostly torn off, and it hung from her face by a short, sinewy string. One eye was caked with blood. She was shuddering and emitting a high pitched, wavering wheeze. I began to try to kill her with my fists, to put her out of her misery. And she wouldn't die.

And so I knelt in the dirt, holding her throat tight with my left hand, punching with my right, screaming and blubbering and weeping. Then I stood and began stomping on her head and neck. I heard the cracking of a twig and looked up to see Jack staring at me from the back porch. My waking coincided with a sound somewhere in the house, a sound that reminded me of a tree cracking in a Fall Nor'Easter. I narrowed my eyes to force the red glow from the clock radio into focus. It was 1:51 a.m. I got up quietly, grabbed my flashlight from the nightstand, and went from room to room, seeking the source of the sound.

When I got to the study, I saw that the drawer that had held the egg was open, the metal tracks that held it in place bent, the lock mechanism askew, torn neatly from the wood. In the drawer, atop my t-shirts, rested two cracked halves of the egg. Blood was smeared on the egg's curved interior. I reached in to run my finger along the cracked edge, and drew it back, hissing. The shell was as hot as a coil on an electric stove. A white blister began to form on my fingertip. I looked around the room. Nothing else had been disturbed. I wedged the drawer back in crookedly. Then I scooped up the shirts with the shells on top and carried the bundle out to the road, where I tipped the hot shells onto the storm drain. The topmost shirt, a blue sleep tee, was scorched where the egg had sat, black-tipped blue threads pointing this way and that like alien grasses. It was a moonless night, still and quiet. Tucking the t-shirts under my arm, I looked at the windows of the house, the streetlights reflected in the panes, and wondered what, exactly, had hatched from within its walls, and where exactly *it* was.

I nestled back into bed and fell right back into dreams. This time, it was one of my endless and episodic sagas, the kind that seems like it lasts all night without respite, broken down into unrelated scenes. In one, my mother, who gets around now with the assistance of walkers and wheelchairs, stacked dishes for me in an apartment I lived in five years ago. She could move around with ease and I felt a surge of relief just seeing it. In the next sequence, I was downstairs in the kitchen, the refrigerator open, spilling a wedge of light onto the night-grey tiles. I was using our butcher knife to cut into a sizeable hunk of flesh on the floor, and angrily shooing away an army of chickens as they edged near the bleeding thing. Rivulets of blood flowed along the spaces between tiles, and I was trying to contain the flood with an old washcloth. The eyes of the chickens showed white and they hissed as I swatted at them.

They had human feet, shriveled and grotesque, with unkempt nails. Next, I was naked in a Lebanese restaurant. And so forth.

At 5 a.m., I woke. I looked at Julie. She was sleeping on her back, which is unusual for her. As I watched, her jaw dropped open and she belched an explosive burst of static. Her eyes opened and she turned to me.

"Did you just say something?"

Then she fell back asleep.

October 1st. I was sprawled out on the couch, one leg forming a bridge over to the coffee table. Jack was at my side, angled up against the back of the couch. My hand cradled the back of his head. He was asleep, his chest moving up and down. I stared at his nose, so like my nose, a little squashed, at his lashes, fine as filaments, and at his brows, furrowed as if he labored under the weight of all the problems of the world. After he'd been born and for his first few years, I was horrified to discover that I felt nothing for him. He was just a baby, a nuisance. He grew until he was… well, he was just some kid. This I hid from Julie, fearing for our marriage. I went through the motions, though, emulating other dads, real fathers and fathers from television shows and movies. Sometimes I thought I'd missed my calling as an actor.

The awful truth is that I didn't know if I'd come to love him, or if I got so good at pretending that I had tricked myself into love. I supposed it didn't matter—there, on the couch, my heart swelled with love for the boy. It certainly *felt* real.

Then a terrible thought occurred to me. I could, in a matter of seconds, grab his head between my hands and bash it against the coffee table. Fast as a flash, I could end his life, plunge my family into horror, into tragedy, drag everyone who knew me into a nightmare. It would be so easy to summon ruin like it was some scaly, horned demon. No murmured incantations, no chalk-scrawled pentagram: just one act of brutality, over in an instant and then carved into eternity's wall as a thing that had been done and could not be reversed.

Instead, I pulled Jack over closer, squeezed his shoulders until he whined in protest. But I didn't stop thinking about it.

"What are you thinking about?" Julie asked that evening at dinner.

I didn't like how quickly the lie came.

"Just work," I said. "They're very big on reorganization right now, and I'm worried they might stick me with a new supervisor, or—and I don't think it will really come to this—eliminate my position altogether."

"You have a pretty good thing going now as it is," she said.

"Jerry knows the job," I said. "People who don't know the job, they get bad ideas, get fixated on them, and they bristle at the idea that an underling might just know better."

And that was that. All the while, the images flashed behind my eyes. The knives in the kitchen, so sharp. A shed full of hedge clippers, shovels, and axes. It would be so easy. So awfully easy. It wasn't that I wanted to do it, but the thought that I could…it gave me a low-grade buzz, a thrill not unlike the one when I got when as a pre-teen I found a pile of water-bloated dirty magazines under a peeling log in the woods behind Andy Gross's house.

Jack had fallen ill. He pouted, rubbing his tummy, mooning around the house like a depressive.

"Do you think we should take him to Urgent Care?" Julie said, which translated to "We should take him to Urgent Care."

"I don't," I said. He'd done this before. He'd say his stomach was upset, refuse food. He was in a funk, that was all. I did the same thing when I was a boy.

She hadn't seen the cut.

I saw it earlier that day when he was tromping down the hall to the laundry to grab a freshly cleaned pajama shirt. It was a thin pink vertical line, about three inches over his navel.

"Buddy," I said. I knelt down before him and ran my index finger down the length of the line. "What is this?"

He shook his head.

"Well, when did you first notice it?"

"Dad," he said, "can spiders crawl into your mouth when you're asleep?"

"Where did that come from?"

"Just answer? Okay?"

"Geez, bub, sure. They can. But nothing would happen. You'd never know it. Plus, buddy, and I don't know if you know this, but you drool like a fool. The poor thing would drown before it got anywhere near your lips."

He touched the tip of his finger to the pink line.

"Don't tell mom," he said.

Of course I had to tell Julie. He was her son, too. It didn't matter that he may have been hurt by the thing from the egg I'd brought into the house. No one knew about that but me. Of course I had to tell her.

I did not tell her.

That night, once again, I dreamed. I was kneeling at the foot of the bed, watching Jack sleep. He was on his side, his face on the bed, his mouth hanging open. A foul thing crouched by his head, multi-legged, fat, hairy, eyes like pustules all over its cephalothorax. With pincers dripping with poison or some numbing agent, it separated Jack's lips, wrenched open his jaw, and climbed over his teeth and into his palate like a child climbing into the trunk of a car. Before it reached out to shut Jack's mouth, all of the eyes on the left of its body blinked, a cruel and terrible wink.

A bulge moved down Jack's neck, down his breastbone, and his belly began to swell like one of those Ethiopian kids they used to show on public service announcements on television. I stood and turned back into the hall, swinging my flashlight round, and Julie was at the top of the stairs at the end, a few yards away. She was floating there in her white bedclothes, her toes curling and uncurling. She had speakers for eyes and a long segmented antenna hung obscenely from the junction of her thighs. Sickly green sparks of light flickered in her ears, her nostrils, her open mouth.

"Free Money Friday," she bellowed in the tone of a rock DJ. And then her belly burst, spraying the room with tattered flesh and a tsunami of miniscule red bugs. I felt them moving along my eyes.

I woke. Julie wasn't in the room, and somehow one of the chickens had gotten into the house. It was Frankenstine. She was nestled like a cat on the folded blanket at the foot of the bed, still as a stone, staring at me. When my eyes met hers, she screamed. I did too. She jumped up in a storm of feathers, hopped off the bed, and hobbled out of the room. I followed.

(((ı)))

The chicken led me to the kitchen, where Julie crouched in a spreading pool of blood.

"Honey," I said. My voice was trembling. She rose to a kneel. Behind her was Jack... Jack's body. His torso had been torn open vertically, his ribcage opened up like French Doors. His insides were a ruin—walls of yellow fat, flattened intestines, ruptured organs, torn and ragged. I fell to my knees and howled. Frankenstine clucked and tittered and cooed.

And then I saw Julie's hands. Her fingertips were burned red and blistered. She saw that I saw, and she raised her hands to me, her lip trembling. From behind me loomed a huge shadow. It fell over Julie, over what remained of Jack. Julie looked behind me and went white, all the way to her hair. I turned, giving in to horror. There was nothing there that could have produced a shadow that large.

"Don't move," I said.

I backed up to the knife drawer, keeping my eyes on Julie.

I plucked out the Wusthof paring knife and slit horizontally across my eyelids so that I could never shut them again.

I watched as the thing emerged from the shadows of the pantry.

And that was how they found us. Jack cracked wide open on the floor, and Julie, crushed as though put through a compactor, purple and red and white and still against the radiator. And a naked, bloody-eyed madman with a knife in his lap, gagging and choking and screaming about chickens and eggs and flesh and love. The radio blared in the yard. It was once again tuned to WMUA. I think they were playing Brahms.

THE PHOTOGRAPH OF MARCUS WILY

Marcus Wily didn't know he had died until he saw the photograph.

My God, I'm gone, I'm gone, he said, and then he settled into a dank, dusty collection of crumbling bones in his very easy chair. He had been in a gun fight, if it can be called that when only one man has a gun and the other only legs with which to flee. The incident was over a woman and her kiss, which he recalled as wet and warm and somehow overwhelming. Her husband—Wily hadn't even noted the ring!—had burst raging out of the bar, shooting. Not afraid of being called a coward, Wily flung away the woman and ran. He felt a jolt as he ran, he felt his head open like a flower, but still he ran, feeling as though he were leaving some great weight behind him. Marcus Wily went on. He tended to his garden; he fed his cat; he was a guest at a wedding and in the audience at plays and concerts. Marcus Wily didn't know he had died until he saw the photograph.

UNCLE ROTTFIELD'S BLACK GLOVES

2015

On a recent rain-soaked Saturday I walked into the Hospice Shop and put four sodden dollars on its counter. The clerk, a fussy, large woman with blue eyelids and a shrill voice, seemed afraid to look at me; the more she averted her eyes, the more I tried to force eye contact. To no avail, but fun nonetheless, oh yes, oh yes.

I emerged with a small bag concealing a pair of long, black gloves. I walked through the Bridge Street cemetery, reading the names on the stones, some of which I knew, and climbed the fence, emerging between a pair of three-story apartment houses on Orchard Street. I ducked into a basement window, ascended three flights of dusty stairs. Turning the ancient and befogged fluted crystal doorknob, I entered an apartment with a cluttered kitchen, traversed a narrow hall lined with wallpaper peeling like burned skin, and found myself in a modest room housing only a twin bed, an antique hutch, and a nightstand bearing a lamp and an alarm clock.

I removed the gloves from their bag and placed them gently under a pillow yellowed from decades of perspiration and saliva. Then I exited. I was not seen. The street was quiet. Cars whispered wetly by on Route 9, and I went under the fence and back amongst the damp headstones.

1942

Though my father's brother Rottfield was a singularly ugly man—each of his features seemed to be on loan from some other face—he was a Lothario of epic proportions. His conquests were women of every age, from teenagers to dowagers; of every class, from the starving wisp to the mansion-dweller. At University he was as sought-after as a Lord. The townspeople wondered aloud: Was it his voice, or the force of his personality, perhaps his confidence? But I knew. It was all of that… and his hands. Women, you see, adored my uncle's hands. They were large but well formed; they looked rough, but were soft to the touch, and he was skilled with them in every manner.

A curious affliction struck Rottfield when he was on break from University. It is thought to have happened as a result of a dalliance with a wretched, decrepit wisp of a woman who lived in a dilapidated shed adjacent to a South Hadley pig farm. Within hours he developed something akin to a whooping cough. He was bedridden for weeks, each inhalation producing a hollow howl, each exhalation a cacophony of coughs that wracked his poor young body. He emerged from the sickness with no color to his eyes—only whites—and a shrunken and discolored tongue. He was taut and strong, however, his muscles having repeatedly torn and healed, torn and healed, torn and healed from the strain of his struggles against his mother's makeshift restraints.

On the occasion of his first trip outside, he had palpitations of the heart of such intensity that his mother, ambling a few yards behind him, swore she heard them with her own ears. He collapsed on the walk, his hands fleeing from his pockets to tear at his chest. On the leaf-covered ground he writhed, twitching and pulling at his clothes as though he meant to free his panicked heart from its bony cage. It was then that his mother heard a sound like a skillet popping and spattering with grease. Rottfield shrieked as his hooked hands burnt and blistered and popped.

Uncle Rottfield's hands couldn't be exposed to sunlight or they would redden, break out into poisonous translucent blisters, and finally emit a malodorous brown smoke. Only black gloves, it turns out, could protect him. He attempted some other pair but once, some cheap tan things, and still has patches of scorched and melted suede enmeshed with the ruined skin of his left palm.

Since that terrible day, his protective mother kept him inside, with nary a book nor any considerable company to entertain him. When she died of shigellosis, he had the run of the house, and he destroyed its insides utterly. He emerged wearing her long black gloves, and even then he never strayed past the borders of Hadley. He would sit in one of the few eateries that would have him, awaiting the scraps left behind by other diners. When, in his forties, he took to bestowing grim and bloody prognostications upon unwitting diners, the staff ejected him and forbade him entry. It is said that he survived on a diet of berries, squirrels, stray cats, and unnamed creatures that made their home in tangled brambles and expansive underbrush of the state forest.

On three separate occasions, Rottfield shuddered, collapsed, and fell to the floor. There being no sign of life, we buried him in the same pine box. But each time, he rose again. Uncle Rottfield has clawed through three pine boxes, each time caterwauling as he staggered headlong through the town in search of gloves to replace the ones that frayed and split due to his exertions, exposing his gnarled and ruined fingers. Father said what we were all thinking: Old Rottfield wasn't done conquesting. He will never be done.

2015

It is Rottfield who manages collections from WXXT's recalcitrant, stubborn advertisers, those who hear our broadcasts and pull their ads in paroxysms of morality, refusing payment and threatening censure.

One such woman dealt with us in such a manner last Friday. I descend to the cellar, where Uncle Rottfield still writhes and weeps in his sodden box.

Gloves, uncle, I whisper. *I know where you can find long, black gloves. I will show you the house. I will point you to the room. The woman sleeps with black gloves under her pillow. Wake her up. Put your hands on her face and whisper her awake.*

Uncle Rottfield needs gloves. He needs gloves that have warmed the hands of a woman the way his hands used to in his youth.

Tonight the sad remnants of those large, rough, well-formed hands will perform vile atrocities, looked upon impassively by empty white eyes.

WILLIAM DITHER (PART 1)

The man with the hat appeared in my window last night. It was silent in my house, and I rolled over, and there he was. I woke up with a jolt. I recognized him immediately.

The man with the hat was—is—William Dither. Ages ago we tore apart all we saw, made people fear to walk the streets unless they were in a mob, even made them fear walking in the light of day. This town has all kinds of corners, alleys, alcoves, all manner of shadows. We were feared. The subject of bedtime stories with which only the cruelest fathers would dare burden their mewling brats. Ages ago, we were giants.

Dither gave me such a start. I didn't know I still had it in me: being afraid. Afraid of what, I wonder? It's been so long since I felt physical pain that I can say the word aloud—*pain*—and still not know how to explain it, to really define the word in its truest sense. I know I delight in causing it, but so much of that delight is gone now because when I dig into the soft belly of a young woman and she screams, I cannot begin to imagine why. Oh, I know what pain *is*, I just can't enjoy it because I can't empathize. No, I don't fear physical pain.

Maybe I fear not existing. Obliteration. Desolation. Not being able to touch or see or hear or taste. All my memories, fair and foul, just... gone. I'm halfway there, of course, but that's a damn sight from all the way there. I don't want to disappear.

Dither talked to me for a while, through the panes of my window. He still knows pain. He says that I can feel it through him. He has invited me out for the evening. Rain is falling out there, but it can't make me colder than I already am.

People rush around in the rain, their peripheral vision truncated by raincoat hoods and umbrellas. Dither told me. He told me we can snatch someone right from the sidewalk, pull them into a doorway, and gnaw into their stomachs like starving rats. He told me that if I don't feed, I will fade.

I have no taste buds, but I remember the taste of mutton, of mead, of blood, of a still-living liver. I can still feel the muscle of a still-beating heart pulsing against my black tongue. I can still feel sinewy rubbery innards between my grey teeth. I can taste wine and worms and mud. Maybe these are phantom tastes, but when they're in me, I feel whole. Like I can't disappear. I can seize a young Smith girl, a sulking linebacker, a cringing store clerk.

But I. Cannot. Die.

Tonight, Old Bill and I shall rampage.

You're listening to WXXT, Marconi's nightmare, the bane of Leeds, the soundtrack that's a death rattle, a last breath, an eaten scream. Today is no-repeat Thursday. Don't look out your window tonight. You might see old Dither, encased in bars of falling rain, now breaking through, his grey hands burrowing bloodlessly through your very walls and into the cavity of your ribcage, his mouth gaping into a vast, foul cave to engulf your collapsing head, forever silencing you.

And I shall be with him.

LITTLE LEEDS

I met Finn at the right time, just the right time. He was sitting cross-legged on a bench outside of the Haymarket Café and the hippie store with mannequins in the window, the ones with the distorted faces stretched into shrieks. A drum sat wedged in the pretzel of his legs and he was beating it with his palms, his fingers bent like claws. He was dressed in dirt and clothes the color of dirt, and dirt was the color of his dreads. He had a sharp angled jawline, the skin taut to his skull. He had a stub of a nose and eyes that encompassed all the colors of every eye ever, before or since. A kaleidoscope. He flashed a yellow smile at me, and so I sat down next to him and moistened my index finger with my tongue. I slowly raised it to his forehead and wrote "HI."

I pulled my finger back and wiped the dirt on the sidewalk.

"What did I just write?" I said.

And he said, "A valentine."

It was the right time, just exactly the right time. Things had come to a head with my folks. I'd grown tired of living in their antiseptic mini-mansion near the women's college, all white walls and everything folded tight and square. Army corners. Central air. Maids and servants like the place was some kind of plantation. The white glove test, straight A's, every time. I felt like a germ, and I knew in my heart that every system in that house had been manufactured to eject me. And yet, there I went, every day, for meals, for laundry. I could afford rent six hundred times over in any apartment in any complex or house in the city, but my folks, they'd be so lonely. In that big house by themselves, Kayla having flounced out at the end of the nineties and Rickman, my half-brother, having drunk himself to a middle-aged grave.

I dressed like a crusty punk, and I refused to shower, and still they clung. I played death metal at deafening levels and they slammed shut their soundproofed doors and watched old movie musicals. I brought dudes around, scary dudes, the fucked up users who sprawled around Tremens Terrace and dealt and hustled and worse, and my folks talked to them like they were any other kids, gave them iced tea and peanut butter cookies. Even when I'd take them to my bed, and, dude, I was *loud*, my folks would greet them in the dawn with a box of donuts and a pot of good coffee. My morning greeting was Fuck Off and my nighttime benediction was Suck My Ass and still I was coddled and tended to and pampered.

Fuck that.

Finn was my out. He lived in the woods. If there ever had been a more poetic refutation of my parents and their lifestyle, I couldn't imagine it. I packed up a Gucci suitcase with two pairs of jeans, some underwear, a bra, and a t-shirt or two, and I went into the woods.

I hadn't known so many kids lived in the woods. The tent city, the newspapers called it, but they just called it home. I thought of it as Little Leeds. They even had a community garden, with basil and rosemary and green onions and tomatoes. I met Hailey, who was the best thief I've ever met. She might as well have been a magician. You'd be chatting with her and she'd reach into her back pocket and hand you the necklace you thought you still had on. Between stuff I grabbed from my folks from time to time and the stuff she shoplifted, no one in Little Leeds ever wanted for food. I met Bricker, who drew the coolest pictures ever, monsters he'd invented, people with feet where their eyes should be, with rudimentary hands for nipples, with teeth lining their eyelids. I met Winnie, obese and depressed and eternally teary-eyed, but her one-liners could just double you over. These were my people. I felt safe here. I only hoped that they saw something in me. I worried about it. Did *I* have anything of worth to offer *them*? It helped that they seemed to accept me right off. There was no discord.

Finn and I shared a tent. He made me my own drum, using some kind of weird skin I'd never seen before—he had sheaths of it in his backpack—stretched over the end of a hollowed out section of log and sewn on with leather tassels. We drummed madly until the other kids told us to shut the fuck up, and then we rolled around in the leaves and laughed.

It was all good. Until Eric came back.

It had been a mantra around the camp: *Just wait until Eric comes back*, they'd say, if someone said something shitty or if a tussle broke out. Eric was their ambassador, they said, but they wouldn't say to whom he'd been sent nor for what purpose. *Don't you want to be part of something bigger than yourself?* Hailey would say. *But not, like, God or any of that ridiculous nonsense? Something you can* believe *in? Because it is real? Just wait. Wait until* Eric *comes back.*

It was a quiet blue morning, waking with tentative birdsong, the cusp of dawn, cool and humid. I woke to a sound I couldn't identify. It sounded like when Fluffernutter, my parents' cat, used to lick the window shade: a repetitive rasp. I opened my eyes. Finn wasn't in the tent. I pushed myself up to sit.

Something was pawing at the flap. The shadow on the tent wall wouldn't resolve itself into anything identifiable: it looked for all the world like a shrub was trying to get in. I yanked down the zipper and saw what it was, and even then my eyes couldn't send sufficient information to my brain. I stepped out quickly, shook the tent off me like a coat, and I backed up until my shoulders came into contact with a tree. In the half-light, I could tell it was a man, or it had been a man. Naked, mostly, browned by time and by terra. Thorny vines ran out of his nose and into his mouth and down, threading through his skin like laces, into the purple tangle at his awful groin. *Down there* was either a harvest of tumors or a cluster of testicles, around which were the browned and tangled remnants of briefs. They swarmed with miniscule insects like magnetic filings in a kid's toy. From his underarms grew foul mushrooms, webbed and caked and sending spores into the air around him. The fungus had taken hold in the webbing of his fingers as well, and sprouted like foul grey wings from behind his ears. His eye sockets bulged with berries, giving his face a top-heavy, bulging, alien aspect.

He lurched forward and opened his mouth to speak. I pressed my back hard against the tree and pulled my penknife from my pocket. I pointed it at him, my hand trembling. Beetles poured from his mouth like tokens from a slot machine. Then the mother of all beetles, this black and cracked giant, poked out from the middle of them. It wasn't a beetle. It was his tongue. It curled around his lips, circling, pushing the beetles away. And then he sang. It was the most mournful, unaffected, beautiful voice I'd ever heard.

Mary, sit with me by the river
We'll pull the stars from the sky

We'll pull down the moon
and we'll pull down the sun
We'll pull down the shade of the eye

"Eric," I said, and he crumpled as though a puppeteer had let go the control bar. I dropped into a crouch and approached him. As the sun began to rise in the sky, I studied the twigs and vines that lay under his skin, some just visible under a thin patina of pale flesh. Some poked out like searching phalanges. From his collarbone extended a shorn spike of wood, its edge as sharp as a blade. And fused with his skin, meshed with it, *part* of it, were flaps and folds of a yellow nylon tent.

I was pulled up by the back of the collar, and spun around. It was Finn. His face was alight with rage, red as a berry. He wheeled his arm around and slapped me hard on the cheek, open-handed. I had never been hit before. Never. I fell on my butt on the cold ground and burst into tears. That didn't stop him. He advanced, his fists clenched and red.

"Don't you talk to Eric," he said. "Don't you dare ever, *ever* talk to Eric."

I scrambled to my feet and grabbed Finn's neck with both hands. His eyes bugged, and he punched wildly at my chest and neck. Still gripping his neck, I walked him backwards until his back pushed up against a tree. I released my grip and he began wheezing, choking for air. I wasn't me. I wasn't *me.* I flailed at him, a mad volley, my fists landing on his eye, on his nose—I heard the bone crunch—on his cheekbone, his Adam's apple, his temple. I was crying, screaming. I don't know what I was saying. Somewhere in my frenzy I discovered that my penknife was in my hand. He fell to the ground, screaming my name until the blade found a home in his throat, silencing his voice.

As I stabbed and swiped and carved, as I tore Finn open, I saw something. In the wounds, in the gashes and gouges where I should have seen organs, innards, and fat, was an alien sky framed by the ragged, red-ringed walls of flesh, a distant horizon, a color I could not and cannot now name. I was looking down, but through the tattered flesh I saw *up*. Through the sky swam monstrous things, blistered and winged and framed in bubbling mist. The things were dropping blue gelatinous blobs from their undersides, like bombs from the belly of a plane, like turds from a horse. The things pulsed sickly, like disease. I thought of cancer. Of spores that take hold and corrupt. One of them sailed up… *down*… toward me, through Finn's opened-up belly. I rolled him over onto his stomach and stepped back. Finn lurched upward at the midsection, his arms twitching as they tried to get under him to grab at his gut. Then he collapsed. A roar came from beneath him, like the guttural growl of some impossibly large beast. The roar faded and went silent. I flipped Finn onto his back again, and all was as normal.

Except this: there was a hole in the ground where his body had lain, a hole with no bottom that I could see. Something had burrowed into the earth. Deep.

But it was gone, and now I stood there stunned, looking at what remained. I had destroyed my friend, my love, the boy I'd found at just the right time. I had taken apart his face like a jigsaw puzzle and crushed to dust and jelly all that had been beneath it, his lovely head ruined, split eight ways like the husk of a firecracker, his dreads spread out on the ground like a many-pointed star.

Crushed and ruined and split open by me, by *me*, who'd never so much as touched someone in anger.

It was then that the applause started. The kids of Little Leeds were surrounding us, standing in a loose circle. Winnie's fist was at her mouth, her eyes gleaming. Bricker was grinning. Hailey bounced on her heels, clapping soundlessly, using just the tips of her fingers. I heard a rustling behind me and turned. Eric, all twigs and vines and leaves, was hoisting Finn from the ground. He propped Finn's corpse up against the tree, the tree I'd pushed him into, the tree at the base of which I'd pummeled and stabbed away his life.

Eric dug at Finn's insides, tore at the cadaver with nails as thick as a dog's. I wanted to shout *no*… to warn Eric of the sick world that was in Finn somewhere, for fear he would get pulled in, when I heard faint drumming, as though Finn's ghost was still pounding out beats on drums of dried flesh somewhere.

When Eric opened Finn's rib cage like it was a book of bone and marrow, I saw the source of the sound. There was no weird sky, no monstrous things, no horizon. There was only a transistor radio in there, clothed in gore, wound in muscle, shot through with bone. It throbbed like a heart.

Eric began to sing, and the speakers of the transistor radio echoed him.

Mary, sit with me by the river
We'll pull the stars from the sky
We'll pull down the moon
and we'll pull down the sun
We'll pull down the shade of the eye

The kids sang along. Leaves rustled. Something—a lot of somethings—were descending from the treetops. I held out my hand as if to catch a raindrop, and a leech landed with a *thwap* on my palm.

You're listening to WXXT, the suppurating sun in the blood-blackened sky.

THE PURGING OF MY UNCLE'S HOUSE (THE TIME OF THE BLACK TENTS)

Through the barren November landscape my mother piloted the old Ford station wagon. The radio wheezed out some 1920's ragtime thing. Tinny trumpets, whimpering clarinets, an unctuous singer pleading with a woman to defrock and, later, to decamp to a place with red skylines and surging surf and natives drumming out frenetic beats. In the background, men chuckled and chortled, clinked their glasses. A woman retched raucous laughter.

A picture materialized in my mind of a bustling bar in black and white. A city of bottles, some squat, some reaching out to touch the brown polished sky above. Sailors in striped collars, belting back cocktails and slapping each other on the back. Women with dramatic eyes, ringed black as coal, lashes like the tines of black forks. Men in sack coats and pleated pants, thin mustaches, oiled hair, blasé eyebrows. I pictured a barkeep with rolled up shirtsleeves polishing a glass with a white rag, surveying the room, shaking his head, a gesture of contempt with a chaser of wistfulness. A couple leaning over their table for a chaste kiss. A large man in the back corner, very still, engaged for the purpose of cracking skulls, should skulls need cracking.

Outside my window streamed in grey and black blurs a bleak afternoon, everything dwelling in a gauze of mist. The sun was a ghost trapped in quicksand made of clouds, emitting only a dull glow, no more powerful than a streetlight. Trees huddled in profuse clusters—forlorn, tall, whiskered things embedded in wormy earth. The last of the leaves twirled down to light on the packed-dirt road, the graceful suicides of the already dead. They skittered across the road, here in great surges, there in fitful migrations. Mother chewed her fingernails. The song faded. Twigs snapped under the wheels and gravel jumped up to rattle against the car's undercarriage.

We've just heard Slinky Salvatore and the Under-tones, a DJ said, his voice a ventricular rasp, as though decades of brown cigarette smoke had accumulated in his vocal folds like an eclipse of moths. *Before that, it was Muggsy Dogswater and his Ragtime Band with "Pancakes and Rye" and Livia Lankweather singing us to sleep with "Dust on my Pillow." It's time for me to once again descend the earthen staircase down into darkness. I've been Nicholas Ripsternum Lusk. After the break, won't you join Jake Rottfield for* The Dreaming Hour? *I know I will.*

Mother switched off the radio. She had had some involvement with Rottfield, long ago, one involving sex or debt, or both, I knew, and there was rancor there, even still. We sat in what passed for silence: the rattle of pebbles, the sound of Mother's teeth biting at her red nails, the twigs cracking and snapping like radio static.

After a time, the thick forest that lined the road gave way to sparser woods. Thin trees stood like follicles on a balding head. Far off, near the glowing horizon, something black fluttered in the distance.

"Is that…?

"Yes," Mother said, sounding like she'd rather not have to talk. "It's the third November."

I stifled my joy, forcing my mouth into a straight, thin line. I loved the Time of the Black Tents. It was better than Halloween even, although maybe I appreciated the anticipation, having to wait three years instead of just one. It was just so blackly exciting to think that in one of the many tents that filled the woods for those three beautiful days there would be…

Mother steered the car sharply to the right, off of the road, and the car rumbled along over the bumpy ground, over leaf-littered hillocks, down steep and root-strewn muddy grades. My teeth clacked with each jounce of the car. I rolled down my window and stuck out my head. In the distance another tent fluttered, the size of a small house, a pointed peak at its top. They were so shiny, so new, untouched, it seemed, by weather, and the flapping of the canvas was like enthusiastic applause. It was as though they were alien things that could be seen, but not affected by the physical, not truly there, but somehow *more* there, like they were from the Leeds from my dreams, the Leeds of red-lit skyscrapers, Satanic cathedrals, and great hulking things just out of sight, and that was the Real Leeds.

We crested a hill and there were more, so many more, strewn for miles amongst the thin trees like silent ghosts. I'd never seen that many. I looked at Mother to remark upon it, but she had that look on her face, the look that told she'd brook no further conversation. At one point we passed so close by a tent I could have reached out and touched it. I caught a smell that reminded me of shooting cap guns when I was a boy: sulfur and phosphorous. It stood my arm hairs on end.

We drove down, down, further down, the grade so steep I was afraid the car might flip end over end, but then the ground leveled off and there by the crest of a trickling brook sat the house, as something spat up from the water to squat at its shore, a modest old log cabin with a smoking chimney and a slight sag at the center of the roof. The logs were scuffed with shoe-marks and hand prints, and the windows squinted like slit eyes against the faltering afternoon light. A few cars lolled at odd angles among the trees, their doors open, their alarms dinging fruitlessly. Alongside the house, like a leech about to latch on, squatted a big blue dumpster.

We got out of the car. From off in the distance, the flapping of black tents, for it was the Time of the Black Tents, all hail and bow to the Black Tents, and maybe this year, maybe three years from now, or six, I would get the invitation, and get to take my chance.

Uncle Bozrah was laid out on the oak table in the dining room. That was not what I expected, but that's what was. I'd seen dead bodies before, more than one, but this was the first blood relative. For a time I felt as though I could not get a full breath. His bathrobe was open to the navel, the lump of his breastbone prominent and pink. At first I thought he was still alive, that there'd been some mistake. His jaw hung low, in a frozen bid for air, and no one had yet bothered to shut his eyes, which, though unseeing, burned with life, staring avidly at the cobweb-clad bulb that poked out from a rusted sconce in the ceiling. His teeth were a dentist's dream. One leg dangled from the table, pale and long and hairless, crisscrossed with old scars at the calf.

Around the table stood his brothers, my other uncles. I recognized them from weddings, infrequent family reunions, and a seemingly endless litany of funerals, and from dreams. Uncle Eltweed was there, thin as a finger, bald on top, long greying hair hanging down to frame his sucked-in cheeks, a toothy grin, low-slung brows ridged with tangles, a chin like a witch's nose. Uncle Randall, too, similar face, also thin, but with a basketball belly—today, as on many days, he was shirtless, with nipples like little wads of chewed up gum—baldheaded and bowlegged and ripe. And Uncle Walter, fat as a tick, in an untucked shirt and loose, wrinkled brown tie, hair sticking up everywhere on his plump head, who slammed shut a large old book when Mother led me in through the open door.

"The kid heard?" Randall said.

Eltweed said, "Kid don't know shit from apple butter. Give him another year."

"He's right here," said Mother. Then she looked at old Bozrah's face and clasped her hands over her mouth to stifle a shocked sob. I *was* right there. And I was 13, a man. I thought they should be able to say anything in front of me, anything at all, but I was afraid of them, and I kept mum.

"D'ja see the tents, kid?" said Walter, the words riding on a wave of the nose-stabbing scent of some sickly-sweet liquor.

"The Black Tents," I affirmed, and the brothers gave each other looks I couldn't understand, much to my frustration, but each look was different, and freighted with dark things in multitudes. It was a conversation in a foreign language. Even poor, dead Uncle Bozrah seemed more attuned to it than I.

Eltweed looked at Mother, and then down at the knot in my dead Uncle's bathrobe, and Mother looked at him with eyes that burned with anger, and with something else I could not name. After a beat of pregnant silence, Walter said, "Kid, let's get you started downstairs."

"Is my father coming?" I asked, trying, but failing, to sound neutral.

Looks all around. Eltweed cleared his throat. Randall spoke up.

"Your father rarely comes to this Leeds," he said, and Walter put his hand on my shoulder and we walked to the door that stood ajar atop the cellar stairs. For a terrifying, irrational moment I feared that he might push me down. Instead, we descended. I thought I heard Mother cry out as Walter shut the door, and I looked at him. He looked at me.

We descended into the basement.

Books. Books everywhere. Books in askew towers and unruly piles. Resting uneasily on scattered magazines. On shelves, atop shelves, leaning on shelves, and at the feet of shelves. Piled on chairs and couches. Climbing the walls like staircases, coffee table books at the bottom, small books at the top. Mass market paperbacks fat and thin, with and without covers. Hardcovers, some in jackets pristine, others in tatters.

"Quit your gawking," Walter said. "Pick what's good, and make your own pile. Pick what's in good condition, and put it on the porch. The shit—the busted spines, the bent and dented—those are for the dumpster, unless you want 'em. Get started."

With that, he tramped up the stairs. The creak of a door, the sounds of scuffling and whispering and cooing, and the creak again, the *chuk* of the door closing. I heard more scuffing of shoes on wood, the floor creaking. It sounded as though there were some sort of muted fight going on. Adults struck me as creatures of infinite mystery. I shrugged there in the silence, for no one but myself. Or maybe for the invisible watchers I assumed were always there, always staring. I went to work.

I had assembled my stacks, enjoyed the satisfaction of hurling books into the metal dumpster that sprawled outside the bulkhead doors, the clatter and the anarchy of it. So many books. Cookbooks with garish colors, full of pictures of plump brown birds and things mummy-wrapped in bandages of bacon. Plays and slender volumes of poetry with surnames I didn't recognize. Endless books on World War II and Adolf Hitler, branded with the ubiquitous stark and menacing swastika. *The Joy Of Sex*, *Ribald Rhymes*, *Dirty Limericks*, Hemingway, Mailer, Fitzgerald, Salinger. Montague Summers. Wheatley, Crowley, Castaneda. Manson. Edgar Cayce, LaVey, Margaret Murray. Abrecan Geist. Colin Wilson. *Uncle John's Bathroom Reader*, many volumes. *Dirty*

Jokes—hundreds of paperbacks with spines whitened with a thousand cracks. Lovecraft, Kuttner, Silverberg, Heinlein, and Sturgeon. Vonnegut. Older books whose names had long been rubbed from their ancient covers.

I cleared from the shelves of a towering hutch a random selection of books (*Shamans of Modern Egypt*, *Plagues of the Near and Distant Future*, *Space-Worms*, *The Barkerton Parade and Others*, *Diseases of the Goat*) from the shelves of a towering hutch. When I had them sorted, I opened the slatted double doors at the bottom. Within was a stack of magazines. I pulled out the topmost, and on the cover was the blurred and flash-bulb lit image of a woman whose denim pantsuit was being pulled apart by many male hands. Most of the males' faces were obscured, just beyond the outer curve of the light. The only one whose face I could see, a grinning, sadistic looking gaunt thing whose slack eyes bore an undeniable resemblance to those of the males in my family, was wearing her colorful sash around his elongated and profusely bruised neck. The title of the magazine consisted of a series of unfathomable characters composed of tapering white lines, similar to *kanji,* in curious patterns—each one appeared to be some variation on one of two themes: a collapsed structure or a cramped creature. I pulled out the magazines and put them with the books to be discarded. Beneath them sprawled a haphazard pile of Polaroids. I extracted one. I looked at it for a long time. Then I flung it back into the hutch and slammed shut the doors.

I crossed the room to clear away the stacks of books against the west wall, and when I got to the midsized books I saw that behind the stacks gaped a ragged-edged cutaway in the wall. I pulled away more books, scattering them behind me on the rug. I peered in. The light from the room made it about a foot in before fading to an impenetrable black. Then, from somewhere back there, somewhere far, I heard a whisper. Maybe my uncles, upstairs, talking. I'd never heard them speak candidly; they always hushed up when I came in the room. My curiosity grabbing hold and squeezing tight, I pulled from my pocket my penlight, and entered. On my hands and knees I crawled. It got colder as I went, and I shivered. The whispers continued, almost, but not quite, separating into understandable words. The narrow light bounced as I moved forward, occasionally switching hands when one got tired.

I stopped.

Ahead in the half-light loomed something made of skin, folded like a bedsheet. In one of the folds opened a wet red eye. I gasped and recoiled, and then saw another fold below open to reveal two rows each of top and bottom teeth. A grey tongue appeared, slid over them, and retreated. The thing whispered. It whispered my name. A shadow moved across that face… no, a silhouette. As my penlight swept, swooped, stopping here, stopping there, I saw my father—the slicked back, toothsome father from my dark dreams of red-lit cities and decrepit angels returning from battle on the backs of leering goats.

He was wrapped around a whip-thin grey husk of a living human, or perhaps two humans. Their limbs were intertwined like the chains when you spin the seat of a swing set. At the end of each arm, a wild asterisk of bony fingers grasped at nothing. At the end of each leg twitched several swollen, dry feet with cracked heels and claw-like yellowed nails. The toes, fused together with mold and white fungi, curled and uncurled. I heard a nauseous slurping sound, and my father fattened even as his hosts shrunk like cellophane pulled taut over weakened bones.

From behind this apparition came a terrible sound, an eerie high-pitched chorus, moving closer, a slithering and bubbling. It was children, by the sound of it, some moaning, keening mass of infants, toddlers. Some sang. Others sobbed. The darkness beyond my father and his victims—a darkness I'd thought was ultimate and inviolate—grew darker.

In my dreams, my father had been a powerful figure, slim but sinewy, fierce eyes and fast mouth, energy thrumming like heat haze all about him. Here, now, he was a coffin-worm, a deep-sea creature, something that had never known sunlight, never felt the touch of anything but dirt and stone.

A hand reached for mine, and took it, cold, a burning cold, and my instinct was to yank my own hand away, but he held my hand fast, tight as a vise. I felt blood rushing under his skin like a subcutaneous river, tumultuous and deadly and somehow colder still than the flesh that kept it at bay.

Dream with me, he said. *Close your eyes and dream with me.*

… and then I stood in a house somewhere, old, all peeling wallpaper and cobwebs, sagging couches and rickety, ancient chairs, the only light streaming in from cracked and dust-caked windows. The ticking of a clock provided the only sound. I needed to know the time, I felt, to be sure that this was real. I turned and found a wall clock directly behind me, above a decrepit armoire, and recoiled in horror. Behind the round glass leered the squashed head of my poor Uncle Bozrah, purple eyelids, shut; whiskey-pocked nose pushed leftward; lips a flat, pink oval in which a grey tongue lay curled like a sleeping slug. The arms of the clock were severed fingers, short, but with long, browned nails. One of them bore a pronounced callus at the first joint. They dangled limp and twitching. 6:30, then, or else the clock simply ticked brainlessly, keeping the time a secret. One eye opened and found me, then looked beyond me.

I turned, and before me stood my father, looking strong and sunburnt and alive, to my relief, my uncles on either side of him, slightly crouched as though in supplication, their skin-wrapped skulls grinning.

"Where's Mother?" I said, but the words came out as though shouted from yards away, the syllables fragmented, rendered nonsensical by clicks and clacks of static. They laughed at me, all of them. Their raucous laughter filled the room like smoke. Walter slapped his knee with a large, flat hand. Their bodies began to bulge and ripple. Father's head ballooned, his brow emerging from curtains of hair, pushing them to either side like curtains. Horns burst from his head, sending torn flesh and sprays of blood to the walls and ceiling. His teeth grew, splitting his lips, causing them to fall away. Two hooves pushed from his chest and parted, splitting his torso like a coat, spilling worms on the carpet in a great wriggling glut. Scrawny, furred, bent legs pulled themselves out from pants of human flesh, casting them aside like macabre trousers. My uncles followed suit, and they stood before me, their human shells piled like bloody jetsam on the floorboards. Goats with wild eyes, fur in patches over skin textured like burlap, signs and symbols branded pink and black into their flesh.

They turned from me and crouched, their asterisk assholes staring me down. My father looked back and gestured with strange, alien eyes, and I climbed atop his back. I grabbed his shoulder blades with my hands as the walls of the house fell to the earth, spitting dirt clouds in all directions. We galloped away over fallow meadows, past stove-in barns and the smoking, burnt skeletons of ruined houses, past leaning silos and crumpled tenements.

Walter brayed, and the other goats joined in. I threw my head back and howled, a wavering falsetto my lame contribution to the hellish chorus, and I saw that above me the sky was crowded with bruised cherubim, pink and purple, their weak, worn wings working hard to keep them aloft. Their features were contorted with the effort, many of their faces swollen like the bulging visages of the drowned. Some held in their hands the toes of thin, stringy, naked bodies of elderly women, blue-veined and whiter than snow-clad icicles. Here and there one slipped from a cherub's grasp and crashed to the earth with bone-cracking impact. Bereft, those cherubim wailed like sirens, fat little hands grasping at nothing. One, whose mouth had been sewn shut with wet black thread, shat out a volley of clumped pellets in a rain of green gruel, which Eltweed deftly avoided, his hooves furrowing the earth as he dug in and broke right. One bobbing cherub whizzed among the others like a fly, looking down at the crushed women, enthusiastically stroking its long, thin erection. Its wheeze cut like the buzz of a bee through the sound of flapping wings, a sound that evoked the wind-stoked flapping of the glorious Black Tents.

And then we crested a hill and before us stood the biggest, blackest tent of them all. It spanned my very consciousness, disappearing beyond my range of sight on either side. Above it, some pale white worm slid in and out of this world, appearing and reappearing as though the sky were the surface of an impossibly blue pond, here a twitching, tapered end, there a furrowed midsection. It reeked of abandoned dumpsters, of meat under a cruel and close-by sun. I gagged as we stormed at the tent. I saw before me no door, no entrance of any kind. Then Father braked, back hooves sliding between front hooves, dirt kicking up in half-circles on either side of him. I lost my grip and went aloft. I blacked out… or, no… it was the beckoning blackness of the tent and maybe—I could not tell—a window had opened into the tent, revealing the cancerous dark inside. My eyes filled with tears as I struggled to keep them open.

Impact.

I was back in the dank tunnel.

My father had let go of my now-numb hand and was spinning his own, untwining the two limbless arms that had wound around his. They fell away like snakes. He reached out to me again, turned his hand palm up, and beckoned with his fingers. Something gave way in my stomach. I felt it move up into my gullet, moving toward my palate. I retched, and reached a hand up to my mouth. Hanging over my lip was a thin hair. I pulled at it, and retched again. I wound my finger 'round and pulled harder. Something was coming up from inside me, something at the end of that hair. I felt it in the wet bag of my gut, felt it rise as I pulled. I opened my mouth as far as I could go, straining muscles in my neck, in my jaw.

Then I vomited it in clumps onto the packed-dirt floor of the passageway, pulling at it with both hands as it emerged, trying to leave space for air. It was a terrible clump of hair and mucus, more than I could have thought would fit in me. Its aroma was sepsis and grog, laced through with metallic blood and toxic smoke. I pulled and retched, pulled and retched, until it was all out, and then I vomited a stream of brown water. My father's hand found the mass, plunged into it. It emerged with a long, ancient key between index finger and forefinger. A three-looped bow, a shaft, an intricate bit like some elaborate sigil.

Through the tattered flesh of the nearly dead, he sang, a wavering, somehow vulnerable falsetto, *in a child's disordered dreams. There are seven and thirty ways (by my count) to get to the Real Leeds.* The children behind him moaned in tune. Rising, becoming deafening. He pulled free of the desiccated corpses on which he'd been feeding and lurched forward, his grinning, fanged face looming right before mine. I turned, and the faces of my uncles crowded the crawlspace, larger than life, smushed in, hair intertwined, old teeth, rust and whiskey, and I knew that they would take me, take me to the Black Tents, and I knew that Mother was dead, violated, bled, and that she littered the floor of the kitchen like discarded clothing and that all I had known up until now would soon be just a memory, and I felt hungry now, thirsty, as though I'd never tasted food, as though liquid had never rushed over my tongue, and we went, the dead and the living, the Stocktons, the Swift River Stocktons, to the Black Tents, to *the* Black Tent, and the things within finally showed us their secrets.

REGINA, REGINA

My first lady friend, Regina, had a taste for the macabre and for morbid experimentation. It was she who cut off the tips of her ring fingers and sautéed them in her mother's skillet for us to taste with cherry wine. It was she who joined me in mocking, torturing, and teasing a bird who'd injured itself flying into a willow tree.

Regina burned and bit me and poked at my eyes with sharpened spoons. She woke me up by pouring syrup in my eyes or walloping me with a wheelbarrow. If I said I had a headache, she'd box my ears; if I was nauseated, she'd sock me a good one to the solar plexus. She stole her parents' money, set things afire, vomited on purpose at inappropriate occasions, soiled herself at funerals and, at the tender age of 13, attempted a bit of amateur grave digging that eventually evolved into a full-blown avocation.

Her eyes were milky white; she was photophobic and suffered from cataracts and corneal ulcers. Her tongue was dry, white, and cracked. She had distended black nipples and thick, wiry hair grew out of control on her toes. I will never lust again like I lusted for Old Regina.

This is WXXT, the Voice from the Ass Hole of the Commonwealth. Join us on Sundays for *Jazz Jackals* with Cecil Trunk in the mornings and the *Tragedy Hour* with your host Lard Scotch in the evenings. WXXT—the dignity of a hard chancre.

ANNE GARE'S RARE BOOK & EPHEMERA CATALOGUE #697969-F

THE LIBELLUS VOX LARVA

The last weeks have brought us an unprecedented run on grimoires. The customers sent emissaries or else arrived with their features obscured by black veils. They paid in cash and were just a mite impatient. All of this is likely an indication that something is about to happen, perhaps something earth altering.

At any rate, for the fan of those musty magical tomes of dubious authorship, we do still have a copy of The Libellus Vox Larva. The unique quality of this particular book is that if the owner is to drop it on the floor, the words and characters and illustrations and diagrams within rearrange and re-form, resulting in an entirely new book of spells and enchantments and invocations.

The owner is strongly cautioned against dropping it outdoors, however. The most recent owner tripped over the carcass of a hog in Rodgeville, north of Shelburne, and the words… well, the words were RELEASED.

News reports from the town paper were necessarily circumspect, so not much is known about the particulars, but after all the chaos had abated and the red dust had settled and the blood had dried, the town was abandoned and disincorporated and all its houses and buildings razed and cleared away. All that remains is barren earth.

Contemporary full mottled calf, spine gilt in six compartments, title in gilt on lettering-piece. Corners bumped, short split to upper joint. Foxed, few stains. Six hundred pages. Fourteen thousand, five hundred dollars.

The Homily

Ladies and gentlemen. Brothers, sisters. Wives and daughters and cousins and friends. It's a cold night, I know, and I've turned down the thermostat. I want you to get close to one another, as I am close to you, among you. I want us to be a single living organism tonight, to be as one, for my voice to speak your thoughts.

When I was a boy, some friends and I, well, we snuck into an abandoned house after school. "Sneaking in" is what you call it when you're a boy. Adults, who are known for their lack of adventurous instinct, and of humor, call it "breaking and entering." But we were boys, with nothing to fear from the law. We snuck in.

While the others explored the bedrooms and the kitchen, I found myself in the bathroom, looking at what the people who had lived there had left behind. There were crumpled and waterlogged boxes of Q-tips on the window sill. Husks of soap, with hairs burrowed into them, clinging like barnacles to the surface of the claw foot tub. Flattened tubes of toothpaste in cocoons of dust and hair. And a washcloth, caked in filth and dried soap scum and dead skin, stained brown to such a degree that its original color was difficult to discern. And hard as an anchor.

I held that washcloth up to my nose and I inhaled. I took in its essence, introduced its secrets into my system as you allow my words into your ears… into your brain… into your heart. Now, did I see you wince, Mary-Lou? Come on, now, sweetheart. I know for a fact that you yourself aren't afraid to try new things. I put that washcloth in my backpack and brought it home with me. I wanted to see whether it could be saved. First, I ran it under hot water, and I watched as the brown liquid swirled around the drain. I pulled off the hair, the insect eggs, the dirt and the dust, and I spread them out before me on the tiled floor of our bathroom. I formed them into patterns, into cities, into patchwork countryside, into suburbs. And then I laid them to waste with the fury of a betrayed and abandoned God.

The washcloth? I buried it in Ma's laundry basket. I found it a day later, in the linen closet, folded into a perfect square. It was a beautiful light blue, almost white. I held it to my nose. It smelled faintly of detergent and fabric softener. It was reborn.

Humanity itself is a washcloth. A disgusting old washcloth in an abandoned house.

It's hard as bark and it smells bad and it's caked in the filth of sin. And we must not simply wash away the sin. We must muck about in it. Engage with it. Before one casts aside one's garbage, one must wrestle with the deep down questions: What is this, really? Is this useful? Is there anything here from which I can learn?

Tonight we shall bathe together, and we shall examine that which runs off of our bodies before we simply let it slip away down the drain. There is no more intimate bond a man and woman can share with his creator than that which we shall forge tonight. It is my Special Work.

Under your chair you will find a towel and what very well may be a newly bought washcloth.

Let us away to the showers.

FESTUS AND JULES

Friday nights in Leeds, in the houses of certain men, one is likely to encounter treacherous things. So it was at Venom Hall at the crest of Round Hill Road, where on one cloud-cloaked September evening Festus Leigh hunched over his stove, stirring and stirring something that curdled and bubbled and burped in a giant black cauldron. His clairaudience held sway over him; he heard singing, as of the choir at St. Mary's, but in a language of antiquity, unknown to him, and slowed down, then sped up, unable to find its true cadence. He stirred in time, faster, slower. When it went backwards, he reversed his stirring. He slobbered brainlessly into the pot, a long clear tendril of saliva laying itself down on the surface in concentric circles across the brown broth. One eyelid twitched and fluttered.

Shhhh, he said to the voices whispering, getting in the way of the sweet and wild chorus. *Shhhh.*

Jules, Festus's brother, older, tireder, shuffled into the room. He pulled his white hair from in front of his eyes. It fell back. Impatiently, he tucked it all behind a wax-caked and slightly swollen ear.

"Festus," he said. "The river has climbed up over its banks. Let us go and see."

"Where's Maw?" Festus asked. "Maw'd like this stew I'm doing."

"Maw passed back last 'vember," said Jules.

Festus drew in all the air in the room with a whistle and let it out in a roar. He gibbered and blubbered and dropped the spoon, making a racket. His fingers, wet and pink, grasped at the air like those of a newborn. His tears salted the stew.

"Oh, for *Christ*," Jules said.

Festus didn't like it when Jules got mad. He brought himself around, but it wasn't easy. The whispers got louder in his head and he shoved them back. He leaned over and picked up the spoon, now festooned with cobwebs and hair. He plunged it back into the cauldron.

"How's them hogs?" he said hopefully, between snuffles.

"Ain't got no hogs no more, remember?" Jules braced himself for another outburst, but Festus just sighed a long, long sigh. Jules tried again. "Let's go down them flood waters."

What Festus heard was, "Fifth caller wins Dither's voice on his answering machine," words that didn't make no damn sense, because only Mr. Whitenose, not him and Jules, ever got callers, because there wasn't no kind of machine that could answer a damned thing, and because old Dither down on Crescent Street lost his voice and never got it back after he'd come down with the typhus. As Jules continued to speak, Festus heard not his words, but instead all kinds of suggestions, things he could do that night, places he could go, windows where he could see things forbidden to him, windows with bushes below where he could secret himself. He liked the whispers better than he liked the nonsense out of Jules, most times.

The steam was really pouring from the pot now. It obscured the things reaching out with many-jointed fingers.

Jules said, "Good on you, you just stay and tend to the guests. I'm gonna help the fellows dam it up. The river, that is."

Festus remembered something. He said, "Not if Mr. Whitenose has anything to say about it," and as though in a scene from some degraded comedy, the door swung open to reveal Mr. Whitenose himself. Festus and Jules turned to the master of the house and bowed their heads as they had been taught.

Shhh, said Festus to the whispering voices that bade him look up. *Shhh*. He dare not look up, no matter what the whispers said. They'd had a third brother, Jules and Festus had, and Festus was afraid to admit he'd forgot the poor fucker's name.

"Gentlemen," said Mr. Whitenose, and his voice was a gob of blood-veined pus sliding down a wall of marble, "I do hope the soup is near to completion. My guests are growing restless, and the bread is rather nearly spent." He walked to the pot and stuck a hand in, ignoring the long grey fingers that poked at his cuff and tickled at his wrist. He drew back his hand, bright red, the skin bubbling and blistering. He ran a long tongue up and down the zig-zag of his fingers. "Mmmmmm," he said. "Yes."

A rose-red infant curled up like a cashew bobbed to the surface, and Mr. Whitenose scooped it up in his equally red hand. Burnt hairs clung to the surface of the child's wrinkled head. He plucked them out, flicking them to the floor. He looked at Festus, looked at Jules, shaking his head. Then he bit off the feet and chewed them like a horse chews roughage, his jaw gyrating, bones crunching between his substantial brown teeth. He flung the rest back into the bubbling soup.

Then he sank into a crouch, lifted the pot with both hands, and swept it away, bending backwards and resting it on his belly in order to bear its significant weight. Curls of brown smoke squeezed out from between the cauldron and his belly as his shirt began to brown. He pushed through the door, and then through the curtains into the dining hall. Jules heard the clamoring of the guests. Festus did not. Festus heard only whispers crawling like worms over a beach of static. They said such wonderful things. And when Jules departed the house to make eyes at the fattening river, Festus took up his master's cane and strode down into the belly of Leeds to look in some windows.

The moon lounged among the clouds, an obese king swaddled in black robes. Festus looked in the window of Mary, generously endowed and blessed with skin so smooth and so white as to seem unreal. How large and inviting her pale pink nipples! How her breasts moved when she brushed her long hair! He looked in the window of Samanta, too young to look at, or so he'd been admonished. How skinny she was and how unbroken! He looked in the window of Sithyl and of Persis and of Katharine. None saw his eyes in the darkness outside their windows. And in the morning, the sunlight rolled down the red-orange mountain like something spilled by a careless child, and pooled in the valley, setting alight the town common, and the screams of the men rose into the morning like the calls of limpkins, and the broken glass glittered on the dewy lawns, imitating the dewdrops with its own malevolent sparkling.

The Weird House

The house crouched, set back from the road, one-story, rectangular, brown with white trim. No light ever shone from its windows; the bulb to the right of the front door hung eternally dark. But someone lived there. Or maybe more than just one. Cars came and went; sometimes four or five at a time sat in the long, gravel driveway; most times just one car, a nondescript silver Nissan sedan with Massachusetts plates.

Bill St. Clair walked by the house at least twice a day, weekdays, going to and from school. He called it the Weird House. It was a sunny, early summer afternoon when he and Tim McLellan, who lived three doors down from Bill, saw that the driveway sat untenanted by cars.

"Let's look in the windows," said Tim.

"Absolutely no way," said Bill.

"Chicken," said Tim. And that settled that.

They walked up the driveway, crunching gravel, then turned, crossed the overgrown lawn, and made their way along the hedgerow that bordered the house on the east. They reached the first window and cupped their hands against its surface. Pressed against the glass from top to bottom, from left to right, were fine lines of patterns and whorls in browns and silvers.

"What *is* that?" Bill said.

"I think that's hair," Tim said in a whisper.

"Let's *go*," Bill said. "I'm done."

"*Chicken*."

They walked to the second window, cupped their hands. The bottoms of grey feet crowded the window from left to right, from top to bottom. Creased soles, flattened toes with tips white against the glass, dry and cracked heels. Some were yellowed. Some were small, terribly small. One had a plantar wart. Then one of the feet shifted position, squeaking against the glass. Bill and Tim jumped back and turned to flee. The man blocking the way to the road was tall, unnaturally tall. He had long, wispy white hair and a liver-spotted, ancient face with a nose like a chisel. In his hands he held an ancient wooden radio receiver with a yellowed plastic face and a silver knob.

"Brown haired boy," he said in a cracked and choked voice. "Turn it on."

Tim reached out a trembling hand and turned the knob to the right.

Aromatic snuff for the headache, spoke a tinny, jubilant voice, *is available at Purseglove's Pharmacy on Pleasant Street. It's just the key for the gentleman or lady with nervous headaches. The price is reasonable, and the proprietor is always on hand for consultations. I am a physician who commands respect for my steady hand and my knowledge of the newest advances in modern medicine. I eat them, eat them alive. From the toes up. Using my clamps and torches and my powders and pills, I can keep them alive for days and days. One fine young lady, well, I got as far as her heart before she expired. Oh, she was very vocal. I like it when they cry. When they plead. Tell me, Bill, tell me, Tim. What are you doing for the next three weeks?*

Tim whipped out his hand and turned off the radio. The man grinned, blood lining his teeth. The boys turned to run toward the back of the house, and froze.

The tall men advanced, holding out their many arms, their long, dead fingers shimmering and twisting. The sun ducked behind a cloud and refused to return.

Creeping Waves

You're listening to WXXT—the plump, tart tongue in the ass-hole of the Pioneer Valley.

WANTED

As an apprentice to a Man of Unacknowledged Sciences, a lad of regular habits, to whom the best encouragement and the highest wages will be given. Boarding included. Fair hair and an unencumbered spirit strongly desired. Interview will be extensive and exhaustive. Apply alone at 333 Pomeroy Terrace when the moon waxes gibbous and the shadow of Tattletale Hill obscures the cross atop the spire of the church on Purgatory Road.

BAAL PROTECTS THE KING (PART 1)

The priest stood in the center aisle of the convenience store, staring down at his shoes. His reflection in the fish-eye mirror formed a slightly curved black blur, like a parenthesis. After a time, he walked to the counter, where a brunette pig-tailed girl with a black baseball cap sat on her stool and looked out the window at the afternoon traffic, her elbow on her knee, her chin on her fist. She turned to him, glanced up. The sun was behind him, punching in through the glass double-doors and framing his head. She closed one eye, still couldn't make out his features. He asked for a pack of Marlboros. She pulled one down from the rack. He pushed it into his pocket, threw a crumpled ten onto the counter. It slid across and over the edge. The girl sighed dramatically and made no attempt to retrieve it.

Box of matches, he said, and she slid it back along the path the ten had traversed. After he left, the echo of the door chime fading, she bent with an exaggerated groan and retrieved the bill, only to find it damp. She made a face and threw it into the till. She wiped her fingers on her jeans.

Outside, holding up a hand to shield his eyes from the punishing sun, the priest waited for a break in the traffic. When it came, he ran across the street hunched over, as though ducking a volley of arrows. The sound of a car horn tore after him, followed by a torrent of incomprehensible syllables. He walked along the shoulder of the road, breathing heavily, looking down at the gravel, the pinched, pink-tipped cigarette butts, the stained and sun-faded receipts, the squashed fast food containers. The wind from the traffic buffeted him, causing his clothes to flap like a flag atop a tall mast. The sweat-soaked lower back of his shirt touched him again and again like a cold, insistent hand.

Finally he stood at the gate to the church. For the first time in his tenure at Leeds Catholic Church, he was afraid to go in. The exterior of the building hadn't changed. Stucco and white brick. Black iron bars guarding stained glass windows of red and gold and white. Arched red doors. Denuded bushes on either side of the stone staircase with black metal railings tarnished here and there with scabs of rust. It was a far sight from St. Mary's in the affluent downtown, with its tall steeples and Gothic Revival architecture, but what Leeds Catholic lacked in grandiosity, it made up for in modesty, in simplicity.

It was welcoming, why, everyone said so. Now, however, everything within had been corrupted. He opened the gate, and walked with great reluctance to the stone steps. He sat on the bottom step, lit a cigarette, and scanned the suburban houses across the street. They squatted, shuttered and silent, their occupants elsewhere, in offices, behind cash registers, in cubicles, standing in classrooms. The sky was a grey carpet hanging low, almost touching the treetops. In the front window of a white Cape directly across from the church, a grey cat stared at him with narrowed eyes, accusing eyes, a bright and alien green. It yawned, its tongue a lick of flame. It looked like it was screaming. A sound like a thunderclap came from behind him, from inside the church.

There was no more putting it off. He stood and wet his fingers, pinched out the red ember at the tip of the cigarette. He put it in his pants pocket, climbed the steps, and entered.

The wooden Christ still hanged affixed to his ornate crucifix high on the wall. Its feet kicked, trying to push them free of the nail. The wood of the front-most foot, the right foot, had begun to splinter, spilling down onto the carpet in shards of brown, white, and red. The priest could see blue muscle in the foot, tendons shifting like piano wires.

Look upon me, my child, the Christ said, and his voice was syrup and strychnine.

"I'd really rather not," said the priest.

Oh, do. We're going to have such fun today, you and me. Acknowledge your Lord.

"You are not Him."

I Am, *my child, as sure as the sun stains the sky, as sure as the rain pulls the filth from the ground. Test me in this.*

Go ahead: ask me anything.

It kicked its right foot free and tucked it behind its left ankle, to pry it away in turn.

The priest could watch no more. He walked down the aisle—his legs weak and wobbly—and sat in the front-most pew. The votive candles flickered like a city on fire, a city of circular glass hovels. Sparks jumped into the air. The priest covered his eyes with his hands and recited The Lord's Prayer over and over until he heard the wooden feet cross the floor, and felt the bench bow and crack when the wooden Jesus sat down next to him.

The priest knew a little of the history of the wooden Christ. It had been commissioned by the church's pastor in 1926 and built by a woodcarver in Nutley, New Jersey. It was fashioned from carved blocks of linden wood, colored with oil-based paints, and sealed with a glossy finish. The woodcarver had personally delivered the Christ to the church. He affixed the cross to the wall and affixed the Christ to the cross, a workaday Pilate in a rumpled suit. In the early sixties, the church dug into its coffers and paid a substantial sum for a restoration; the paint had started to chip and peel. The restoration had been an expensive proposition, but worth it. The Christ had gleamed as if brand new. How its eyes had shone.

Afraid to turn his head, the priest stared straight forward.

Look upon me.

The priest squeezed shut his eyes and shook his head back and forth.

I command it.

There was nowhere to go. He turned in the pew and looked. Never before had he been afforded the opportunity to see the Christ up close. The flickering candlelight reflected in the lacquer lent the carven face the aspect of an old movie or a hologram, animating the features, making the Christ appear to be grinning, then leering, then furious, then despondent. It reminded him of the chipped and corroded horses at the carousel at Paragon Park, as his face and theirs were similarly gaunt, gape-mouthed, and cadaverous.

There was a rustling in the rafters. Shadows swarmed among the wooden beams and spiraled down like black ribbons to gather behind the rood screen. The priest could see through the narrow windows tattered vestments, raiment of the grave, elongated white faces with hollows for eyes. They glided out then, horrible robed things with their heads thrust up into the skulls of animals that looked like nothing of this earth. Feet dangled from the robes, toes huddled as though glued together, swollen and bruised and webbed with dead skin. Their nails were painted ruby red. Erections jutted at their midsections.

The priest reached out and touched the cold arm of Christ, and Christ turned his head and thrust it toward the priest's face, hissing like a cornered possum. Frozen, the priest stared at the wooden tongue vibrating over wooden teeth, and the wooden Christ grabbed him by the shoulders and pulled him over until they were chest to chest. The priest gave in to the terrible kiss as the holy water boiled in its stoup and the flames rose from their candles like hands clawing their way out of crypts. The robed things descended upon the two, and within the walls of that modest church on a suburban street in Leeds commenced hours of obscenity, of desecration, of abomination.

MAMIE

I was, I confess, something of a scrapper as a boy, an inveterate fighter and a scamp.

I would lift our old terrier Roger for hours, staring into the mirror and saying things of a masculine and steely nature. After Mother sent Roger for an indefinite vacation on a faraway farm, I would instead lift our young neighbor Michael, until his mother forbade him entrance into our home for reasons utterly unknown to me.

In my teens, my face and trunk bore the bruises of countless puerile skirmishes among the trees by the river. At some point it occurred to me that I might in fact have been engaging not in wrongdoing, but in that thing called "sport," and so I thought I might evade discipline both parental and parochial by formalizing the affairs.

My first boxing match took place against Mamie Marchequestelique on a platform fashioned from several pallets covered with a tarpaulin. Mamie was a tomboy and each of her legs was as thick as my trunk. I feared her greatly, for there were rumors that she drank bitters and spat and picked her nose like a roughneck.

When young Phillip Rippingcoat rang the bicycle bell, Mamie hit me so hard that two of my teeth had to be extracted from my earlobe by our family surgeon, Dr. Gladmost Alespiller. While I sat on his table, the Good Doctor also checked my lower parts for "distemper."

Having failed to find any, he then checked his own. I tried to stare at a small plaque above the doctor's desk which read, "Everyone is Queer But Me and Thee, and Sometimes I Wonder About Thee," but Dr. Alespiller insisted I instead check my nipples for distemper whilst he checked his own nether parts.

Afterwards he gave me a gumball and a pat on the head and sent me away with a small vial containing my errant teeth.

My next fight was with Father when he was in his cups and tried to slap me. I bruised father's eye, broke his toe, pulled out a handful of his hair, and set his ears alight with a kitchen match. Later, as I lay awake, unable to sleep, I heard Father apologize in the dark doorway, then stumble out into the hall and fall down the stairs.

Years later I asked Mother to allow me to visit Roger on his farm, but she claimed not to know of whom I was speaking. For a time I thought I must have made up the mutt, but I swore I recalled his labored breath which helped lull me to sleep, and the brutish way he'd assert his paw onto my forearm when I would cease scratching his distended belly. I also seem to recall his piercing eyes. Some nights he'd stare at me while I slept, his head tilted in that way that dogs' heads do. I'd peek at him and wonder what dark thoughts tumbled about within his knobby cranium. He looked as though he might be sizing me up.

This is WXXT, radio for the profoundly unsound. Join us after the break for six straight hours of *The Sounds of Innocent Sleep*: a child of but six unknowingly recorded while sleeping, volume forty two.

The Tree

Geoffrey Stanley Raffort's spirit haunts a large tree in Look Park in Leeds. Lonely, location-bound, and miserable, his activities are restricted to dooming young lovers who enjoy the great shade of the tree's many abundant branches, cutting the skin of boys who climb its trunk, and, on one black, black day, sapping all the moisture from a 9 year old girl named Mary Weatherstorm Notchkill, turning her body to a cracked white husk which flaked and blew away in wisps and strings with every breeze, leaving only her pretty purple dress behind.

Carl Stalkflank, a dim groundskeeper with a harelip and a difficulty with Schnapps, was indicted in poor Mary's disappearance. An angry, bloodthirsty mob hanged him from the very tree under which her dress was found. Thus was Raffort provided with a companion. Stalkflank, however, was so stultifyingly dull that Raffort willed the tree to burst into flames, and with that he disappeared into the dusk, dancing and twisting along the wisps of black smoke that left jagged trails across the Leeds sky.

You're listening to WXXT, the malady in the valley, the voice of unreason, the cadaver in the crawlspace, the pox in the fruit punch, the nunchuks in the nave, the pestilence in the pews, the carrion in the catechism, the body, the blood, the baseball bats and blasphemies, the bigotry and blastcaps; the blisters, bludgeonings, bile and binge-killings; the bloodbaths, boondoggles, and broken backs.

You're listening to Nicolas Ripsternum Lusk and this is Free-Range Fungus Friday. If you're the third caller, you can be the proud owner of 17 pounds of tainted ground chuck if you can just provide an answer to the following question: just what is that lump below your right ear?

THE APPLE

Most lives are never touched directly by the macabre. All of our stories, of course, end with our demise—the waste!—and many souls plunge into darkness after a frightening disease or suddenly, in a burst of unexpected violence. But words like "evil" to most seem exaggerated, melodramatic, childish.

Most children look out their bedroom windows at night, but almost none see a pale face, mouth agape, staring at them from the woods. All men get up to use the bathroom in the middle of the night and almost none step out of their bedroom only to confront a faceless cadaver with outstretched arms. Most women drive alone at night, but few are lured by their radios to a boarded-up house with trees growing up through the floors and branches reaching for help from broken windows.

And most young mothers walk their babies in strollers through crowded streets, but few—well, one, so far—have their infants scooped from the safety of the stroller by a grey man in a suit, who then disappears down a side street and out of sight. This happened. This happened in Leeds, Massachusetts. This happened in Leeds, Massachusetts on a Fall day in 1959 to a young woman named Mariette Langfort.

What was unreported was the single item left behind by the grey man in her stroller. It was an apple. Mariette Langfort, while waiting for the police, ate the apple, core and all, effectively eliminating the only piece of tangible evidence. She was aware of this but did not seem affected by it. When questioned, the numb young woman said only that the man had apologized even as he was kidnapping her only child, a young boy who had been born with one brown eye and one blue, and with a smile that could dispel shadows from the dingiest of rooms.

Mariette divorced not long after and left Leeds, never to return. A year to the day after her departure, her husband was felled by a brain hemorrhage. He was discovered at the kitchen table, his face in his cereal bowl, pictures of his wife and baby boy tacked to the wall beside him. Over time, the disappearance of the boy was long forgotten, just another among the missing and the lost of Leeds.

Somewhere in the deep woods, watched over by silent and looming beings, by monkey-faced creatures and long-fingered humanoids with oblong heads split down the middle as though by a hatchet, the boy learned many things, secret things, and on the thirteenth year of his life he was given the gift of a new body. A costume, as for Halloween.

Sitting on a high branch now, the boy digs his teeth into a shiny red apple. Birds wheel madly above. Something in the woods screams, something else, something far off, laughs a deranged laugh. The boy chucks the core down through the branches, and he follows it down, jumping from branch to branch. He reaches the ground, where with his new hands he straightens his new hair and tucks in his new shirt. It is a big day today. For the first time, young Andrew, for that is the boy's name, is going on a trip. Andrew is going to be escorted by his dark keepers to the secret Leeds, the hidden Leeds. Andrew is going to see for the first time the place of which he's been told for all of his sentient life. Andrew is going to see the Real Leeds.

HAVE YOU SEEN THIS MAN? (3)

Have you seen this man? He escaped from the Northampton Lunatic Asylum, killing a guard and eating his eyes. He may sink into cement. He paints his face. He carries a .38 snub-nose and answers to Rexroth Slaughton. He doesn't like the curious or the obese. He doesn't care for fornicators or the French. He likes to hide in clothing racks at department stores. He likes to peek in windows. He likes the backseats of Hondas. He likes women's necks. He likes Root Beer and lurid photographs. He sobs in hotel foyers. Do not give him a ride. Do not tell him your name. Do not reveal to him the names of your children.

Have you
seen
this man?

Have Have you seen this man?

seen this

HABE OYU SEN THIIS M

THE PARKED CAR

"All right. Are you ready?"

"I'm ready."

"Turn it on."

Vernon Golden had pulled the car over to the shoulder of Northampton Street, just south of Leeds. To our right was the Connecticut River, houses on the opposite side blinking in the afternoon sunlight, docks like long wooden tongues tasting the water. To our left squatted a shabby little motel, consisting of ugly tan huts in a half-assed half-circle around a hybrid convenience store-office-apartment with a red and blue neon OPEN sign hanging crookedly in a cracked window.

"What are you waiting for?" Vernon said.

I turned on the radio. It spit a loud burst of static and I spun down the volume.

"Eighty-eight point one," Vernon said. "Or point three. Just... move it around."

I turned the dial down past easy listening, past bleating techno, past a sugar-bloated right-wing host, and then rolled the dial between my thumb and forefinger in tiny increments until a voice boomed in the car and we both jumped in our seats.

HALL! LAY! LUJAH!

The voice seemed to emanate from between our heads. Reflexively, we turned toward the center of the car and leaned just slightly back. So as not to be touched, maybe.

OH DEAR BROTHERS (the voice said) *AND SISTERS. HERE ON THE CUSP OF THE NEW TIME, WE BOW IN SUPPLICATION, WE SUP AT THE BLACK, BLOODIED DIRT OF EARTH. HERE, WHERE ONCE DINOSAURS FED AND UNKNOWN THINGS SWARMED AND SLITHERED AND HOVERED, WE GATHER OUR ARMY. YOUR CHILDREN COME BACK...*

And here the announcer began to lose his voice, to cough, to sputter. He wheezed and croaked, his breath whistling like a teakettle. I could hear the sounds of fists slamming down on a table, a glass tipping and rolling, liquid pouring off the edge of the desk, then just dripping as the choking sounds faded, the announcer falling away from the microphone, fingernails scratching the floor. The sounds of vomiting, retching. Shoes drumming arhythmically. Then silence. Vernon peered at the radio, his eyes narrowing.

"Turn it up," he said, "and listen."

It was there, far in the background, someone whispering, tongue scraping teeth, lips parting with a *p* sound, a joyful, capering whisper, liturgical and rapturous.

The car started to shake, just slightly, and a dark liquid poured over the roof and dripped down the windows, blotting out the sun, painting the windows black until I could see nothing, the darkest dark I've ever experienced before or since. The dark of the grave, of a sealed casket in a cemented mausoleum at two in the morning on a cloud-crowded, starless night. I reached up and felt around until I found the dome light. I hit the button. Vernon's face was a forefinger's length from mine. He was grinning like a devil. The dome-light brought out terrible things in his face. He began to whisper. I leaned in closer so as to hear.

THE BALLAD OF JOHNNYPANTS GORSTED

Johnston Gorsted was a bellman at Northampton's John Fitch Hotel. He was known for his quick wit, his capacity for imbibing biblical quantities of wine, and his skeletal frame. But mostly he was known for the pants he wore, which were far, far too large for him. He would cinch neckties around the cuffs and buckle a belt tightly about his waist—so tightly, in fact, most of his otherwise immaculate white Arrow shirts bore a faint horizontal stain that was unmistakably blood.

Gorsted did not socialize with the other staff of the hotel, and reserved his jibes and banter for the hotel's infrequent lone female guests. Despite his angular body and his curious visage and the aforementioned inelegance of haberdashery, women would invariably fall for his firm but obsequious requests to let him touch their faces and, finally, to be his dance partner.

He would then flee, claiming to first require use of a restroom. When he returned, his pants would be stuffed full with what most assumed were other clothes or perhaps balls for sporting. They would think it odd, and some would leave, shamed and red-faced. Others, though, took Gorsted in a joking spirit and danced boldly, pushing at his sunken chest and jutting out their breasts provocatively until the sweat soaked Gorsted's brow. Then he would spirit them off to his room and they would never be seen again.

I was living in the hotel at the time and had a room adjacent to Gorsted's. He worked there for six years and seduced, by my count, one sweet young thing every four months. In the morning, the women's lodgings would be emptied of their personal effects, and they were assumed to have fled without checking out, ashamed of having been so showy, and so readily taken. It happened so infrequently it was not remarked upon. I, of course, took an interest.

I made Mr. Gorsted an offer, one he staunchly and vociferously refused, pretending offence. But I knew, because his room reeked in a way that I would note and others would not. I am a reasonable man, and I repeated my offer and was again stubbornly refused.

Three weeks later to the night, I saw Mr. Gorsted emerge, flushed, from his room, pants stuffed full. I followed him to the ballroom and peeled off to the kitchen, where I found a Negro toiling sweaty over a mountain of encrusted dishes. I promised the Negro a substantial wad of cash and a long, sharp knife in return for a brief but vital favor. The young man accepted—all young men accept—and, as Gorsted twirled his date, the Negro bolted to the dancefloor and struck, slicing a long slit down the seam of Gorsted's pants. The young man then threw the knife to the ground and ran.

Out of Gorsted's pants rolled and bounced seventeen pretty blond heads. The guests shrieked and stampeded, some tearing right through me as though I weren't there. Gorsted's date shrieked and began to faint and, before the police arrived, he took her life with his boot on her neck while simultaneously warding off several strong-stomached would-be heroes, some of whom swore that Gorsted bared very sharp fangs at them.

Gorsted did not die in a hush. Surrounded by the police, he charged at them with the young man's knife, hissing, and they cut him nearly in two with their pistols. No one ever ascertained his final tally.

No bodies were ever found. To this day, some residents of Main Street claim to see headless beauties twirling in the streets late, late at night, still in their gowns, blood spouting like fountains from their ruined necks.

The final victim's name was Mary. The Negro's name was Charles. Gorsted's nickname was Johnnypants. My name is Benjamin Scratch Stockton, founder and director of WXXT radio, one time resident of the John Fitch Hotel, multiple murderer, chronic sadist, unrepentant ghoul, bastard, and very driven dead man.

THE LEEDS WORD AROUND TOWN (2)

by Miss Margaret Maughbrook
From Ms. Maughbrook's column in the *Leeds Weekly*

Mr. Wallace Dogswater piloted his car into the Mill River after seeing a goat adorned in the vestments of an earlier age cross a Leeds street on its hind legs, says my well-regarded source. Mr. Dogswater did recently (I must dutifully note) purchase a quantity of dubious bourbon at a rock-bottom price, and that comes from no source other than my Very Own Self, (who was at Morley's Liquors merely for a chaste tonic)! He emerged from the river alive, but drenched and in the grip of a mortal ague, and is said to have taken to his bed.

* * *

Several school-age children report that Mr. Guy Stanton, recently returned to the sweet haven of Leeds from the-Devil-knows-where, said improper things whilst fast asleep on one of the benches that line the sporting fields. The constabulary apprehended Mister Stanton who, in one voice, denied all wrongdoing, whilst in a second voice, told the police exactly where they could go and on specifically what sort of conveyance. He is due to appear before a judge before the week is out.

* * *

A bridge game whose participants were Constance Goodrich, Carol Myer Waters, Helen Lightstep, and Wilhelmina Futz ended in a flurry of blue-veined fists and ineffectually-swung canes after an accusation of cheating, reports my all-seeing source. Ms. Goodrich (the accused, to the disbelieving surprise of precisely no-one) uttered such language as to be unfit even for the books she secrets on the shelf in the crawlspace below her stairs, and, as her sons will verify, is wickeder than the wickedest demon in the sub-basement of the lowest and cruelest level of Hell; is a vicious, cancerous lesion taken hold in the very soul of the city, and no greater gift could be received by the Commonwealth than that of her capture, encagement, prolonged suffering, and eventual extinction.

* * *

Mr. Daniel Coulton, local saddler and harness maker, was sued for divorce by his wife, Susan J. of Haydenville. She charges him with deviltry, drunkenness, goat-worship, excessive book reading, and having annexed her kitchen for experiments that generate intolerable odors and terrible voices that offer suggestions most noxious from bubbling cauldrons, over which Mr. Coulton labors without end, having turned over the running of his business "on a temporary basis" to his harried assistants. The complainant asks the reinstatement of her maiden name and the attachment of Mr. Coulton's wages so that she might continue to live in the elevated station to which she is irretrievably accustomed.

THE MASSACHUSETTS STATE TROOPER

Mickey was on one of his tears again, really ripping into this one.

Here we are with the soapbox, Sara thought. This one was his current go-to: the government, their spies, their secret systems. She did up a quick and dirty ponytail with a hair tie she'd pulled off of her wrist and leaned her head against the window. The heat had turned the little Datsun into a damned oven, and the prick refused to turn on the A.C. Bad for the environment or some such. It was going to be bad for *his* environment if she couldn't pry him away from that little principle. His window sat open a crack, letting air in just enough for it to whistle, providing a background for his excited monologue. The car was speeding along at a hell of a clip now, the trees a continuous blur of greens and browns.

Mid-July had swaggered in, sweaty and hot to fight, and the afternoon storms had once again brought only humidity, no cool-down. Sara watched a stray raindrop shimmy on the windshield, a dancing ghost, clear, but with tinges of red and blue. It split into five smaller drops, each of which leapt over the back of the car. She looked into the side mirror to see if she could see the drops airborne, and that's when she noticed the lights.

"Cop," she said, not bothering to try to find an entry point in his spiel.

"Christ," he said, looking up to the rearview. "Christ." He pulled the Datsun to the shoulder, popped the glove box, and pulled out his registration. He was digging in his back pocket for his wallet when the cop opened the back door and slid into the seat behind him.

"The *fuck*," Mickey said, turning around. A state trooper stared back at him, the goddamned dictionary definition. Absurdly big hat. Mirrored sunglasses. Ears like jug handles and a jaw carved into straight lines.

"Mickey!" said Sara.

"Hush, now," the trooper said. A slight tremor shook his unexpectedly gentle-sounding voice. "Can we all just be quiet for a minute?"

And so they sat in the hot little car, potato chip bags and straw wrappers and mud on the floor mats, the engine clicking inanely as though to fill the silence: the man, the woman, and the Massachusetts state trooper. No traffic passed. Clouds stood still in the sky. If the earth was still in fact moving, there was no way to tell. In the distance on the tarmac shimmered puddles or the illusions of puddles.

Mickey couldn't let the silence stand. "Can we… can we *go*, officer?"

Sara remained silent.

The trooper doffed his hat and placed it upside down on the seat next to him, as though providing a vessel for an invisible offering. His damp hair stuck to his scalp in little waves, like a kid's drawing of an ocean, but inverted. A horizontal red line creased his forehead. He exhaled. Then he laughed, a funerary laugh, a charnel laugh.

"When we go, sir, ma'am, we go for *good.* There are all kinds of vows, you know. All kinds of contracts, and some don't involve a pen and paper. But they're binding."

Sara dared a glance into the rearview mirror. The cop's broad grin was such that she could see every one of his teeth.

He's crazy.

"How about a little radio?" the trooper said, and lurched forward. His muscled arm thrust between the seats. He tapped the 'on' button and wound the dial down to the left, all the way. Mickey smelled Old Spice and perspiration. The trooper withdrew his arm, fell heavily back into the seat.

Smoke started pouring from the speakers—red, a blood mist. A voice bounced around the car—the strained and tired voice of a woman.

His body was just riddled *with cancer.*

An audience, thousands strong, laughed raucously and applauded.

It was three weeks from diagnosis to death.

The applause swelled.

I loved him more than I'd ever loved anything, but once I knew he was dying, I cast him away. I couldn't look at the face I adored. I cursed him and shamed him. I did the worst thing you can do: in his last days on earth I proved to him that his greatest fear was real: he was alone. He left this earth shunned and despised by the last person who'd loved him.

The cheers and applause reached a crescendo, and the trooper began slamming his palms together, causing Mickey and Sara to jump in their seats. Sara burst into helpless tears. The audience's roar began to subside; in its wake remained only a few hand-claps, some amused tittering… and one person who seemed tickled beyond repair, a mad cackling that rose and fell, shrieked and gamboled, fluttered and soared. The trooper joined in, snorting and giggling helplessly. He slammed his hands mirthfully onto his knees, then against the headrests. Sara and Mickey leaned forward in their seats and glanced at each other with fear.

The audio faded and an announcer noisily cleared his throat.

"You're just heard "A Mother's Lament," by Lorraine Amaral. Before that was the Savage Sisters with "Menses on Parade"—dang it,

I just *love* those Savage Sisters. On the heels of the Sisters was Reginald Hammer regaling us with "Lost Children in Drainage Ditches," a real favorite around the station, I can tell you. And that about does it for me. Coming up is *Mad Ronnie's Laughing Hour*; actually, it's three hours, but who's counting…"

"Turn it off," the trooper said from the back seat. It sounded like a warning. Mickey silenced the radio.

The sun stabbed its knives through the trees, turning the leaves a brilliant orange. The car had cooled just slightly.

The trooper said, "Turn and face me. Do you have eyes to see, children?"

Sara and Mickey turned around in their seats to look at him, and he removed his mirrored glasses. Sara shrieked. Mickey just stared. The officer's lids had been torn from his eyes and hung down on either side like curtains with lashes for fringe. His pupils loomed huge and blacker than a thrice-veiled forest midnight, the bags under his eyes split and blistered. Some of the blisters had burst.

Gangrene, thought Mickey, *Gangrene and fungus*. Miniscule bugs swarmed in the man's eye sockets like static.

Without warning Sara flung her door open and ran around the front of the car into the highway, heading for the woods on the other side. Mickey just stared. The 18-wheeler burst from a cloud of blue diesel smoke as though roaring in from another dimension. She saw it at the last second and tried to double back, but the right passenger side tires caught her at the ankle, crushing her feet and rolling her legs until they were intertwined like a French braid. The rear tires hit her at the midsection. The impact was devastating; it exposed Sara's interior walls and tore them up like cardboard, propelling her insides out, reducing her to purple threads and red ribbons and brown tatters in an instant; scattered her across a hundred yards, painting the asphalt red. Mickey grabbed his hair with both hands and opened his mouth as wide as it could go. His jaw cracked. No sound came out. The radio clicked back on. A man, cackling and cooing and gibbering and chortling.

The backward leaning letters along the length of the trailer read ANNELID INDUSTRIES INTERNATIONAL. A fat-necked trucker in overalls and a black t-shirt clambered laboriously down from the cab's passenger side and walked over to examine the human wreckage. He walked through the blood like it was nothing, even as it soaked his white New Balance sneakers and snaked up his socks like brown vines. He fell to his knees and began to feed.

The trooper exited the car. His head was open at the back, flesh torn away to the skull. Maggots were widening the bloodless hole, squirming and roiling and frenzied. The trooper's biceps trembled as he walked toward the scene, trembled and… and split vertically. From the slits slithered two wet pink things that looked like elongated rats. They slid to the tarmac. When they began to pull their limbs from their sides and stretch them, Mickey saw they were in fact girls, mortally thin, snake-jawed, floss-fingered. They slither-clawed their way to the trucker, climbed his legs, and affixed themselves to his back. They began to feed on him even as he fed on Sara, their bodies puffing like balloons as his withered and shrank. The trooper fell to one knee, splayed a hand on the pavement, arranged himself cross-legged, and began to clap enthusiastically, flaps of skin waving like flags at the backs of his arms.

Mickey heard a rustling and turned to his left. A grey man lolled in the passenger seat, hollow cheeked and dead-eyed. His nostrils hung distended and crawling with maggots. A mephitic stench filled the car, nauseating and inescapable. It intertwined with odors of the excrement and urine in which the cadaver sat. A fat, bulging microphone hung in front of the thing.

"Do you have any requests?" he asked, turning his head to Mickey, his eyes fixed on nothing. A maggot fell from his nostril and landed in his lap.

Mickey felt put on the spot. He stammered. He tried to speak and gagged, a wretched, eye-bulging *gack*. He choked it back. He could think only to say the last thing he'd said, the only thing he wanted, the only thing he'd ever wanted.

"Can… can I *go*?"

"*Can* you?" the corpse-DJ sang, and the maggots rained from his nostrils as he laughed and laughed, gibbered and tittered and chuckled. The wind kicked up and the trees danced madly, lashing each other with their branches, as the audience emerged from the woods. In grass-stained tuxedos and dirt-smeared dresses they came, applauding and cheering and drooling and stomping in the mud. They walked through the remains and they walked past the feeding creatures. The streetlights came on, turning everything yellow. Mickey could see something was very wrong with the people's faces. He covered his eyes with his hands. For a long time all was still and quiet. He wondered whether he should pull away his hands.

ANNE GARE'S RARE BOOK & EPHEMERA CATALOGUE #4444499-Z

Vistas of Carrion by Carp Tarscallion

Carp Tarscallion worked as a bank teller at the Northampton National Bank at the time of its robbery in 1876. Though he witnessed nothing—the robbers rousted from bed a cashier and tortured him until he revealed the combination to the safe; they robbed the bank in the wee hours of the morning—the fact of the robbery is said to have caused him substantial emotional trauma. He began writing furiously and at all hours, filling journal after journal. Previously he had used his journal only to record his meals and the color and volume of his bowel movements. He began missing meals and foregoing sleep. He was eventually fired for writing on the job, ignoring his duties and going to sit in the men's room with his note-books and pen. What he produced was a ragged masterpiece of hallucination. The notes described in great detail a parallel world whose landscapes and vegetation were of raw, red flesh, dotted with mouths ringed with pustules, mouths that shrieked when set upon by humans. And the "humans" as described by Tarscallion were grotesque in and of themselves: composed of brick and wood, with curled wires for limbs. Their faces, located at their posteriors, were the only aspect that resembled humanity. Mouthless, they consisted of six wet eyes ringed around a smattering of hair-clogged nostrils. From the nostrils they occasionally vomited a foul greenish liquid that burned the raw skin of the earth on which they labored, causing the earth's mouths to shriek in a cacophonous chorus. These humans' labors consisted of a variety of endeavors: burning singed roads into the earth's flesh; the construction of rubber vehicles on which they traversed said roads; teaching distorted and patently untrue depictions of the version of earth on which we live; space exploration; and the production of bestial pornography, which was odd, as these creatures were sexless, devoid of genitalia, and reproduced asexually by the laying of eggs from their eye sockets. Tarscallion published his work through a vanity press. Twenty five copies were made.

Hard bound, in pristine condition. Two thousand three hundred and thirty dollars.

THUNDER

They'd been talking up the storm all day on the news. It was all the talk at the Finast and along the counter at the Bluebonnet and in the hardware store and out front of the bank. Tornados, they said, and hail the size of oranges. Damaging winds. Outages and trees down.

Ah, they always hype it up, *Jacob*, Mom said over the sound of the knife sawing through crust as she sliced the bread for dinner. I'd curled up in the recliner across from Pop, who sprawled out on the sofa, his legs all over the room, white and hairless. The radio played the Sunday evening service. The homily was about family and forgiveness.

Simultaneously came a clap of thunder, the extinguishing of all the lights, and a small shriek from mom in the kitchen.

Jeepers, Mother, called Dad. *It's just thunder.*

No, it ain't that, Pa. I cut myself.

Bad?

Pretty bad. I can feel it coming out. I think I'm. I think.

I heard the knife hit the counter and then the floor. I jumped up and went into the kitchen to feel around for a candle and I stepped in wet. Flowing wet. It coursed under my toes, warm and sticky.

The power ain't all the way out, Pa called from the living room. *The radio's still going.*

Over the shrieking wind and the sky-spanning, rolling, grumbling thunder and the pouring rain, a voice spoke somberly and without pause in a language I had never heard, though the rhythms and cadences were clearly those of a preacher, more strident than Father Mike from St. Mary's, and more serious, almost angry, but a held-in anger. Like stepped-on.

Turn it down, I called, *I think Mom might be hurt bad.*

What?

TURN IT DOWN. I reached out in front of me and shuffled slowly forward, calling out for my mother, yelling over the rain. My hand encountered something wet… slimy. The voice on the radio increased in volume.

I'm turning it down, I swear, said Pa, *but it keeps going up!*

I heard the door in the living fly open, slamming against the wall. A flash of lightning illuminated the house, casting large, looming shadows over everything. I looked at what my hand was in and part of my mind just shut down. I withdrew my hand and walked slowly into the living room, thinking of how to tell Pa… of *what* to tell him.

He was standing in the doorway, and something stood in the yard, facing him. Something tall. I could see only the bottom of legs, furred and matted. It had to be taller than the house, taller than the oak that punctuated our yard. A massive hand snatched Pa up out of the frame, fast as you please. One second there, then next gone. His slipper fell onto the front step. I went to the doorway. And standing in our very yard, soaking in rain, was none other than the Lord Jesus, in a tattered and bloody robe, taller than the sky itself. Pa was screaming from up somewhere in the clouds like a baby getting born and the voice on the radio said *turn around, Jacob, turn around, turn around, turn around.*

UNCLE RED READS TO-DAY'S NEWS (3)

To-day in Hadley, a man found his wife with her throat a gaping maw and filled with what looked like honey, oozing from between her large, flat breasts and pooling in the dark divot below the proscenium arch of her rib cage. Marbles of swirling, unearthly hues had been inserted in place of her eyes, which were not to be found, and her mouth was filled with an abundance of filthy coins of unknown origin. The man was brought to the Northampton Hospital for the Mentally Insane, whereupon he killed an orderly and committed a most unholy suicide by banging his fore-head repeatedly and without restraint upon the unyielding brick corner of the venerable edifice.

To-day in Leeds a boy of no more years than six, naked and bleeding a profuse river that followed him like a copper snake, collapsed in the door-way of Mikelson's General Store. Upon close inspection, no wound was found, and the boy, before expiring, claimed to be a 72 year old woman named Darlenia, explaining in specific detail the names and qualities of the medicines she needed to take for her ailing heart. Upon dying, he pawed with violence at his nether parts and begged for a "Mr. Riles." There was to be no one of that name found in the city or its surrounding regions.

Last night in Amherst a creature with the body of a mutt dog but with the head of a dead man was found shambling in clumsy circles by the pond. It landed heavily on its rear leg, causing the bone to snap with a startlingly loud report. It took no less than eight men to subdue the beast, whose head lolled grotesquely, a low and baleful humming growl emanating from its slack, black lips. The man's eyes were grey and glassy, and no breath came from his mouth. He was identified by his wife, who later required sedation for her hysteria, as Mr. Daigle Skinter Maas, a local grocer. Dr. Paulus Reige was unable to provide an explanation for the creature. Sherriff Daniel R. Wills shot the beast in its foul heart. Coroner Warren P. Causton and his men severed the head and buried it in East Cemetery. The body was burnt in a fire presided over by the Honorable Reverend Ezekiel Shineface, who praised God and begged forgiveness for us, wretched sinners.

You are listening to WXXT, the Valley's only pure pestilence. Today is Three-Peat Friday. When you hear Janis Joplin's death rattle, be the ninth caller and you'll win a year's supply of Uncle Mackerel's Anti-Itch Cream for the Male Undercarriage.

DADDY ZEKE

You have surely heard tell of Father Ezekiel Shineface, who ranted fire and brimstone on the same frequency occupied by WXXT. After a few months of battling over the airwaves, I approached the good Father in his den. I had taken to listening to his seething broadcasts, and I knew he would be a boon to our burgeoning concern. We chatted, he and I. He was surrounded by books. Holy texts and scatological picture books and writings by the doomed, the damned, the lost, and the despondent. He was a man not afraid to read that which might shake his beliefs. It did not take much persuasion.

I told him I thought his words might save our unholy remnants and free us from the bonds of the dirty earth. I told him I knew he could speak truth to the faithful. I said many things to him on that rainy night.

The transition was painless, and for a good long time the minister's broadcasts maintained their same tenor and tone. But time and nurturing and surroundings change mortal men, even past their deaths. When the good Father shook off his shabby coil only to find no golden boulevards stretched out before him, only then was his true voice loosed.

Now Shineface, under the name Daddy Zeke, hosts the darkest, foulest filth ever to poison the airwaves. Join him every Wednesday night for the *Shattered Tablets Hour*. WXXT—the drop of blood in your morning milk. The bruised hand reaching up from the toilet. The bathtub filled with teeth.

THE LEEDS GHOST WALK

"Good evening, and welcome," said Merrie Thornbuckle, "to the Leeds Ghost Walk. This will be an extra spooky, um, version, due to, well…" She gestured with plump pink hands at the snuffed streetlights and the darkened shops, above which some of the apartment windows winked with candlelight. This was the third power outage in as many months, and the longest of the three, everything having flickered and died almost five hours earlier.

"My name is Merrie, but I promise you…"—she cleared her throat more noisily than she intended—"this walk will be anything but."

She paused to accommodate the usual chuckle, but received in response only the sounds of dry leaves skittering on the sidewalk. So she chuckled for them, her contrived chirps echoing off the buildings before petering out. Gathered in the shadows on the stairs of the city hall, the crowd loomed, tall and quiet, like corporeal versions of the buildings that crowded the Center City section of Old Leeds. Halloween was weeks away, but at least two in the crowd wore masks: one had donned a skull face under a white wig, and the tallest of the men wore a shaggy goat mask with a black cowl tented by nubby horns. She took a step backward, barely conscious of having done so.

Merrie was in her late thirties, matronly but fallow, a den mother without a den. The Bluebonnet Diner had cut her hours, and the Ghost Walk gig, which she'd seen advertised in the *Gazette* classified section that someone had discarded at the diner's counter, had been a real godsend. Not only did it provide much-needed additional income, it got her out of the damned TV chair and walking. Sure, from time to time she ran out of breath, and had to ask the groups to wait until she could speak again. Certainly she had gone over the allotted time once or twice because of it. But she was new. She'd get better.

The previous Leeds Ghost Walk hostess had been its founder. Susan Dimmsler was slender and petite, and spoke in a helium-tinged version of the mannered tones of a newscaster, which was, in fact, her primary vocation: a morning microphone jockey for 22 News, introducing the meteorologist, standing at the state fair in a noisy chicken pen, interviewing the inexperienced owner of a doomed restaurant venture. "Susie Dim," they called her, and "The Pipsqueak," but the voices hushed after she disappeared while leading a midnight crowd into the Bridge Street cemetery, not officially a part of the ghost tour, having offered to show them something "truly terrifying."

When the Gazette published a feature on her disappearance, only one of the people who'd been on that walk came forward. Reed-thin, unkempt, and a stutterer, he proved not very forthcoming. Susie Dim *had* showed them something terrifying, though he could not recall what it was, and then she'd s-s-sailed up through the treetops and tuh-tuh-turned to starlight. That was the story he gave the police. Then he began to sing: *Through the tattered flesh of the still-living man, on the highways of dead mens' dreams, there are four and twenty ways by my count, to get to the rea-eal Leeds.* He was held, questioned extensively, and finally released. The disappearance remained unsolved.

Merrie's mother had called them Bingo-Wings; Merrie had also heard them referred to as Hi-Helens: those unsightly, sagging sacks of upper-arm flab. She had them now; overnight, it seemed, they had appeared. She fancied herself too young, yet there they hung, emblems of bad choices, of premature aging. Tonight they were secreted behind black silk, so when she gestured upward to the eaves of the section of the city block that had housed the John Fitch Hotel, she fancied herself not a middle-aged waitress gone to fat, but rather some romantic witch, perhaps a fortune teller, a guardian of secrets.

"It was here in this very building, now shops and lofts, but in the 1930s a hotel that drew guests from all over the world due to its refinement and elegance, its large and well-appointed suites, that Robert Barrelforth strangled his young mistress and hurled her body from the 17th floor balcony to the lobby and bar below."

Someone in the assembled crowd tittered madly, a sound like fingers dragging along the rightmost keys of an untuned piano.

"Broke right in two over the balustrade," declaimed the issuer of that horrid laugh, his voice betraying delight. *"The blood turned white wine to blush in more than one glass, and not a tarpaulin in existence could cover the carnage."*

Another voice, this one behind her: *"They were finding bits and pieces a month later! Picking her out from picture frames and fixtures!"*

Not having encountered hecklers before, Merrie pushed ahead with the script.

"Bernice Whittier's ghost …"

"… in halves!"

"… is still said to haunt the shop that now occupies the ground floor. Clerks report a weeping figure, back turned, in the half-light of the corners, and something tugging at the hem of their dresses…"

"That's not Bernice, that's Old Ben, that randy old rascal!"

"Gentlemen, *please*," Merrie said, mindful not to lapse into the whining tone her ex-boyfriend Mitchell had informed her (rather indelicately) that she employed when upset.

"Beg pardon, Madame. Do continue. Your tales are delightful."

"As spun from slivers of gold."

She felt anxiety thread throughout her system, reddening her ears and getting her heart thumping, but she soldiered on, turning on her heel and proceeding to the iron fence that bracketed the ancient courthouse. The crowd shuffled behind her, jostling and whispering and tittering.

"Chased down by a mob and impaled on this very fencepost in 1893…"

"Rexroth Slaughton! Pushed his prominentia laryngea right out like a baby's head through a ripe, red cunt!"

Merrie cried out as if physically stricken. The moon ducked behind a cloud and the shadows of the crowd began to rise, to grow like time-lapse trees. They loomed above her as though about to link heads at the top, as though to form a cage. A cold arm interlocked through Merrie's and she froze. A high-pitched female voice right at her ear said, *"Come with me,"* and tugged. Hard. Merrie went. She found it in her to run for the first time since she was 17.

Merrie collapsed at the gates to the cemetery, pulling down with her the woman who had come to her rescue. The moon dared to peek out now, causing the gate to glow like an apparition. She pulled in air as best she could, and released it in howls. Finally, she said, "What *was* that? *Who were those people?"*

"They're just some very, very naughty boys," came the high-pitched voice. Merrie's eyes had adjusted to the darkness, but she could make out only a petite silhouette, no features. The edges swam in what little light there was. The silhouette approached and again an arm hooked around hers and lifted. Merrie and her new companion slipped through the gate and into the cemetery. They passed among the leaning stones and ascended a hillock where a mausoleum loomed. The arm around

hers loosened and she heard the creak of the ancient door, rusty metal scraping on rusty metal. They entered.

Merrie wondered why they'd entered this place. Was it to avoid the men from the walk? She moved a hand behind her and felt a cold concrete surface. She sat. It was so starkly silent. No cars passed on the nearby road. It occurred to Merrie that she couldn't detect the sound of breathing, save her own. To confirm it, she held her breath. The silence was complete.

"Miss?" she said. "Young woman?"

The answer came in the form of the creaking door, followed by shuffling, fabric on fabric. The sound surrounded her on all sides, a sinister susurrus. The high-pitched voice spoke again, coming from right in front of her.

"It won't be so bad," it said. *"There are children. Lots of them."* Lips touched Merrie's and she flinched. She hesitated, but opened her mouth. Again the lips came, brushing hers, lingering. The tip of a tongue flicked at her upper lip. Then the comforting cocoon of an embrace… and more tongues. Tongues at her legs, at her private places, along the zig-zag of her fingers and between her toes. Sparks of pleasure.

A bulb above her burst into radiance, showed her the thing that held her, revealed that those wet, prodding things were not, in fact, tongues, and the walls were not shrouded with black curtains, but with figures in black robes. In a silent chorus they doffed their hoods and showed her the dead faces of the Dark Lords of Leeds. Their fingers grew, intertwined, like webs they spread, and the petite thing pushed her up and into the sinewy web of fingers and the roof opened as the sky plummeted down in blots and sparks and bloody phosphorescence.

Outside, the light had come back to Leeds. Houses glowed, streetlights pushed back against the night. Cars swept by. An airplane screamed overhead. The mausoleum towered over the dark cemetery like a fat preening god surrounded by leagues of hunched worshipers.

You're listening to WXXT. The moth in the belly of the Pioneer Valley. Up next—

HE HAS TO BE FED

I woke up drowning. I was in warm water—in a bathtub—naked. I must have started out propped up, but I'd slid down until my mouth, then my nose, had slipped under the surface of the lukewarm, soap-scum surface water. The first thing I felt was enormous pressure, as though someone was standing on my ribcage. I opened my mouth to pull in air, and got only lukewarm water. I pushed myself up, ejected a gush of water from my throat. It hit the wall opposite me, ran warm down my chest. I sputtered and spat, hacked and gagged. I howled as I greedily pulled air into my lungs.

The door opened, slammed against the side of the toilet. Golden was there, silhouetted.

"Let's go, bud," he said. "Places to go, people to meet."

I wriggled upwards, hugged my knees to my chest. I spat out more water.

"What the fuck?" I said, regaining my voice in the process of speaking. "What happened?"

Golden shrugged.

"You passed out," he said. "In the car. Can you get yourself ready?" He looked at his watch.

"Hold on a minute," I said. "Slow down. I'm not going anywhere until you tell me exactly—*exactly*—what happened."

Golden whipped a towel off of the wall fixture, threw it at the edge of the tub where it landed in a heap.

"Your clothes are on the toilet," he said. "Get dressed, come out of the bathroom, and I'll tell you."

I dearly hoped I had undressed myself. Golden's smirk suggested otherwise.

I climbed up out of the tub. I felt a pressure at the back of my neck, warm and insistent. For some reason I thought instantly of a leech. I reached back and felt something wet, peeled it off and flung it at the wall. It was just a washcloth, old and blue and stained a light brown. It lay crumpled on the radiator. I stared at it. I rubbed the back of my neck. The washcloth had jolted me, called to mind something just beyond the limits of my reach, something from a long time ago, from childhood. The details wouldn't come.

"Let's *go*," from outside the door.

I stepped into my pants, climbed up through a t-shirt. Since I'd awoken, I'd been semi-aware of a persistent droning that sounded like static. At first I thought it to be water in my ears, but the sound surrounded the house. Rain. Roiling and seething rain.

I walked out into a sparsely furnished living room, lit only by a nightlight behind an easy chair. I had no idea whether we were in a hotel or in someone's house or apartment. The rain fell louder now, blurring the windows, pummeling the house, punishing the trees. There was a closed door across the room, faint light fanning out from the space beneath. I pushed my way into the next room.

At first I thought he was shooting up. He was facing away from me, sitting cross-legged on a bare mattress browned by years of human runoff. The sheets and blankets and pillows had been flung aside. He had his sleeve torn lengthwise and rolled up over his shoulder, his head lolling left, the tatters piled between his neck and his ear. He held his arm out straight before him. As I approached, I heard him whispering in the tone one uses to try to soothe an unsettled infant.

He swiveled on the ottoman and thrust his arm at me, palm out. At the crease of his elbow sat a thick reddish-blue line, bifurcated and swollen. It looked infected. Above it, two puncture marks, and above those, almost at his underarm, two small horizontal scars, the left one about two inches higher up than the right. As I watched, the left scar began to split, a gummy mucous stretching into lines spanning the gap. Then those snapped apart, revealing a horrible eyeball that rolled around madly before settling on my own eye. The pupil dilated, a black orb sailing off into a murky distance. Then the gap at his elbow opened wide. I saw two rows of rotting teeth like stones scattered across a purple dike, and a black, cracked tongue wheeling around in the middle, an antenna seeking a signal. It was peppered with pustules, white and oozing. Outbreaks of spittle formed at the corners of the hellish mouth. I backed up until I hit the chair behind me, and fell into it.

"He has to be fed," Vernon said. His hand—the hand from which he'd been feeding that grotesque mouth—formed a cup in which curled the torn remains of a mouse in a bed of its own droppings. The other eye on his right arm opened. The eyeball within was dead, sightless, cloudy; its colors leeching out beyond its borders. The arm coughed, causing Vernon's whole body to tremble. It began to speak in a rough and raspy baritone.

... One... one hun... one hundred thousand. Thousand watts of Ill. Ill. Ness. From... from Great Barring. Barrington. To New. New Say. Lum... the ti. The time is. The time is 9:29 pee em. You. You are listening. To.

And it began to sob, tears streaming into its nostrils, running over its rotted teeth and down, pooling in Golden's outstretched hand. A gob of mucous rolled out over its bottom teeth and clung to his forearm.

Oh, that horrible mouth said, drawing in a shaking breath. *Is that the time. Is* that *the time? It's too late. Where has the time gone? Oh Sithyl. Oh, old Ben. Oh, Lemuel and Eltweed.* It coughed, spraying spittle, then spoke again in a double voice, like Tuvan throat singers. *Stellan?*

I staggered to my left and grabbed the doorjamb. It was the voice of my father, speaking in duet with that cracked and hollow voice.

All I want is a drink, Stellan. Just. Just a Manhattan. Or… an Old Fashioned.

My father sounded far away, desperate, and sad. The other voice, the foremost voice, was sticky-slick with mockery.

"Make it stop," I whispered. "Vernon, make it stop."

I looked up at Golden's face. His eyes were rolled up to the whites. No… they were rolled *down.* I could just make out the top curves of his eyeballs over his reddened bottom lids, suns setting into a sea of pink. He was mouthing something. The mouth on his arm, the mouth that belonged to that horrid, distended face, began to move in time with Golden's. Then the sound came, as if someone somewhere were turning up a volume knob. It was a grim chorus: my pop, Golden, and that hideous, mocking voice. And they were counting. Counting down.

Ten.

Nine.

Eight.

THE WXXT PERSONALS PAGE

WILLIAM LEONARD UPLAND

Interests: Knee socks, black eyes, lollipops. High-pitch voices and strong twine. Whisky. Bondage and role-play. Dismemberment, Disembowelment, Feces. Flowers and Candy-Canes. Nurses and syringes.

Turn ons: See above.

Turn offs: The Law, Cry-Babys (sic), Doctors. Father and his knife. Mothers who cry at night and hide in daylight.

Seeking: Blonde, free-spirit, rebel. Hates mother. Weak, ineffectual father. Open mind. Friend named Megan desirable, but not necessary. Likes woods and doesn't mind torture play, Mind Games, Whisky. Tattoos a plus, as are piercings and the willingness to acquire more (deleted) piercings.

HASTINGS WARREN BURNCOLT

Interests: Conversation, commiseration, and carnivals. Cold stone walls. Worms. Long walks at night. Crouching among toadstools. The sound of crickets. Cellars and the smell of old books. Cavernous libraries. Abandoned churches and factories. Fog, smoke, and fire. Flannel sheets. Shrouds, sentinels, and sarcophagi.

Turn ons: Does Not Apply.

Turn offs: The living, Big Band music, parades, laughter.

Seeking: I don't want to commune or cohabitate with the living. I don't want warm hands to mutely comment on my coldness or red lips to light upon my dank aveolar process in a sad parody of a kiss. I don't want a warm mouth to house my dry leaf of a tongue. I am looking for a woman who died in her twenties or thirties, one with a strong sense of former self. Looks not important. Let's get together and talk about what we miss. Some days I think I miss coffee, of all things, the most. Not sex or food. Coffee! Strange.

GROVER KINGSLEY PINE

Interests: It is lonely in the woods. I traverse the same paths in maddening patterns, finding and eating crickets and mice and staring at the boxes of light beyond the meadows and the wretched shadows that flit past them. Sometimes round lights come in pairs, and their bouncing unhinges me and I scream. I scream and scream, and I crawl in the dirt, and I am with the night crawlers, and I crawl

Turn ons: Among them and I pile them into my pockets. I seek someone to come walk these woods with me. I cannot offer much but dead fingers and cold breath and the mud that binds my eyelashes. But I will take you everywhere with me. We will walk the sidewalks and

Turn offs: We will break girls open at their hinges like mutton. We will upend automobiles and sleep in the beds of the rich and soak sweet tea in their hot sweat as we suck the eyes from their skulls like sour candies. No one is a romantic like I am, and no one has put more candles in more hollowed out

Seeking: Insects, sinews, pus and pewter. Long scissors and sheets of skin sloughing off the rooftops. Sacrifices and sex and that book and basement smell in my waistcoat. Time and tortures and forceps and frontage roads. Handfuls of guts and yellow and pouring all black ink into your headlamps til the worms and night crawlers and twisted muscle and ganglia

SITHYL

I went around with Sithyl for six months back in 1935. She was an opium hound of the worst kind, all lolling eyes and lazy tongue and flopping hands. Sloth and decay and lost potential all tied up in a plump and pale 5'10" frame. She clung alternately to me and to the drug with the desperation of a child lost in a crowded market. She was 15 and a tedious slattern, a conniving and capricious seductress who had indiscriminately secured the favors of an uncle, two cousins, and her ne'er-do-well brother Jonas. She left them wrecks of men, who wrote her flowery and wretched letters begging for some kind of reinstatement—it curled my very toes to read them. She tossed those letters aside and I lapped them up like curdled cream, nourished somehow by the rank emotions of other, lesser men.

Before I met Sithyl, I was young, and I was despairing for my seeming lack of emotions. I could not feel. Could not laugh or cry, and could not care, not even enough to hate. But she brought out such seething and virulent hatred in me that I sought her company frequently, and she was more than accommodating. I cared not a whit for her, so I risked nothing.

And the times when I indulged in opium with her—I could always give or take the drug; I am far stronger than any narcotic invented or conceived—my hatred bloomed into a rancid black flower. Every time she opened her mouth to speak, I wanted to open it wider with an axe swung horizontal and hard.

One night I did. I chopped her gaping maw straight back to the ears. Sithyl looked like a jack o' lantern, a jack o' lantern vomiting black cider. At that thought, I found myself laughing. It was the first good laugh I'd had in months.

Oh, dear listener, did I howl that night. I shrieked and guffawed and giggled and pounded my one good knee to shit with a hard fist. Then I raised my axe and I hacked and whittled and pounded Sithyl into a stew. Then I made tender love to her, a love drenched in emotion and devotion and tenderness and care and mercy. I sobbed the whole while. When I came, the recoil sent me backwards across her miserable room into a hutch of second-rate China. I slept then, the sleep of the carefree and the content. I was happy. I woke up to the smell of wildflowers.

You're listening to WXXT. This is Ben Stockton. A man in love, with a face full of roses and sweet breath like wildflowers and turpentine and pestilence and rain.

SOUNDS FROM THE CAVES

The northern and western regions of Massachusetts are clotted with forests with all manner of nooks and corners and caverns created by fallen trees and bursts of psychokinetic and ectopsychic energies that blast caves into rock-faced cliffs and blow deep pits into hard packed ground. I stomp these woods at night like God gone mad. I singe the leaves with a stare of fire. I dismantle hikers like toys and ruin the minds of campers in diaphanous tents.

There are armies in these caves: armies of the missing. From Florida and Arizona and Maine, from Prague and Hong Kong and Thailand. Our collectors find them in graffiti-strewn stairwells and bars, in bowling alleys, bordellos, and dugouts, crouching by dirty streams or dancing half-naked in cacophonous discos. They squirm in dirty clusters and gnaw on gravel and fungus, a writhing, wet, blood-soaked ball of your imminent destruction. Their cries are an obscene orchestra, their tears run streams through cracked caverns and drip down massive chasms in an overlapping and complex and torturous beat. There are more every day, toddlers and whores and innocents and brats.

Listen to *Sounds from the Caves* on WXXT Sunday mornings at 10 a.m. and again at 11 p.m. Do not listen while driving. Turn your radio up until the sound is distorted. One day you will turn off your radio and the music will be on your street, up your stairs, splintering your door, and destroying everything you know, everything you love, everything you thought was real and eternal.

WXXT: The Baleful Howl of the Commonwealth.

ANNE GARE'S RARE BOOK & EPHEMERA CATALOGUE #945493-H

Scrapbook

This scrapbook, culled from many papers, snapshots, holiday cards, and letters—some in fragments—and put together by bookshop staff, paints a disturbing picture of a family torn apart by its patriarch's dark obsessions.

"All letters written in the late afternoon are written in desperation," begins one, written by "Rose" to "Dearest Ben." Another letter, the likely reply, though not signed, says: "One must either do one's business on the pot or get off. I would be most sad if we were to part ways because of a thing you think you saw but you know is impossible on its face."

Also, written on a small manila envelope, sealed shut by pressure, and dated January nineteenth, nineteen forty three is the following:

> My name is William Flood. And I wasted two men who are now hunting with Cochise. The third man won't forget me in a hurry. There are many other unmarked envelopes similarly sealed whose contents might only be known to the purchaser.

Among the many snapshots, some of them quite prurient, is a picture taken in a bedroom with light blue wallpaper and adjacent unmade beds. On the bed to the left sits a roll of toilet tissue and a large package of diapers. On the other bed, two young women in rather abbreviated nightgowns and pigtails affect aspects of childhood. One sucks her thumb, the other stares with mock innocence tinged with smoldering curiosity. To their left sits a large stuffed bear whose face betrays an oafish idiocy. The bear… well, we can't give away everything, can we?

Two hundred and fifty dollars. Includes extras.

KNIVES

For a time, in order to work as a broadcaster on WXXT, an applicant would have to absorb a knife attack by my 10-year-old son Richard. Prospective employees had to disarm Richard without causing him injury. Richard was unnaturally strong and suffered from acute manic depression, attention deficit disorder, and highly contagious greyish carbuncles that eternally oozed on his genitals, neck, ankles, and on his wiry arms.

I would watch and laugh. One young fellow who thought himself quite capable ended up losing four fingers on his right hand. He got the job, though, and became quite adept at changing LPs with one thumb. He was also a smooth and captivating monologist. The warts took hold in his ruined hand, though, and he died when they metastasized into his throat, clogging his windpipe.

We buried him under the studio.

This is WXXT, home of the Beckoning Castrato. Stay tuned after the break for a half hour of uninterrupted wailing. WXXT—where the rock never stops.

THE STREETS OF LEEDS

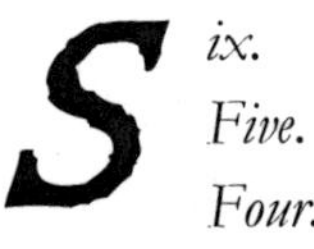

ix.

Five.

Four.

Three.

Two.

ONE.

It was daytime, maybe mid-afternoon. We were strolling the streets of Leeds, Vernon and me and the face on his arm makes three. It was wrapped in a bandage. I felt its presence, a weight between us, as though we had kidnaped some malevolent infant, blindfolded it, and were bringing it somewhere, or it was bringing us somewhere.

Vernon carried a bulging shopping bag, I a battery-powered transistor radio. We made our way around the townies, who loafed and lazed in a postprandial haze. Something was off. They seemed drugged. We turned off the main drag and took a right down an alley between the back side of the apartment-topped shops on Main and a building that housed a steakhouse, a sushi bar, and a psychic. The alley was shaded from the gray light of the day, and dark. I could hear the voice muttering under Vernon's sleeve. Vernon turned.

"Have a seat," he said.

We sat cross-legged on the pavement, opposite one another. Vernon pulled from his shopping bag a few black candles, a pack of matches, a tattered old washcloth, a large, ancient book whose spine was tattered and threadbare, and a small nip bottle whose label had been removed, leaving a ragged patch of white on its plastic surface. Inside was a reddish-brown liquid. When I saw it, saliva flooded my mouth and I felt faint. I hadn't tasted a drop of alcohol in over 24 hours, and I hadn't even *thought* about it. If ever I believed Vernon Golden had any kind of power, I believed it then.

But now I wanted what was in that bottle. I wanted it as the infant wants the breast, as the man wants what lies south thereof, as the addict wants oblivion.

A cloud moved over the sun, and as it did, the sounds of downtown hushed, fell away. I could hear peepers and a rush of wind. A cat turned the corner, black with a bib-like patch of white at its throat. It looked at Vernon, looked at me, blinked, and then turned back the way it came, a little stub of a half-tail waving languidly to-and-fro. I couldn't help but laugh, but I also felt a rush of envy. It could go anywhere. I was lashed to my destiny like an islander to a tree, with a typhoon fast approaching.

Vernon handed me the pack of matches and cupped his hands around one candle—I lit it without trouble—and the other, which took a little more doing. He handed me the bottle and said, "Drink half." I snatched it from his hand. As I drank—it tasted like grape juice gone over—he turned on the radio. A gorgeous voice sang out:

Mister, sit with me by the river
We'll pull the stars from the sky
We'll pull down the moon
and we'll pull down the sun
We'll pull down the shade of the eye

The sky, the very air around us, had gone dull orange, the shade that precedes a fierce and powerful storm. The wind had stopped. The silence was profound, as though the entire town had fled the streets, fled the city. No birdsong. No highway sound—no traffic at all. The only sound was footfalls approaching. My stomach clenched as a shadow rounded the corner, spreading across the pavement like spilled acid. I felt the urge to scuttle back, as though the shadow would burn my skin. The thing that belonged to the shadow turned the corner.

WILLIAM DITHER (PART 2)

William Dither was a man of prodigious polyamorous appetites. As a boy at the turn of the last century, he was beaten severely by the schoolmaster for luring into the Janitor's closet a significant segment of the school's student and administrative population, and, later, was turned out of his home by his scandalized parents after they awoke to find their son ***[1].

He was the scourge of the orphanage, and on a night when the moon was enshrouded in clouds, one of the orderlies unceremoniously dumped him on the street. He made his way through life on the kindnesses of women and of men and of every gender between the two, all of whom found his charms impossible to resist.

He found himself as an adult, reclining in the beds of the most illustrious occultists in Western Massachusetts, and his friendship with Benjamin Stockton, the most elusive and mysterious High Priest (a demon, many claimed) of the Pioneer Valley's covens, resulted in widespread destruction, profound instances of madness, and

---

[1] On the grounds of Godliness and good taste, the editor has demanded the omission of the next several words.

innumerable disappearances of people of a variety of ages, but especially children.

Their falling out, reportedly over differing interpretations of a section of text in *The Libellus Vox Larvae* was equally thunderous: Stockton, a fearsome necromancer, raised an army of corpses to descend upon Dither's Leeds homestead. After they breached Dither's battlements, it is reported, *he* breached *theirs*.

Anne Gare, stopping in for a visit, was heard to shriek, "Is this a harem or an abattoir?" before jumping bodily into the fray. From that unassuming domicile for a fortnight emanated the shrieks and groans and pleadings and blasphemies of a most unspeakable, violent, and unholy orgy.

INTERNS

Every year, the women's college at the crest of the town brings in a new breed of living, breathing human beings that I use to tend to WXXT's technical, electronic, financial, and physical needs. They come from Virginia, from California, from Oregon, from Texas, from China and Iran and India. They cry by the rivers and they wander in the woods. They are tiny wisps of things, hair painted jet black, who float along the sidewalks like wraiths. You can tell them by their large eyes, their twinkling bracelets, and the bolts pushed through their fine, white, lightly-veined flesh. You can tell them by the crisscrosses of self-inflicted cuts on their arms.

They can be moved to commit any act, however foul, however degrading, however putrid, however taboo, when they meet a man who speaks in the same voice they hear on the radio late at night when they are pretending to contemplate suicide.

And I am a ghoul who speaks over radio airwaves, and long ago I was a man who took great, perverse joy in getting his hands dirty, who would often fall asleep with someone else's blood clogging his nostrils and bubbling under his black, hot tongue.

But I cannot meet these young women. Not the way I look now. Not in public, anyway... unless I...

Well.

Have I not told you that it is not my long dead husks of hands that type, that wring, that pummel, that pull and pry and poke and punch? Those wonderful activities require the use of living hands, powered by a beating heart and a functioning brain. I can find those. I can work my way into the weak men, the hungry men, the sick and the dying and the stupid men. I use their arms and their hands and their faces, which are presentable—more so than my ghastly, ruined visage, which has gotten me forcibly ejected from more bars, brothels, and bassinets than you'll ever see in your miserable, trifling lifetimes.

And I meet sweet new prospective WXXT interns at the Woodstar, at Haymarket or the Moan and Dove. I meet them under the awning at Thorne's and by the rocks under South Street. I meet them down Center Street or at a table in the far back of Packard's. I pour beer down someone else's gullet. I take the girls into the woods. I divest them of their beliefs and their faiths and their futures. And the survivors walk amongst you.

UNCLE RED READS TO-DAY'S NEWS (4)

Police have announced the untimely and gruesome death of local poet and Leeds historian Michael Dooley. Mr. Dooley's piteous remains were found in the pond of Langford Primary School, in the lunch bags of four children who attend the self-same school, in the confessional at Leeds Catholic Church, in the lanterns that line the catwalk that stretches between McCauliffe Park and Tremens Terrace, in a collection of small metal lock-boxes owned by local box collector Ruth Swaddleston, and wound around the trunks of ancient trees in the loneliest reaches of Look Park. Two toes each were found in stewpots in the kitchens of Mary Lowerton, Richard Frogtoucher, Susan Diggle, Nathaniel Ronstadt, and Robert Grain-Toggle. The poor man's face was found hanging from a coat-hanger of local doctor Elias Stonehearse. It expected that more of Mr. Dooley will turn up when, once again, spring thaws the rivers and roads of our lovely city.

TAKING THE LADIES OUT

Dither and I like to take the ladies out. Last night Maggie showered her blue-black guts over the barstool at the Dirty Truth while I swung the bartender into the wall-sized mirror by his ankles. Dither put his many fingers into six fraternity brothers while Winnie sucked off the beer spigots, her shattered pelvis undulating obscenely, her hair and dress alive with blood beetles. Then we burst out into the streets. I sliced off heads all down Pleasant while Dither shoved swords up through the seats at the Calvin Theater. Winnie set bassinets afire at Cooley Dickinson while Maggie squatted to piss in the lobster tank in the Stop & Shop. We pinwheeled through the Bridge Street cemetery, upending ancient caskets and sending their contents into the grey sky until it looked like smoke from a great fire. It was a beautiful night; we poured wine into our lungs like drowning sots. In the pink morning we were stacked on the benches like cordwood. The sky was a sick yellow bruise. The sun was a cold dead eye. The winds raised up and shook the houses and thrashed the trees. A great fire is coming to Leeds. Pneumonic plagues and blood from the faucets and worms exploding up into bath tubs from the drains.

You're listening to WXXT. The time is 6:16 a.m. It is not too late to rise, rise and do what needs to be done. Up next, we've got Burton

Stallhearse and the Grappling Grannies performing their version of "Dark Was the Night, Cold Was the Ground."

Baal Protects the King (Part 2)

Alex knelt, the marker tight in his fist, thickening the lines on his sign. His tongue jutted from of the corner of his mouth like a peeking worm. The marker squeaked and squealed on the sheen of the board.

"Cut it *out*," Bonnie said.

The worm retreated into its cave.

"I'm almost done." He held the sign out before him. GET OUT OF LEEDS, it read, in an all-caps slanted scrawl. The capital D had been scribbled heavily over a lowercase version.

Bonnie screwed up her face.

"You messed up the 'D.' Do it over."

A half hour later, they each grabbed an iced tea from the refrigerator. Alex was 37, clad in a red and white plaid shirt and cargo shorts. He had the beginning of a round, firm belly that rode high on his torso. Bonnie wore black tights and a grey hooded sweatshirt. She had tied back her hair, dyed a curious and jarring shade of red, in a ponytail so tight that it crimped the skin at her hairline. They loaded the signs into the back of the Saturn, leaving their half-empty plastic iced tea bottles on the roof. As they drove off to the protest, the bottles slid from the car and landed in the road. The bottles looked somehow forlorn, abandoned. They faced each other in their despair, their contents settling along their lengths like blood in fresh corpses.

They hadn't expected so many cars, such a large crowd. People lined the fence, sat cross-legged in clusters on the walk, and leaned against cars and chattered excitedly. The ages ranged from infancy to decrepitude, the clothing from sweats to suits. Children squawked and babbled. Bonnie searched up and down the roads surrounding the church until she found a spot along the road a quarter mile up and drove up over the curb.

"If that many people actually showed up every Sunday, they never would've closed the place down."

"That isn't why," Alex said. "The Vatican closed it."

"Yeah, because of poor attendance, like I just said."

"I don't... I think it was more complicated than that."

"Was it?" Bonnie said.

The church itself looked much as it had before it had been shut down; someone had kept the bushes trimmed, hosed down the brick walls, swept its walkways and its porches. It stood starkly against the sky, a brick Victorian edifice with two steeples, one large and one small, on either side of a central arch topped with two crosses. Arched windows in layered recesses, a broad staircase spanning the front. Four arched entrances mirrored the windows, and a central pattern of tracery vaguely reminiscent of a four-eyed skull with gritted teeth. But the stained glass, once multicolored and beautiful, had been replaced with reds and blacks, in shapes suggesting grasping claws, feminine curves, slitted eyes, and thirsty mouths. The small flower gardens that ringed the church, imprisoned behind iron bars, sprawled overgrown and tangled, littered with obscene statuary: dancing elves; legless things with long fingers and flat heads; snarling dogs, two headed and without pupils. Grinning, many-handed homunculi grappled with their comically enormous genitalia.

The cameraman trained his lens on the mayor, and the blonde reporter held out her microphone.

"This is a city," the mayor said, "known for its diversity and for its tolerance. And what we're witnessing here today is democracy in action. The freedom of religion we are afforded in the country does not limit itself to religions we find 'acceptable.' The people who are protesting today are doing so in good faith, I think. They, too, have the right to express their disapproval. As long as it doesn't extend to harassment."

As if summoned by that statement, a red and rotten tomato sailed over the crowd and smashed into one of the great black doors. It hit the ornate pull and its gore rolled down the door and piled in a pink puddle. Two policemen reluctantly left a conversation with a teenage girl in a tank top to grab the miscreant and haul him away, to a mixture of cheers and boos. The girl sneered when they left, and tugged down the bottom of her skirt, scanning the crowd behind her to see if any perverts were looking.

A shriek pealed out over the crowd. Conversations staggered to a stop as people looked around for the source. The mayor, startled into dropping his guard, emitted a shriek of his own. It echoed off the buildings. A young girl in an icing-pink jumper dropped her ice cream cone.

"There!" shouted a man in a cape whose face was painted like that of an owl. The tall front door had been pushed open; that was all. A man strode out onto the walk. Dressed in white down to the shoes, with a black square at his throat, he was young, square jawed, his black hair parted on the side and wet, as though freshly washed. His mouth was wide, almost preternaturally so. His eyes gleamed. His skin glowed as if lacquered.

Signs were hoisted and bobbed. Some people booed. A few turned and left in a rush. From one section of the crowd, a blossom of arms shot out, crucifixes in their fists. He approached a seated group and he crouched, his arms crossed over his knees, hands hanging limply, and began to speak. A titter of laughter spread through the group like a fast-moving virus.

"What's he saying?" Alex said.

"Ooh, he's cute," said Bonnie. "Let's get closer."

Alex rolled his eyes.

The man extricated himself from a small crowd gathered alongside a huge RV and jogged back up the steps.

"Coward," someone called out.

He turned at the top of the steps and surveyed the crowd.

"Good people of Leeds," he said, in the firm and polished tones of an old-time politician, or perhaps a carnival barker, "You have come here to protest our presence in your city. I'm sorry to inform you that you are over three-hundred and fifty years too late. But the last thing I want is for you to feel you have wasted your time in gathering here today. I speak to you now not out of defiance nor bitterness, but in the spirit of fellowship. Of community. In a few moments, the doors behind me will open. I invite you to enter and to face what you fear, to see for yourselves what you have come here to banish. If, after you see, you still object, well, my door is always open. You may come and speak to me directly."

The doors behind him opened inward.

"Who will be the first?"

Bonnie grabbed Alex's hand and led him up the steps. They ran into the darkness beyond the doorway, and the doors shut behind them.

Alex had never known such darkness. He could not even see the ghosts of colors that usually floated before him when he closed his eyes. From somewhere deep in the church sounded the somber, low, meandering notes of a pipe organ. Bonnie's hand slipped from his and he reached out to reestablish contact… but she was gone.

Bon? he whispered, and the whisper echoed back at him, bending and changing as it faded. Bon*? Bon?*

Baal?

Bah?

Baa.

Ba.

The music from the organ grew louder, began to pick up in tempo, to morph into a raucous march.

From the darkness, five blurred pale orbs emerged. As they approached, they formed into skin-colored blobs stained red, then into kewpie doll masks shrouded in hoods somehow blacker than the darkness that framed them. The faces floated off the ground at about knee level. The eyes, rounded at the tops, flat across the bottoms, were painted with huge blue pupils looking leftward over two puckered red dots forming the rudiments of a nose, bracketed by circular cheeks like subcutaneous bruises. Below puckered a cupid's bow mouth. They gathered at his feet.

Cold, two-fingered hands grabbed at Alex's fingers and he pulled away, frightened. Then he felt a pressure at his lower back, and something pulled and twisted the hem of his shirt and shoved him forward, hard. He was propelled through thick curtains and into the nave of the church.

Before him stood a tall, colorful carousel, lit by red and white spotlights mounted in the high rafters. Green neon shone from under the slowly spinning platform. The rounding boards that topped the carousel formed a panoramic mural. Painted in garish colors, they depicted a nightmare Leeds as seen from above: wilted buildings, degraded vegetation, bridges crumbled into roadways and rivers, spiky church spires crowned with red eyeballs, and many-legged insectoid vehicles, all of it watched over by a gang of drooling, dead-eyed, banana-breasted cherubs perched atop black clouds strewn like turds across a chemical-orange sky. Below, the colorfully caparison-clad bodies of horses, muscular and brown, slid up and down on the blood-smeared steel columns on which they'd been impaled. Their heads had been severed and replaced with wooden Jesus heads, agonized eyes rolled heavenward, thorns from their crowns drawing blood drops on sweat-slicked foreheads, mouths agape. Bloody sandals occupied the horses' stirrups, facing rearward.

Alex circled the carousel, avoiding the pleading eyes of the Christs as they bobbed up and down in his periphery. To his left, the pews had been piled up against the wall. As he moved deeper into the church, a chorus of shrieks rose above the cacophony of the pipe organ, and he recoiled in horror when he spied the altar, topped with a bloody pile of horses' heads in a maelstrom of buzzing flies. The mouths of the horses opened and closed, baring teeth like tombstones, emitting ragged, high-pitched shrieks over pink pimpled tongues. Their eyes, reflecting the red from the spotlights, rolled wildly in their sockets. Among them, cross-legged, smeared so heavily with blood that Alex hadn't seen him at first, sat someone he recognized—it was the priest from Leeds Congregational, the one who had presided over his Confirmation, the one who always had funny sermons, more like stand-up comedy than preaching. The priest was naked, and he was weeping. From a wooden bowl in his lap he pulled out and ate communion wafers like they were popcorn, licking his fingers with avid thoroughness.

Body of Christ? he called out to Alex, as he clambered to rise, reaching out with a fist full of wafers. *Body of Christ?*

Alex backed away until his calves hit the carousel platform, and he fell backwards, landing on his butt. For a few moments, he could not process what he saw above him. At the ceiling of the carousel churned gears made of bone and muscle, lashed to the pipes, spraying with blood the glittering underside of the carousel ceiling. Straight above him, stretched out into a flat white rectangle, was Bonnie's face. Her eyeballs dangled like grotesque ornaments. He could see straight through her mouth and her nostrils to the ceiling.

A voice boomed out over the cacophony of the pipe organ, and Bonnie's lips, manipulated by the bones that had once occupied her fingers, moved in time with the voice.

Welcome, young Alex, to the Leeds County Carnival and Old Time Circus Show! Such treats we have for you! Visit the midway and try your luck! Ride the rides! It's an ancient tradition! Stroll the grounds! See the sights! Get a Leeds Sausage Special at Foxcroft's Tent of Meat! Behold the forbidden magic of The Great Spettrini, performing every two hours at the Pavilion of Perversion! Delights await around every corner! In every tent and exhibition hall and pavilion! Games of skill and games of chance await!

The carousel began to sink, as though screwing itself into the ground. Dazed, Alex scuttled backward and watched as the parquet floor gave way to strata of wood, concrete, pipes, black and insect-twitching earth veined with the roots of trees, and then an azure sky striped with streaking black clouds, as though a comb dipped in black ink had been dragged across the deep blue dusk, all of it lit from below as by a landscape of fire. He climbed to his knees, crawled to the edge, and looked down upon a vast carnival that stretched from horizon to horizon: exhibition halls; ticket booths; rides; tents, red asterisks on white, broad pavilions; illuminated fountains, lit red, blue, yellow, and green; all of it bisected by a limitless midway. The carousel landed with a squelching sound on a muddy circle cut into grass greener than he'd ever seen. He scrambled to his feet and jumped off of the carousel.

Before him gaped the open rear entrance of a food stand; within which toiled white-aproned teens, their necks slick with sweat and grease, tending to griddles piled high with long, curled sausages in beds of sizzling peppers and onions. Ordering the teens about was a broad-backed bald man whose mustache Alex could see jutting out from either side of his furrowed head. The end of one of the sausages, he saw, formed a tiny grey fist. From the ceiling, hanging from thick brown string, were clusters of small, curled bodies, fetal, glistening in bodysuits of newly fried batter. One of the workers, a girl with ginger pigtails, walked into his line of sight and wrung a blood-sopping washcloth into a large white bucket. She caught him looking and winked. Her eyes were red marbles, her teeth yellow and disarrayed. Alex smiled politely and turned away.

I've been drugged, he thought. *Or… I passed out. I'll wake up on the church steps, surrounded by EMTs. Bonnie and I will go home. We'll watch* Hoarders *and get pizzas from The Hungry Ghost. I'll keep dozing off, and finally I'll come to bed. I won't have any dreams.*

He walked along the side of the stand to the main thoroughfare of the midway. Crowds milled about or strolled in groups, families and couples, arms entwined, groups of kids, gangs of teenagers, all toting inflated rubber aliens, amorphous clouds of cotton candy rising from paper cones, stuffed bears with frozen grimaces, damp sausage sandwiches in paper holders stained see-through with grease. It was all too real to be a dream; everything was too vivid, his senses were too engaged: the smells of sizzling meat, frying grease, sheep braying, the distant shrieks from the thrill rides, lights in primary colors stretching off in all directions.

Making his way down the lantern-lit dirt road, he stared unbelievingly at the game booths manned with bellowing barkers and framed with arrays of bizarre prizes: plush-furred homunculi; blood-smeared shrunken heads, giant inflated genitalia; banners and flags depicting inscrutable symbols or detailed paintings of savage gore-orgies.

He walked up to one of the stands to get a closer look at the shrunken heads. They were horrifyingly realistic. One wore glasses whose twisted stems had penetrated into the skin above its wax-plugged ears. Its lips were pulled back over clenched teeth, full-sized and bulging and lined with plaque. Three of the teeth bore silver fillings. Its blue eyes rolled toward his and locked in, pupils dilating.

"He can be yours," called the barker, a skinny, toothless man with a straw-broom mustache and ears like chewed up bubblegum. "All yours. To do with as. You. Please." He winked a lurid wink. Alex turned away. Across the road, howling teenagers stood hurling darts into an azure wading pool full of miniature boats on which diapered pink infants sat, looking all about them like little lost captains or staring confusedly over the edges of their crafts. The surface of the water was filthy, and here and there floated expansive tangles of hair. One of the teens, a pudgy, pale kid in nylon shorts and a t-shirt with the number 8 on the back, held up his arms in victory as a stricken baby slid off its boat and into the water, blood billowing to the surface and spreading like an oil slick. He jumped up and down, his thin braided ponytail swinging left and right.

"Direct hit!" he bellowed. "Right to the heart! Real Leeds repre*sent!*"

The others hooted and clapped him on the back as the irritated attendant fetched his prize.

I'll just go back to the carousel, Alex thought. Maybe it would take him back up… take him home, where real carnivals awaited, with tan-skinned farm girls and normal merry-go-rounds and plastic trinkets and gimcrack shacks proffering beer and hot dogs. But now he couldn't remember which way he'd come. Fighting panic, he turned toward the lights of the swinging and surging rides that lit up the sky to his right and headed in that direction.

A tall man in a seersucker suit sidled up alongside him, slender as stereo wire, with bulging cloudy eyes ringed with pink mucous, a mouth that stretched almost to his ears.

Games of skill, games of chance, the apparition hissed. *Games of skill, games of chance.* The man's lips were as white and dry as sun-bleached worms, his tongue cloaked in cobwebs. He walked so terribly close to Alex, giving off waves of corruption and illness, that Alex finally shoved the man away. When he did, the man's body went all fluid, as though boneless. He wriggled off, leapt upon a little girl eating cotton candy on a patch of dirt, and enveloped her in his grotesque limbs. Alex limped away as quickly as he could, not daring to look back.

Before him, reaching up into the sky, towered a massive guillotine, ancient, its wood splintered and cracking. A small boy with a blonde crewcut lay face-up on the wooden bascule, his neck in the loose grip of the lunette. He was drooling, his head tilted back so that the saliva ran along his cheeks, pooled in his open eyes, which betrayed a profound idiocy, and dripped down the sides of his head into the skull-hungry bucket that waited below. The blade rested inches above his scrawny neck. Another boy in a striped shirt swung a giant mallet into the air and down onto a padded lever, causing the blade to shoot skyward. The weighted blade hit the bell that dangled from the crossbar at the guillotine's apex, causing the boy to hoot and to fling his mallet in the air with triumphant abandon, and then the blade descended in free-fall, reflecting both starlight and the lights of the carnival as hurtled to the earth.

Alex turned away, but he heard everything. The iced tea went sour in his stomach, and he stumbled over to a garbage can abuzz with bees. He put his hands on the edge and puked into it. When he pulled back, still retching, he saw four fat, gelatinous flies the size of baseballs, bracketed by blurs of wings, descend into the barrel and begin to slurp at his mess.

He stumbled out into the main thoroughfare of the midway, wiping his mouth with his sleeve, crossed, and made his way through the darkened path behind the food stands. It reeked of stale beer and fried batter.

He emerged into a colorful corridor of Dark Rides: Freak Houses, Funhouses, Haunted Houses, Slaughterhouses from behind whose walls emanated horrific screams, Houses of Ill Repute walled with gossamer curtains of pink and white behind which cavorted curvy shadows. The walls towered above him—looking up, angling his hand at his brow, he could barely see the façades of turrets that topped them. On the shining walls of purple and red and black loomed painted ghouls and gypsies and strongmen, monsters and magicians, giant spiders, drooling ghouls. To his left and his right, people crowded into carriages and locked themselves in with bars across their chests. To a person they wept, tearing at their clothes, inconsolable.

"*Al-ex!*"

A female voice, young, saying his name in singsong. Stricken, he kept walking, afraid, somehow, of looking foolish.

"*Al-ex!*"

Commanding and maternal. It stopped him cold. He turned.

Tucked between a Freak House and a ride called Stockton's Radio Rumpus sat a small wooden stand with a red-curtained window. A hand emerged from the curtains, small and white. It curled a red-tipped finger, beckoning. He walked towards the stand and it retreated into the darkness as though on wheels. He followed it between the buildings, into the darkness.

He emerged, blinking, in downtown Leeds, drenched in daylight, but deserted. No cars, no people. Not the peep of a bird nor the bark of a dog. The digital clock atop the jewelers at the main intersection read 0:00. The clouds stood still as though stricken. The windows, all closed, reflected the sky, making the buildings look hollow. Alex walked dazed down the center of Main Street, staring at the closed shops, the empty benches and crosswalks, the still trees. Behind him came a sigh. He stiffened, then turned.

In the road stood a wooden Jesus, warped and fissured and naked, taller than two men. It had flat breasts and a sagging gut, a curved wooden pecker hanging down to its knees. The white-suited priest stood on its foot, humping its leg. He turned his head and grinned at Alex. The wooden Jesus opened its mouth to speak.

OLD BEN AND THE MONTAGUE HOUSE

At the end of a day of broadcasting, it is important for me to go to a place that has dark corners. A place the owners keep dim, whether for atmosphere or to save on the electricity bill. A place with a cat or two. A place with books. A place with a television, which is an invention that I still find baffling, mystifying, and a little frightening. I can't take my old eyes off of it.

It is not easy to do what I used to do—to dwell under lean-tos, in crypts and musty basements buried under dirt. It is too much like being dead. Nor is it easy to wander endlessly. But a few years back, as I meandered along the paths and the thoroughfares, through the dingles and along the silent walks, I found myself in Montague, a small village in the north of Leeds, a place where it looks like October even in starkest, sunniest May.

And in Montague I found a house. I stood outside its windows and watched a grey cat endlessly lick his paw and run it down his head in that familiar, welcome, almost mechanical motion. A kitten skittered into the room and pulled a book from a set of shelves that covered a full wall. A fire died and popped in a brown brick alcove. A man leaned forward in a chair, immersed in bluish light. Light that seemed to swirl out the window and gather in a warm pool at my cold feet.

In order to enter a house, I must be invited. But no matter how convincing a mask, no grown man or woman would extend a word of invite if they could detect me at all. I dwelt on these matters a moment, and then a woman entered that warm room with a child of maybe five holding her hand. I grinned until I thought the corners of my mouth might meet at the back of my head.

If you are a father or a mother and you have a child—

If that child takes a sudden and unabating interest in looking out the windows at night—

If you hear a knock, late, and hear your child answer the door—

If your child says, "Yes," or "Come in—"

Then I am home.

Four months later, the child drowned in its bath. Its attentions had overly vexed me and had worried the man and woman. They pulled the child from the tub. They were singing a raucous duet. As they cawed and choked and bellowed, descending the stairs, their arms around the dripping dead thing, I drank the water, lapping furiously, my mouth a gaping well, my snorts and exaltations echoing throughout the house and exciting me further.

The cats mourned along with the man and the woman, but then they came to care very much for me. They climbed the walls to find me. They sat where I sat, in any one of a number of comfortable chairs. They yowled at me and purred when I passed by.

Strangely, I came to care for the bereaved couple. The man would sit in darkness. The wife would weep in her bed and refuse to leave it for days at a time.

I did things for them. I gnawed at their curtains, pulled their plugs, and yanked their toes under the bedsheets. I ran the bath. I sought their attentions, but in their grief I was ignored. Finally I sat in their company and enjoyed their shivering around their tiny kitchen table. I bathed in their moans whilst they watched the television.

Several weeks ago, the woman took her own life and the man moved away. I find myself missing them. New people come and go and look at the house and frown and consult one another in hushed voices. Who-ever moves in, I hope they have books. I hope they have cats. I do not require their invitation. This is my house.

You are listening to WXXT. The centipede in the ear of the Pioneer Valley.

THE REAL LEEDS

It was an old man. His left hand gripped a cane. His shoes were oddly shaped; it was as though someone had cut off the front of his feet and then folded the sole upward. His mouth curled downward and his eyes blazed.

"I brought him to you," said Golden to the old man, "so you must give me back that which is mine," and I scrambled to my feet and bolted. It had been a sham. Whoever this old, evil man was, Golden was working *for* him, not against him. I'm no gift, no bargaining piece, not to anyone. I ran. And my footsteps made no sound.

I turned the corner onto the main thoroughfare and stopped cold. It was night. There were no people on the street. It was silent as the tomb. Everything was wrong, the angles, the light, the sky. The windows were black holes, the benches hungry jaws, the road a river of liquefied bone, molten hot. I had often wondered what became of Golden's followers, and now I knew they'd all come here. Vernon hadn't come to confront some devil. He had hosted the bugger. If I went any further I might meet that devil, unfettered and unmasked, and see a face that would drive me mad.

I heard the old man shout, a voice like poisoned thunder:

"No returns," he said. "And no exchanges."

I turned back just in time to see the first hit. The old man crashed his cane down on Golden's skull, shearing off half his face, causing it to flop like an untethered curtain against his neck. He struck again, this time a killing blow, breaking open Golden's skull like the shell of an egg. Teeth tumbled across the pavement. His eye lolled. And still Golden stood. The old man bashed him again, and once more. He approached Vernon and with his left hand, a wrinkled, arthritic claw, gripped Golden's collar, letting his cane fall to the ground. With his right hand he scooped Golden's brain from the shattered skull that could no longer protect it. He opened his mouth impossibly wide, his chin bouncing against his sternum, and he ate it in a frenzy, grey matter falling onto his shirt. He gnashed and smacked his lips and swirled his tongue this way and that, catching the detritus, sucking it into his palate, choking it down his throat.

The whole time, his eyes were locked on mine, no longer blazing, but serene, blue marbles in twin pools of milk.

And still Vernon Golden stood. The old man tore the sleeve from Golden's arm, stripped away the bandages. The face in Golden's arm blinked to life. Its nostrils dilated and contracted, dilated and contracted. Its dead eye sat as its live one found me. The mouth pursed and parted and the lips smacked.

"Oh," it said. "Oh, oh. There are such sights in store for you. Can you open your eyes to the *real Leeds*?"

Golden's body staggered toward me. The old man retrieved his cane, gripped it again in his left hand. With his right he grabbed the back of Golden's collar, walked him on a straight path, straight to me. We three stood in a tight circle and they told me everything, everything, the face in Golden's arm and the old man. They sang to me, they sang so sweetly. Darkness, black as coffee, gathered around us as we walked back to the main thoroughfare. I could hear whispering from the windows above the shops, from the trees lining the walks, from the gutters and the alleys. I craved nothing more than a drink. A drink would make everything make sense, would gather the whispers into one, and I would finally understand. I would see the Real Leeds.

The old man reached into his jacket pocket and pulled from it a flask. I took it from him—his hand brushed mine and it was hot and wet—and poured its contents into my throat, squeezing my eyes shut. It was as though I had been drained of blood, and now I was getting it back. The flask seemed as though it would never empty. Its river warmed me from the center out as it refilled my veins, fresh blood pumped through my starving heart.

When I opened my eyes, my father stood before me. He was grey-blue, torn up. His hair was standing in spikes, caked with graveyard dirt. His gut hung obscenely before him, a bag of yellowed fat. I could see the fat through his skin, clumps of curdled buttermilk, as I could see his muscles and veins. He glowed with demon alcohol, with yet-unspent power. A grin stretched across his face.

My boy, he said. And I was.

It's… you know, I'm not sure what time it is. You're listening to WXXT, the murmur in the heart of Leeds. Sweet Leeds. Leeds has leant down to kiss my lips, the tops of its buildings become walls, its streets become trenches, its rain become vodka. I wear leeches as my clothing, even as I pale and contract, they redden and swell. When the sun comes, it will bring with it a brisk and bright Halloween Day. I'm told there will be a parade. I'm told I will meet the Halloween Queen, the Queen, the Queen of Halloween, and if I'm a lucky dog she'll provide the tipple that will take me spiraling up into eternity and silence and forgetting.

Up next, we'll hear a little Vasterian Cull with his one-hit wonder, "The Century of Rot," that spry little number that rocketed up the charts in middle of the rockin' '50s. Turn up your radio. Turn it up all the way.

ANNE GARE'S RARE BOOK & EPHEMERA CATALOGUE #NIL

"..."

I wish I knew what to say about this book that sits before me on my desk as I type these words. Do I tell you that it somehow sucks the very light from the room? That it smells like a recently lit match? That when you open it, when you touch the cover, look at the frontispiece, turn its pages, that shadows gather about you, attached to nothing, landing upon sheets of air you would otherwise have thought invisible? Do I tell you of the susurrus that fills the room, sets the curtains in motion, causes the shadows to flinch and hunch as though in terror? I do. I do. All the sounds of traffic outside have ceased. The sidewalks have emptied of people. Everything is still and sepia, the way it is before a thunderstorm. The book contains poems, written by a woman. Her name appears nowhere and the book has no title. The words are nonsense until you read them aloud. Then even the birds flee. Then the night shadows everything, even though it is barely after noon. The stars are differently arranged, the constellations demoniac and… and getting closer? Even my hands are unrecognizable to me, the fingers longer, the nails gone, the whorls of my fingerprints worn away. The mirrors in this room reveal yawning chasms of nothingness, and they have never not reflected reality. The bell downstairs has rung, indicating that someone has come through the front door. There are footsteps on the stairs, many of them, legions, as if the whole of the town has come to wrest this book from these unfamiliar hands at the ends of my slender arms. They can't have it. They won't have it.

You can have it for two hundred dollars.

Red boards, gilt decoration. Fine.

EPILOGUE

In the Winter of 1654, when half the Leeds settlers disappeared.

WXXT WAS THERE.

When in 1906, the first radio broadcast of voice and music was heard in Brant Rock, Massachusetts.

WXXT WAS THERE.

When in 1920, the very first radio station presented the results of the Harding-Cox election.

WXXT WAS THERE.

When your father fell to his knees before tall and stately Satan in the Holyoke woods.

WXXT WAS THERE.

When your father vowed allegiance to the Master of Worms, forsaking all other gods and loyalties to men.

WXXT WAS THERE.

When he arrived home and howled in the basement, pleading with the walls for forgiveness.

WXXT WAS THERE.

WXXT. The Worm. The Woods. The Will. The Way.

We will always be here.

ACKNOWLEDGMENTS

While writing is generally a solitary enterprise, no book exists in a vacuum. Not even a self-published book like my debut collection, *Gateways to Abomination*. For that book, my wife did the cover art. My friend Tom Pappalardo, a graphic designer who works under the name "Standard Design," put together the cover in exchange for my dropping off beer from time to time. In fact, he's about due another six-pack. My wife gamely took on copy-editing duty, but bailed when the accumulation of horrors triggered her anxiety. My co-worker Todd Jansen stepped in, and then my brother Jonathan gave it a go.

Creeping Waves is no different, other than the fact that since the release of *Gateways*, there has been a long, long list of people who have helped put the book in the hands of readers.

Let me start from the beginning. I must thank:

My parents, Mark and Juneal, for bringing me up to appreciate words. My brother Jonathan, for being a friend as much as a brother. Lindsey Blount, for encouraging words.

My mother-in-law Penelope and my wife Katie. Katie's sister Alison and Alison's son Victor. Your support means the world.

The unholy trinity: Tom Breen, who was reading my stories when I first started writing them in 2005, and who since then has encouraged me to try to get them published. S.J. Bagley, who encouraged me to send *Gateways* to the *Arkham Digest*, despite the fact that as a rule they did not review self-published books. And the *Arkham Digest's* Justin Steele, who wrote a wonderful review. Without these three, I would not have a writing career. Simple as that.

For their hard work and camaraderie: the men and women of the New England Horror Writers.

For first publishing "Rangel" as a chapbook and showcasing it beautifully: Sam Cowan.

For an introduction that I must have read a thousand times, and for tremendous stories: Nathan Ballingrud.

For the cover, oh, the cover: Nick Gucker.

For everything, including but not limited to kind words, good advice, and inspiration: Michael Adams, Catherine Albert, Michael Aronovitz, Meghan Barnes, Laird Barron, Max Booth III, Mike Breen, Thomas Broadbent, Michael Bukowski, Christopher Burke, Liz Nixon Carrubba, Lou Columbus, Kelsey Cropp, Jose Cruz, Thom Davidsohn, Mike Davis, Barry Lee DeJasu, Kristi DeMeester, Peter DiCrescenzo, Scott Dwyer, Andy Enjaune, Dave Felton, Alex Fienemann, David Garrity, Amy Gohlke, Anna Gohlke, Sylvia Gott, Catherine Grant, Orrin Grey, Lena Griffin, Mike Griffin, Acep Hale, Clint Hale, Curtis Hawkes, Niels Hobbs, Christopher Houck, Angela Hunt, Timothy Jarvis, Scott R. Jones, Michael Kelly, Leeman Kessler, Jordan Krall, James Krstulovich, Des Lewis, John Langan, Robert Levy, Brian Lillie, Ross E. Lockhart, Tom Lynch, Karen Michaud Mann, Raymond Majerski, Anya Martin, Erik Merkosh, Adrean Messmer, Charles Meyer, Gina Miller, S.P. Miskowski, Daniel Mills, Edward Morris, CM Muller, Adam Nevill, Scott Nicolay, Jeff O'Brien, Brian O'Connell, Jimmy J. Pack Jr., Joseph Pastula, Duane Pesice, Chad Garrett Pilcher, Joe Pulver, Matthew Warren Richey, Ian Rogers, Christopher Ropes, Jayaprakash Satyamurthy, Susan Schaeffer, Lisa Shiota, Robert Slack, Christopher Slatsky, Clint Smith, John Claude Smith, Soren Sorenson, Simon Strantzas, Jeffrey Thomas, Scott Thomas, Sean Thompson, Dawn Thornton, Paul Tremblay, Kenneth Vaughan, Michael Wehunt, Heather Whamond, Kevin Wright, Kelly Young, Joe Zannetti, and so many more.

For helping to shape this book and for editing prowess above and beyond the call of duty: Jonathan Raab.

For those I neglected to name here.
Thank you, thank you, thank you.

ABOUT THE AUTHOR

Matthew M. Bartlett is the author of *Gateways to Abomination*, *Anne Gare's Rare Book and Ephemera Catalogue*, and *The Witch-Cult in Western Massachusetts*. His short stories have appeared in such anthologies as *Xnyobis #1*, *Resonator: New Lovecraftian Tales From Beyond*, *Faed*, and *High Strange Horror*. He lives in Northampton, Massachusetts with his wife Katie Saulnier and their cats Phoebe, Peach Pie, and Larry.

You can follow him on Twitter at @MattMBartlett.

He blogs at www.matthewmbartlett.com.

CPSIA information can be obtained at www.ICGtesting.com
Printed in the USA
LVOW11s1532040816

499078LV00003B/542/P